ABE

ABE

D.J. MOLLES
THE REMAINING
UNIVERSE

D.J. MOLLES

Book Cover by Tara Molles

ISBN Print Paperback: 9798323786343

ASIN: B0CZ4PK185

First edition 2024

The Remaining Universe

It began with a bacteria called Febrile Urocanic Reactive Yersinia. When exposed to a host's blood or mucous membrane, the bacteria would burrow holes through the frontal lobe, destroying the host's ability to reason and speak.

The FURY bacteria spread so rapidly that it burned itself out in a matter of months. But by then, the damage had been done. 9 out of 10 people had been infected by it. Many of those infected experienced a massive spike in their metabolic rates, causing them to feel insatiably hungry. Due to their damaged frontal lobes, these infected turned hyper-aggressive, and preyed on anything they could get their hands on--including other humans.

After a year, most of the infected died out due to starvation and exposure. But of those billions, a few were gifted–or cursed–with genetics that favored extreme adaptability. These individuals not only survived, but began to thrive. Their bodies underwent a period of macroevolution, resulting in morphological changes that made them better suited to be an apex predator: elongated forelimbs, hardening of the fingernails, widening of the mandible, and lengthening of the canine teeth. These came to be known as primals.

In the aftermath of societal collapse, several factions vie for control of dwindling resources. One of the most precious resources is fuel for vehicles. Along the Gulf Coast, the United Eastern States battles with the *Nuevas Fronteras* cartel for control of the oil fields and refineries in that region.

After several months of fighting *Nuevas Fronteras*, Abe Darabie, an operative working for the United Eastern States, is given a new mission: Find and rescue the families of several refinery workers, currently being held hostage by the cartel, somewhere in Mexico...

PROLOGUE

I'LL BE THE FIRST to admit that killing women isn't easy.

Killing a guy? I don't know. It's just different. I mean, sometimes you still feel bad for the fucker, and other times you barely even think twice.

There's been a lot of guys like that recently—guys whose faces I won't remember, because I felt absolutely nothing when I took them out. Like I was just squashing bugs.

And there's something about that—the killing without feeling anything—that worries me. Makes me wonder if I've lost a piece of myself somewhere along the way. Or maybe broke some part of my brain that should feel guilty for taking life.

But women? No, killing women always sucks.

Yes, I've done it before.

And yes, I'll do it again if I have to.

This woman—the one I've got pinned to the wall and am holding at gunpoint—I think she gets that.

My left hand has her by the throat. My right hand has my little Sig P365 tucked tight into retention, but the woman sees the direction of the muzzle, and she knows I'll punch holes in her pelvis if she gets squirrelly again. That'd be a bad day for her, so she goes very still.

Just in case there's any lack of clarity, I tell her, "Don't push it, señora. I will kill you."

I can feel her carotid pulse bumping rabbit-quick against my fingertips. Her shallow, rapid respirations are warm against my wrist. Straight, coal-black hair hangs disheveled in front of her wide, dark eyes.

She glances down at the pistol-grip shotgun that lies on the dirty linoleum floor. She'd been trying to yank it out of a kitchen cabinet just before I rammed her into the wall. I can tell by the look in her eyes that she wouldn't have hesitated to load my face up with buckshot.

I kick the shotgun a bit further away, and then jerk her off the wall. A picture of the Virgin Mary, which dislodged from its hangings when I slammed the woman into it, drops to the floor. The cheap, pinewood frame fractures. Mary tilts forward and faceplants.

Better that Jesus's mom doesn't see this.

I grab the woman by the collar of her denim shirt and drag her to the little square table we'd been sitting at only moments before. I force her down into the chair she'd just vacated when she'd gone for the shotgun.

"Hands on the table," I order, positioning myself behind her and pressing her face down onto the crumb-strewn wood. "Don't fucking move."

She slaps both hands down to either side of her head and goes rigidly still.

I guess she understands more English than she speaks.

I snap my gaze up and scan the environment.

The house isn't big, but it's spacious enough. The kitchen is open to the living room, where there's a musty brown sofa facing a boxy TV that was ancient even before the world went to shit. A hall leads back, presumably to the bedrooms. The front door stands to my left, between the kitchen and living room.

That's where Menendez is, peering through the wire-mesh security door, a Glock 19 in his hands.

"Dez!" I get his attention, then nod at the table. "Check the underside for me."

Menendez, face tense and eyes sharp, gives the outside one more glance, then hustles over and bends down, checking under the table to make sure our hostess doesn't have another surprise duct-taped there.

"It's clear," Menendez says, straightening and orienting himself to the door again.

"Where's your kids?" I ask the woman.

She rattles something off in Spanish, her voice quaking and muffled as she speaks into the wood.

Menendez says something back, his tone making it clear that we're not fucking around.

She responds, and it sounds like begging.

Still watching the door, Menendez translates for me: "She says they're out doing chores."

"They gonna show up with guns and start shooting at us?"

Menendez repeats some version of my question in Spanish. The woman responds in the negative, then begs again. I don't speak the language, but I get the gist, even before Menendez makes it clear.

"She says they don't have guns. She asks us not to shoot them."

"Well, that's entirely up to them, isn't it?" I growl back, then crane my head to try to see out the front door where, about thirty seconds ago, we heard a gunshot, and what should've been a low-profile intel-gathering op turned into this shitshow.

The front door has two parts. The weathered wooden one, which is hanging open right now; and the wire-mesh security door, which is closed. Through the security door, I can only see a few of the outbuildings that surround this little homestead, out in the middle of Buttfuck-Nowhere, Mexico. But I can't see anything that explains the gunshot.

Actually, it was just the crack of a supersonic bullet. The rifle report itself was suppressed.

"Had to be Branch," Menendez voices my own thoughts.

Branch is our designated marksman. We put him on overwatch as me and Menendez approached this little settlement. The other three members of our team are with him.

If it was Branch, that means he saw a threat somewhere on the grounds.

And who might that threat have been?

The woman begins to shake under my grip. I realize she's starting to sob.

There's a part of me—a little holdover from the Abram Darabie of times past—that waits to feel some stirring of pity. I'm almost disappointed that I feel absolutely nothing. Whatever mystical organ in the human body produces the sensation of empathy...well, it's dried up or burned out.

The woman's sobs aren't out of fear—there's a quality to them that is scared, yes, but not for herself.

When did I become such a connoisseur of people's weeping?

The woman has realized what I just realized: One gunshot, most likely from our overwatch, and most likely into her husband, who'd departed the house just a few minutes before this all went down.

Yeah, I can extrapolate that well enough. But I still need to make contact with Branch and the others. Unfortunately, me and Menendez came in stripped down—wearing civvies, with only our backup pistols stuffed into our waistbands. No comms with the team, because discrete earpieces aren't something we're equipped with.

We do have radios, and decidedly-*not*-discrete earpieces to go with them. But in the interests of me and Menendez posing like a pair of common nomads, I left my radio locked up in the center console of the old Toyota 4Runner that's parked out front.

This is why I hate undercover shit.

"Take her," I snap at Menendez. "I'm gonna slip out and try to make contact."

Menendez makes an uncertain face, but complies, taking my position behind the woman.

I glance behind me and realize there's a window. I can just imagine one of the kids creeping up to that window with an AK and plugging Menendez while he's focused on the woman.

"Scratch that," I say, moving quickly into the living room. "Pull her in here."

There are windows to either side of the defunct TV, but if Menendez sits the woman on the couch and stands behind her, at least he'll be facing them.

I rip the cushions off the old sofa. The fabric has that feel to it like it's been waxed by decades of dirt, body oils, and skin cells. I jam my fingers down in the cracks, stifling a shudder as I feel petrified crumbs, and God-knows what else. I've got a thing about gross tactile textures.

When I find no weapons stuffed down in the sofa's disgusting nooks, I declare it clear, and Menendez pushes the crying woman down and stands behind her, his pistol trained on the base of her skull.

"Hold tight," I say, moving towards the door, and keeping well-clear of the windows. They afford me a glimpse of the green bumper of our Toyota, off to the right. "Back in a jiff."

"Watch out for those kids," Menendez warns.

The woman explodes into more begging.

Menendez grabs a handful of her hair and doubles her over so her head is nearly between her knees. "*Cállate!*" he snaps.

I know that word well enough. My knowledge of Spanish is limited to such timeless phrases as "hands up," "get on the ground," "shut up," and "fuck your mother."

I pie off the door as much as I can, getting a decent view of our vehicle. It's parked about twenty yards away, more or less in the middle of this little compound. My first instinct is that maybe the woman's husband was messing around with our vehicle, and Branch had taken him out. While speaking with the couple in their kitchen, I'd got the distinct sense that the man wasn't buying our cover story, and when he excused himself, I felt strongly he was going to go snooping.

But the vehicle looks secure. And I don't see a body near it.

I ease the security door open and clear the unknown left, but there's nothing there but dusty hard-pack and a few slim chickens scratching at the dirt.

Besides the house, there's four other structures. Directly across from the house sits a small, weather-beaten barn, its planks a sallow gray and its corrugated metal roof rusty-red. More chickens congregate there, as well as a skinny, black and white goat with engorged udders that stands there and watches me with a sort of accusing silence.

To the left of the barn, there is a rather large chicken coop that makes me think these folks used to have a lot more than the dozen or so chickens I'm seeing. To the right of the barn, a slightly-newer-looking shed of indeterminate purpose.

The fourth building is way off to the right, maybe thirty yards back from our vehicle. This one outsizes even the house and the barn. Metal sided, with a big, bay door that's currently rolled up, revealing a dim interior. I get the sense of a mechanic's garage.

There's no one to be seen.

Not the kids. And not the man.

I punch through the door, hang a right, and head towards the 4Runner. Eyes on corners. Windows. Doors.

I reach the edge of the house and clear the corner. No one's there, except for some gray-scaled lizard that disappears into a hole under the house's foundation.

I'm just a few strides from the Toyota. I kick it across the open space and seize the cover of the engine block. Take another second to make sure some ten-year-old isn't about to blast me, then rip open the driver's side door. I keep my eyes up and scanning three-sixty as I reach in and pop the center console. Inside, lies the radio.

I grab it, retreating to the engine block again and clicking the radio on as I go. Squatting at the front tire, I slip the earpiece in and immediately hear one of Menendez's guys transmitting, his voice slightly keyed-up.

"Abe, you copy? It's Lucky."

"I copy," I transmit as soon as his voice cuts out. "We heard a shot. Talk to me."

"Cover your three," Lucky says, and I immediately pivot, bringing my pistol up to cover the big mechanic's garage. "Branch had to take the dude out."

My heart finally begins to make its palpitations known. Of course, I'd suspected as much, but hearing it said and realizing that our little operation had indeed gone tits up still hits me unpleasantly.

Lucky does not elaborate on why Branch chose to put a hole in "the dude."

"Is the target down?" I ask.

"Confirmed down," Branch's voice breaks in. There's not a breath of emotion in it, but that's not unusual for him. Then he begins to recite to me what led him to make that decision, his voice as rote as if he were in a review board with a bunch of military brass. "Target exited the west side of Structure E holding what appeared to be a large, handheld radio. I believed he might be attempting to communicate with the cartel. So I eliminated him."

Shit, shit, shit.

"You know if he got a transmission off?" I demand.

"Negative. I took the shot as soon as he lifted it to his mouth."

Right. The main threat was down—and hopefully before he could call in the cavalry on us, though that remains to be seen. Now I need to know about all the other potential threats.

"Where're the kids?"

There were three of them. I saw them myself when we reconned this place, just prior to making contact. Two girls and one boy. The boy looked to be around maybe six or seven, and was the youngest. The eldest of the three girls looked to be in her teens. I hadn't seen them since their mother shooed them out of the house after welcoming me and Menendez in.

"Younger two are holed up in Structure C," Branch says—Structure C being the barn. "Older girl squirted around the back of the house after I took the shot. Lost sight of her."

Well, that's alarming.

If she's still around the back of the house, then I'm entirely exposed in my current position. Unfortunately, I'll be exposed no matter *what* position I'm in. The whole center of the settlement has become the killbox in my mind. And I very much want to remove myself from it.

Best option at this precise moment? Move to the other side of the garage, presumably where the man's body is.

"Roger," I transmit, getting to my feet and covering the back corner of the house as I push out towards the garage. "Branch, keep me covered. Lucky, watch Branch's six. Marty and EZ—move in on my location. Dez is in the house with the woman."

They're still about five hundred yards away. Even hauling ass, it'll take them a few minutes to reach me.

I get to the cover of the garage's metal walls. Metal siding doesn't stop shit, but there's lots of other big, metal stuff in there that hopefully will. I keep moving, all the way along the wall to the back end of the structure, which faces west.

Clearing the corner, little needles of adrenaline prickle my fingertips as I spot the body, and think, somewhat nonsensically, *By the pricking of my thumbs, something wicked this way comes.*

I'm not a Shakespeare or literature whiz, so I find the thought unsettling. I don't like how unexplainable thoughts sometimes feel like portents dropped into your mind by some sixth sense, or perhaps a higher power.

The man lies on his side, facing me. His pose is typical—body loosely curled, arms and legs roughly pointing in Branch's direction. Nine times out of ten, a body falls with its feet pointing towards the shooter.

Branch took him in the chest. I can't see the hole, but I can see the blood darkening the dust under his torso. The ground around him is undisturbed: He didn't thrash around after getting plugged. Bullet must've punched his heart out and killed him quick.

Branch is an excellent shot.

I don't linger on the body, working a wide angle around it as I keep my pistol's sights on the open man-door in the back of the garage. However, I do note the worrying lack of a large, handheld radio anywhere around the dead body.

Someone took it. And the only other someone that's running around out here is the teenage girl.

Branch must have missed it when he was covering me or searching for additional threats.

Physiologically-speaking, my body is pumping all the stress hormones. But my mind is detached and calm. You learn to do that. The body never stops panicking when shit goes down, but you learn to operate outside of yourself.

The garage. The man-door, still hanging open. The missing radio. The missing girl.

I ease towards the door, taking my support hand from my pistol and keying the radio. "Marty. EZ. ETA?"

It's Marty that responds, his voice breathless and shaking with the exertion of his run. "One minute out. I see you."

I don't look around to try to spot them. I can't take my eyes off the door.

We don't have a minute.

You don't have to be Sherlock to put the pieces together. Missing girl. Missing radio. Why take the radio if she wasn't planning to use it? And I couldn't let her use it, just like Branch hadn't let her dead father use it.

I push to the right side of the open man-door and pie off as much of the interior as I can. As I draw closer to the door, I hear a small noise. Could've been the scuff of a shoe. Could've been a small intake of breath.

It's close. I just don't know which side of the door it came from.

I make a decision, because sometimes urgency demands that you take the quickest viable option that pops into your brain. I punch through the door, moving hard and trying to get clear of the corners before the girl can shoot me, or brain me with a lug wrench.

Twisting right, then left.

And I see her.

Backed into a corner of the shop, her white camisole shirt stands out like a beacon in the dim interior. That, and the whites of her eyes, stretched wide behind a curtain of sweaty, black hair.

In that snapshot of an instant, I can see that she's holding a boxy, handheld radio with a long, whip antenna. Her fingers are on the PTT. Her mouth is open.

My sights are on the bridge of her nose. Just three, subtly-glowing dots, over which her eyes stare right back at me, and she seems to know she's about to die.

What hits me most in that tiny moment is how young she is.

It's not easy to kill a woman.

It's harder still to kill a girl.

Or, at least, I *imagine* it is. Because here's the truth: I've never killed a kid before. I know many an operative that has been forced to take that shot for the sake of a mission. But I've never been in that situation myself.

It is some final, dark frontier in my mind, the borders of which I have yet to cross, though I've always known that I might have to someday. For the sake of the mission.

Odd how a mind can think and perceive so much in such a small flash of time.

Just a fraction of a second, really.

I feel the tingling again in my fingertips, and the thought echoes through me, like picking up some strange radio signal: *By the pricking of my thumbs, something wicked this way comes.*

Is it me? Am I the wicked thing that's coming?

The moment flies by, never to be taken back.

The girl takes in a breath, as though to speak.

Her hand tightens on the radio.

And my finger drops to the trigger.

Physiologically-speaking, my body is pumping all the stress hormones.

But my mind is detached and calm.

Calm enough to wonder, as I take the slack out of my trigger...

How did I come to this?

CHAPTER 1

YOU NEED TO UNDERSTAND something about me.

I want to make it ultra-clear, and banish any misconceptions you might have.

A lot of people think that if you're any kind of special forces, you must inherently be of some high moral caliber. And I guess some guys are. I don't want to make a blanket statement here. I'm only talking about myself.

I. Don't. Care.

Zero fucks to give.

I always have been—and always will be—a black-hearted devil.

But I get shit done.

"Her name is Tracy," the man says, and I can tell his voice remains blank only by an effort of will.

The photograph is a five-by-seven, and in surprisingly good shape. The corners still have tape on them, from being stuck to the inside of his locker all these years he's worked at the oil refinery on the Gulf of Mexico.

It shows the man and his wife, sitting on a blanket in some park-like setting, their two children sitting in front of them, as though the whole family were on a picnic when a photographer just happened by. His wife is a looker—which always strikes me as comical when the husband is not. Though, admittedly, with the guy across from me on the verge of tears, I don't feel much like laughing.

"My daughter's name is Kinley," he goes on, his voice thickening. "And my son is Gauge."

I offer the barest hint of a smile. "That's a good, strong name for a boy."

That's just something I say to every father who tells me their son's name.

I finally look up at him. I've been calling him "Pez" for a while now, because that's what everyone at the refinery calls him. I knew his last name was Pizzuti, but I only just found out his first name was Michael.

It's weird. He doesn't strike me as a Michael. I would've gone with Andy.

Pez isn't a roughneck. He's an engineer, and...yeah, that's pretty much what he looks like. Medium height with a slight build. Big, black-framed, Clark Kent glasses. A worn, blue ballcap that bears the logo of the oil company that owned this refinery once upon a time.

Behind his glasses, his eyes are red-rimmed and watery. He casts them aside.

We're in a bunkroom in the refinery—one that Pez shares with a few others of the skeleton crew that has kept this refinery pumping far past the end of society. It'd lain dormant for a while after the plague hit the United States and everything went down the shitter. Then the *Nuevas Fronteras* cartel seized it in their gambit to control the oil fields around the Gulf.

We'd taken it back two weeks ago. But the cartel still had their hooks in the refinery workers. After all, how do you get a bunch of engineers and roughnecks to do a job for free? Well, if you're a cartel that has the ambition of controlling oil production and using it to bolster an invasion of the Southern United States, then you hold their families hostage.

Guys work real hard when they're afraid their wives, girlfriends, and kids might be returned to them, one piece at a time.

"How long ago was this photo taken?" I ask Pez.

He blinks and swallows. "I think...five years ago? It was two years before the plague and...all that."

I nod, glancing at the photo again. "How old are Kinley and Gauge now?"

"Kinley's eleven now," he says. "Gauge is about to turn nine."

Kids can change a lot in five years. Chances are, they don't look like they did in the photograph anymore. But if Tracy is still alive—if *any of them* are still alive—she'll look more or less the same.

"Thank you," I say, and I mean it, because he's the only one that had a photograph of the people I'm supposed to be extracting. The other six guys could only give me physical descriptions. Then I give him a cautiously-hopeful look. "Can I hold onto this?"

I know I'm asking a lot. Physical photos are a rarity. Anyone that kept all their memories on digital files now has nothing. This bit of glossy paper I have in my fingers is likely all Pez has to remember his family.

Pez considers it for a moment, standing very still. Then he bobs his head up and down. "If it'll help you find them...that's all that matters."

"It'll help us identify them," I say, but leave out what I'm actually thinking. *Or their remains.*

There's no guarantee that any of these families are still alive.

Nuevas Fronteras knew we'd retaken the refinery. We'd even killed the head of the cartel—he'd roasted inside of his getaway car like a marshmallow forgotten in a campfire. But someone new had stepped in. And they'd been using the captive families to get the workers to sabotage the refinery. Several of the workers tried to blow shit up or otherwise ruin equipment. A few others tried to kill me and a handful of other soldiers guarding the refinery.

Those workers were all dead now.

But Pez and six others hadn't caved, and instead had asked for our help getting their families back. That's nice. I'm glad they didn't try to kill me. And I'm willing to help. But I don't know what their refusal to act on the cartel's orders means for their families.

Pez eyes me for a time. “Can you really do this? Can you really find them and get them back?”

I sigh heavily through my nose. “Pez. I’ve just spent the last couple months of my life hunting cartel. They’re tough, but I know what I’m doing. So do Menendez and his boys.” I shift my weight and look once more at the photograph pinched between my fingers. “You know I can’t guarantee you shit, man. That ain’t how this works. All I can promise you is this: If Tracy and Gauge and Kinley are still alive? We’ll find them and get them back to you. Or we’ll die trying.”

“This here’s the Pizzutti family,” I say, and pass the photo around.

I’m doing the briefing outside on a weather-beaten picnic table that used to be a place for refinery workers to take their breaks—and presumably to smoke, if the aged remnants of cigarette filters scattered around the area are any indicator.

This whole plan to rescue the families came about after one of the refinery workers tossed a stolen grenade into the control room a few days back. It hadn’t done that much damage, but they were trying to repair a few of the systems, and had cut the power inside the refinery as they tried to rewire some shit. I’d’ve preferred to do the briefing inside. But we need the light. So outside in the sunshine it is.

It's still morning, and the day hasn't quite gotten to full devil's-asshole heat just yet. The smell coming off the Gulf is a combination of ocean breeze and sulfurous shit-stink from the crude oil lines.

We've all gotten used to it by now.

I'm standing at the end of the picnic table. Menendez is immediately to my right, and he takes the picture of the Pizzuti family and gives it a good, hard inspection, locking those faces into his brain.

"That's the only photo we have of any of the families," I continue. I've already covered the other six families—biographical data and physical descriptors. Menendez and his team each have a sheet of paper in front of them, on which I've hand-written the important info for them.

Menendez nods solemnly and passes the photo to his right.

Branch Douglas takes it and looks it over. He's got olive skin and dark hair, but blue eyes, which makes his ethnicity hard to place at first glance. He tells me his father was half Cherokee. Maybe that explains it.

He's solid. Quiet and introspective. He takes criticism well, and rarely needs it. Former Marine Scout Sniper. Current Designated Marksman for Menendez's rowdy little group of killers.

"Adult female is Tracy Pizzuti," I tell them. "Thirty-eight. Pez says she pretty much looks the same, though her hair is dyed blonde in the photo and she's a natural brunette. Last time he saw her, which was about ten months ago, she'd cut it to shoulder length."

Branch makes no comment, and passes the photo.

Next to take it is Jon McKenna, who everyone calls Lucky, I guess because of his Irish heritage. His pale skin and blonde hair are not getting along with Texas, and his face is just one big, reddish blotch of freckles, despite the fact that he constantly wears a boonie hat to shade him.

"Other identifying marks?" Lucky asks. Still holding the photo, he consults the paper with all the intimate details of the nineteen people we hope to extract. He hasn't come out and said it, but it seems he doesn't think we're going to find any of them alive, and has been focused on identifying marks, in case we find them in pieces.

I can see that Lucky has found his own answer—his index finger is tracing across the bottom of the page, where the details on the Pizzuti family are written. I verbalize it for the sake of the others.

"Butterfly tattoo on her right ankle, and a horizontal C-section scar on her lower pelvis."

"Got it," Lucky says, and holds the photo out across the table.

"Basic bitch, then?" This from Marty Thomas, who's sitting across from Lucky and takes the photo. He's grinning as he says it, looking around for who else might want to get in on the joke.

Menendez's expression just kind of flattens, like a mother who's moderately ashamed of a child too troublesome to bother correcting anymore.

I paste on a flaccid smile. I've worked with this crew before, and deliberate irreverence is par for the course with them. I recognize it for what it is, and I don't begrudge it. When your life is an unending string of brutality, you can either take it seriously and eventually drive yourself mad, or you can make a joke of every sacred thing, to rob it of its power to destroy your mind.

"Nah," EZ says, plucking the photograph deftly from Marty's fingers. "First off, I think you mean basic *white* bitch—don't lump my people in with your women and their tattoos of butterflies and dolphins and sea turtles and shit."

Marty rolls his eyes dramatically. "Yeah? What would a black chick have? Like, a panther crawling up her arm or something?"

EZ is entirely unoffended. Marty Thomas and Ezekial Williams cut an interesting picture. Marty, with his loud, Texas accent and his "God, Guns, and Country" philosophy. And EZ with his Baltimore accent and his street-wise attitude. In a civilian world, they probably would've hated each other. But now, after fighting together for years on end, they're best friends.

These two...they play a lot of games. And this one here is their favorite: dancing across the lines of long-dead social mores, saying the most offensive shit that would've given the politically correct of bygone days an aneurysm.

"Yeah," EZ nods in response to Marty's charge. "A black panther—that shit is hot. Fierce. Or, like..." he gestures to the side of his neck. "A neck tattoo with their own name on it?" He looks skyward with an expression like he's just tasted something incredible. "Mm. God. So hot. I mean, even a cow-fucking Texas cracker like you's gotta admit that's hot."

Marty shrugs. "Hey, don't knock the cow-fucking 'til you try it."

EZ gives the photograph in his fingers a little wrist snap and refocuses. "But this? Oh my. No, this ain't no basic white bitch. This here's a lady, Marty." He turns and looks at me. "Can I keep this? You know. For future research?"

Menendez clears his throat.

EZ and Marty snicker amongst themselves, but they don't keep their gag running. They know play time is over.

Still smiling blandly, I remove the photograph from EZ's fingers. "Nah, I'll hang on to that."

I am completely unfazed by anything they said.

Allow me to explain why.

You see, human beings' chief survival strategy is cooperation. Because of that, over the eons of our evolution, killing your fellow human beings has become the biggest, most instinctive taboo. And when you've spent so many years violating that taboo, then what power can any other taboo have over you?

Being a professional killer makes society and all its taboos seem just a tad farcical.

And yes, they might not look like it, but these guys are professionals. Which is why it only took Menendez clearing his throat to get them back on track.

"And on that note," I say, segueing off of nothing. "Objective is obvious: Find these families, and, if they're still alive, then get 'em out of there, and back to here." I sigh and stretch my back. "And that's literally all I've got for you guys. We are going into this completely blind, unsupported, and with zero intel."

I see a few tired expressions, but none of them are really surprised. This is how they're used to operating. If they had support and intel, it would've seemed like a rare treat.

Menendez shrugs. "We can create intel on the way."

I nod. "That's the plan. Which is why all of you need to beg, borrow, or steal some civvies. When we make contact with locals, we'll be posing as a group of drifters looking for a settlement to call home. Casey from the pump room has given us a working Toyota 4Runner for our transport. We'll have all our guns and gear stowed in the back, but we won't be strapping up until we're going to work. Whole point being, we do *not* want to get on the cartel's radar. We're gray until we go hot. To that end, I kept our cover story very simple—so Marty can remember it."

"Har har," Marty grunts.

I nod to Menendez.

He lifts the hand-written page, reading from the very bottom. "Six months after the outbreak of the plague, we all met in the fictional settlement of Redstone, in central Texas. That settlement disbanded about a year ago, due to starvation, sickness, and infighting. Since then, we've been wandering around the border, doing odd jobs for whoever had enough fuel and food to trade with us. We're now heading further into Mexico, looking for greener pastures."

Menendez lays the paper down. "I'm the only one that speaks Spanish, and Abe here can kinda pass for a Latino, so we'll be the ones making contact."

"Wait..." EZ looks at me, confused. "You're *not* Latino?"

"First generation Pakistani-American."

EZ looks blown away. "No way. Thought you were Puerto Rican or something."

I roll my eyes. "Everyone thinks I'm Puerto Rican or something."

Menendez shakes his head. "So racist, EZ. Anyways—as I was saying—the rest of you, avoid interacting if at all possible, but don't be rude. Be nice and forgettable. If you do have to interact with the locals, keep it short and sweet, and don't get creative. Stick to the cover story. Like Abe said: Gray man. If anyone asks general questions, play ignorant and defer to me or Abe. If anyone asks you about yourself, act sad and say you don't wanna talk about it."

EZ raises a finger. "What if they ask about Marty's bulky ass?"

Menendez eyes go half-lidded.

EZ gets defensive. "No, I'm serious. Look at him. He's clearly not half-starved."

EZ's got a point. Marty is thick-necked and well-muscled. Not body-builder or anything like that, but enough to raise eyebrows amongst people who barely have enough food to keep from starving.

"Maybe I eat people?" Marty offers. "There're cannibals, right? Abe, you ran into some of those a while back, didn't you?"

Menendez shakes his head, adamant. "This is why I told you not to get creative."

I cut a hand through the air. "For the love of God, don't tell anyone you eat people. Me and Dez already talked this over, and the best solution we could come up with is for you to wear loose-fitting clothes. I doubt anyone will push the issue, but hey, here's a learning opportunity. Let's have a role play." I splay my hands on my chest. "I'll be some little señorita that's taken a shine to Marty." I put on a girly, falsetto voice. "Oh, Mr. Marty-Wanderer-Man, why are you so muscly?"

He blinks, but quickly takes the role-play seriously, despite my laughable impression of a female. He averts his gaze, kind of shyly, and murmurs at the table top, "Just big-boned, ma'am."

I give him a beat or two to screw himself over by saying more, but he smartly keeps his mouth shut and his eyes down. I smile appreciatively and go back to my regular voice. "There. See? Perfect. Simple, to the point, and most importantly, forgettable."

Marty gives a stage bow. "Natural thespian."

"Alright." I hike my foot up on the table to stretch my hip and groin. They've been nagging me lately. Perils of being in your late-thirties and still an active operator. "Like I said, overall objective is to extract these families. But first, we have to locate where they're being held. Again, zero intel on that front, so...we're going to have to create our own intel. Which brings us to objective one: We're going to infiltrate cartel territory, locate and identify the highest-ranking cartel member we can find, capture that individual, and extract information."

A stern silence overtakes the guys at the mention of extracting information. They don't balk, but they all know what it means. They know we're going to do some bad shit.

"If we're wildly lucky," I continue. "We might get intel on the families. More likely, we're going to have to start out with a low man, and work our way up the food chain until we can find some higher up that actually knows where they're being held. Point being, when we snatch someone, we need to remember that the clock is ticking for those families."

They know what I'm saying there, too.

We won't have time for a protracted interrogation. Won't have time to build rapport, and make some cartel asshat *want* to talk to us. Whoever we get our hands on gets exactly one chance to talk, and then he's gonna start losing body parts.

"That's about all I can give you guys for a briefing at this point." I pull my foot off the table and shake the leg out. "All other bridges will be crossed as we get to them." I consult my watch. "It's oh-seven-forty now. Go get your gear and find some civvies. Meet back here by oh-nine-thirty for checks. We're enroute by ten-hundred."

CHAPTER 2

"THIS TERRAIN SUCKS BALLS." Branch's words make it seem like he's pissed, but his tone is clinical.

"Yeah." I give the flatness all around us a cursory glance. "But I'm sure you can work with it."

Still squinting over his rifle scope, Branch offers a slight smirk. "Of course I can work with it. Just sayin'—it sucks balls."

We're both sweating bullets in the midday sun, laying on our bellies in a stand of brush. About a mile out from us, the little settlement shimmers with mirage. Midday is when mirage is least likely to affect your accuracy, as the air and ground temperatures have roughly equalized by then. But a mile is still a stretch, no matter how good Branch is with that fancy-ass rifle of his.

And it is fancy. A MacMillan TAC-338, with a Leupold Mark 4 M1 scope. It has the *ability* to hit out to two thousand meters and some change. But I still want Branch to be closer.

I lean into him, laying an arm across his shoulder so he can see where I'm pointing. "How about that swale there? Take it off to the right. You see that little clump of boulders?"

Branch doesn't immediately respond. He reaches over and liberates the combination range finder and spotting scope from my grip, then lases the boulders.

"Four-fifty-one," he murmurs with slight approval, doing the math in his head. "That'll put us within twelve-hundred meters. Very doable."

"Alright." I touch off my PTT. "Abe to Dez."

"Go with it," Menendez transmits back.

"Occupied settlement. Single family. Several structures. Me and you are gonna make contact. Send the others up, but stay with the vehicle. I'll be back with you in about twenty minutes."

"Copy. Sending the others."

I settle back into position. Branch is taking notes in a battered little booklet, the stubby remnants of a pencil scratching out the descriptions of the settlement's occupants. I use the spotting scope to keep an eye on the settlement while he works.

This is our second day on the road. We crossed into Mexico the previous day, but all our time got ate up doing exactly what we're doing now, except the two settlements we reconned yesterday were both abandoned. A waste of time, but then, you never can be too careful. I thought this one was going to be abandoned, too.

I'm not even sure if we're really in cartel territory yet. To hear *Nuevas Fronteras* tell it, they pretty much owned all of Mexico. But that could just be big talk.

Part of me hopes that this settlement is in with the cartel, because, if it is, we might get our first lead on where the families are being held.

Another part of me hopes these are just some random folks, trying to survive. Because...this looks like a family to me. Man, woman, and three kids. What if I have to pull their dad's teeth out? Or their mom's?

What if I have to hurt one of the kids?

Mission first and all that. Yeah, sure. I'll do what I have to do.

Just wish they were all dudes.

But then I have to wonder—am I just thinking that to make myself feel better? Make myself feel like I'm not a sociopath? Because here's the truth: When I imagine shooting one of those kids, the feeling I have is just kind of...

Oh well.

Sucks for you.

Play stupid games, get stupid prizes.

Was I always like this? Or did something turn inside of me over the previous few months? I'd been on a bit of a vendetta against the cartel. Spent a while just hunting them down and slaughtering them. No ROEs. No mercy. Just stacking bodies.

And not once did my conscience prick me. But the more days I put between me and that killing spree, the more I've started to think about why.

When we took that refinery back from the cartel, their leader, Mateo Ibarra, tried to escape in a vehicle. He got shot while he was driving away. Crashed the car. It caught fire. He was pinned inside. We could've pulled him out. Or put him out of his misery.

We didn't.

And you know what I thought, while I watched that guy burn alive?

Fuck you, crispy critter. That's what I thought. Not even bitterly. Just kind of...amused.

I racked out that night, thinking, *crispy critter.*

Crispy critter.

Crispy critter.

You ever turned a thought over and over in your mind, trying to get the measure of its meaning? Like taking repeated bites of something and rolling it around on your tongue, trying to figure out what flavors you're tasting?

When you distill horrific things down to amusing alliterations, they lose context.

I guess I was trying to figure out what *crispy critter* meant.

Charred flesh. Burnt bones. A blackened suggestion of a person who'd died in horrendous pain. A person who had screamed until their upper layer of dermis had cracked and peeled, and the nerve endings had been seared.

That's what *crispy critter* actually means.

And when I realized that, I just...stopped thinking about it. What was the point? To make myself feel bad? To try to empathize with Matteo Ibarra's last moments? What good would that do?

And then I just fell asleep, easy as pie.

But over the last few days, it's all started to make me wonder about myself.

Through the range finder, I see a girl in her mid-teens exit the main house in the settlement, carrying a plastic bucket. I think she's the eldest of the kids we've spotted. She's got straight, black hair, pulled into a sloppy bun to keep it out of her face. She wears a white camisole and jeans that look a bit baggy on her. She goes to an old-school pump-well and begins working the rusty-red handle, while water spurts out into the bucket.

I glance sidelong at Branch. He's riffling through the pages of his DOPE book—Diary Of Previous Engagements—trying to find when he last took a shot in similar atmospheric conditions, so he knows where his first, cold-bore shot will land.

"How you feel about these targets?" I venture.

He doesn't look up. Shrugs. "Is what it is."

"Yup. You ever iced a kid before?"

His finger traces down a page crammed with tiny, handwritten letters. "M-hm." He seems to find the entry he's looking for and reads it over for a moment. Then he sticks his pencil in the spine of the book to keep the page and lashes it closed with a rubber band. "Why? You worried I'm gonna hesitate?"

"Nah. Just curious."

He eyes me, and for a moment I'm certain he's going to challenge me with the same question: *What about you, Abe? You ever killed a kid?* And what would I say about it? An entire imagined conversation plays out in my brain. He and the rest of Menendez's crew have shit-tons of combat experience at this point—some of it from before the world ended, and a whole lot of it from after.

I'm still vastly more experienced than any of them, and they know it. And yet, stupidly, there's a part of me that wonders if my experience will somehow be impugned by the fact that I've never killed a kid before.

There's something wildly fucked up about that.

Branch doesn't challenge me on it. He says, simply, "Gotta do what you gotta do."

"Yup," I say again, and look back through the spotting scope.

You gotta do what you gotta do.

It is what it is.

There's something serene about circular reasoning. A numb sort of comfort in knowing that nothing makes sense anyways, life is illogical, and it's best not to overthink it. That's generally where I like to keep my headspace.

I've been wandering out of that comfort zone lately.

That's dumb. I should stop.

Through the spotting scope, I see the girl finish pumping water. She hefts the bucket, her thin frame straining at the weight. She totters back into the house with it.

I hear the quiet shuffling of multiple pairs of boots behind me.

I hand the spotting scope back to Branch as he begins readying himself to move.

Lucky, Marty, and EZ shuffle into place behind us, squatting or kneeling to stay behind the concealment of the brush.

I roll onto my knees, taking up my rifle and slinging back into it. "Follow Branch," I tell them. "He's got a spot for overwatch. I'mma link back up with Dez. Radio when y'all are set, and we'll head in."

They're in business-mode. Their eyes are focused and hard-set.

"Roger that, Boss-man," Marty says, then gives Branch a pat on the shoulder as the marksman stows his rifle into a drag bag and slings it onto his shoulders. "On you, Branch."

They head off, moving low and single-file towards the swale that will lead to the boulders. I move back, following their tracks all the way back to where Menendez waits with our vehicle.

We sit inside with all the windows down. It's hot, but at least we're out of the sun. We keep the engine off. Can't afford to waste fuel. I give Menendez a more detailed run-down of what we're heading into, as I know Branch will be giving the others.

When I finish, he asks me, "You see any crops?"

He says it with a suspicious glint in his eyes.

I shake my head. "No crops that I could see."

He grunts, looking out the windshield. "How you keep a family of five from starving without any crops?"

I think I know what Menendez is getting at.

"Maybe they've been eating the primals," I offer up, without much conviction.

Menendez makes a face.

"I've seen it before."

"Is that considered cannibalism?" Menendez wonders.

"I guess that depends on whether you consider primals to still be human. I personally don't. But that don't mean I'd eat 'em."

"These people you met that ate the primals...did they get infected from eating them?"

"Nah. I mean, they were crazy as fuck, but not from the plague. I don't think you can get infected from eating primals."

Menendez gets a contemplative look on his face. "So...you don't think of the primals as humans anymore. But you wouldn't eat one?"

I shrug. "Dunno. I've been pretty close to starving to death a few times. But I've never been hungry enough to eat a primal."

"Okay. But let me ask you this, then: would you eat a chimpanzee?"

"Maybe a chimp. But not a primal."

"They're practically the same thing."

I shake my head. "No, they're not. Primals look way more human than chimps do."

"So it's about what they look like?"

"No, it's about the fact that primals *used* to be human."

"You just said you didn't consider them human."

"They're not. *Anymore*. But it's about the fact that they *were*, before they mutated." I frown at him. "Why? You telling me you *would* eat a primal?"

He shifts in his seat. "I dunno. I agree with you—I've never been hungry enough to cross that line." He holds up a finger. "But I can't promise I won't get hungry enough sometime in the future. Know what I'm saying?"

The radio shushes in our earpieces. "Lucky to Dez and Abe."

I nod to Menendez and he answers up. "Go ahead."

"In position. Ready to proceed."

"Roger that," Menendez says, then cranks the Toyota up and pulls the shifter into drive. "Anyways, my original point was this: These folks aren't growing food. Which means they're either cannibals—or primal-eaters, or whatever..." He looks sidelong at me. "...or they're being supplied by the cartel."

I sigh through my nose, as we start to roll towards the settlement. "Yeah. That is a possibility."

I almost hope they're cannibals.

The people are cautious, but that's to be expected. "Stranger danger" takes on a whole new meaning after society crumbles.

Menendez stops the Toyota at the edge of their settlement so as not to spook them unnecessarily. The guy is already on the front porch with a shotgun, watching us. Menendez gets out and raises his hands to show he's unarmed, though that's a lie—we've both got small carry pistols concealed in our waistbands.

They holler back and forth across the hundred yards between them. I don't understand what's being said, but I hear the tone go from suspicious alertness to something bordering on friendly.

Eventually we are allowed to drive the 4Runner closer to the house. The guy on the porch is skinny, with deeply-brown skin and small eyes that squint at us. He's been joined by a woman that I presume is his wife. He doesn't point the shotgun at us, but he keeps it in hand.

There's more talking outside of the house.

I look around, getting the measure of the place, while trying to *not* look like I'm sizing them up.

After another five minutes, we are allowed inside. The three kids are standing behind a battered old sofa, as though they'd intended to take cover there if the shooting started. I smile and nod at them. The two younger ones smile and wave back. The eldest girl only scowls. Apparently, her suspicions have not been allayed as much as the adults.

That makes her the smartest person in the family.

The woman hustles the kids out of the house in a familiar tone I know means, *Go make yourselves useful.*

Me and Menendez are instructed to sit at the kitchen table. I keep an eye on Menendez to gauge where his head's at, since I can't really tell what's being said. He's all smiles. A quick glance lets me know he thinks we're in the clear.

The adults remain standing at the kitchen counter, the man with the shotgun still in his hands, but held low. They're pretty smiley too.

Things are going well. Menendez is turning on the charm, and it's clearly working. The man and woman sit at the table with us. The guy even leaves his shotgun on the kitchen counter. There's lots of grins, and even some laughs.

Then...I don't know what happened. Maybe Menendez put his foot in it. Or maybe they just didn't like something about our cover story. But the man of the house gets pretty quiet, and his smile goes a bit rigid. I detect a flash of eye contact between man and woman that seems to carry some weight.

Then the man excuses himself from the table, and goes outside.

Menendez lets me know that something is up by nudging my foot underneath the table. But he just keeps smiling, and engaging the woman in conversation. I mark her as a pretty good actress, because, aside from that one glance she shared with the man, she's remained warm and welcoming.

Then we hear the crack of a bullet breaking the sound barrier, and a distant *whump* that both me and Menendez immediately know is the sound of a bullet hitting flesh.

And then everything goes to shit.

CHAPTER 3

THERE WAS THE WHOLE scuffle for the shotgun, and me threatening to blow the pelvis out of a little Mexican lady that could barely speak English. A picture of the Virgin Mary got broken. I ran out to make radio contact.

You know the rest.

And now I exist in that little slice of time where I've got three little tritium gun sights lined up neatly across the nose of a teenage girl, and I'm about to cross a line I never wanted to cross.

When your mind is wide open, it can take in some surprisingly pointless details.

In that microsecond of time where the girl's life hangs by just a few more ounces of finger pressure on a trigger, I notice that she's wearing mascara.

Yeah, I know. It's a stupid thing to notice. But it just strikes me as so weird.

Who wears makeup at the end of the world?

Maybe it's providence. Or maybe I just don't want to cross that line. But some instinct tells me to bum rush her, instead of shooting her in the face. She's only two strides away. I'm pretty sure I can slam the fuck out of her before she gets a transmission out.

I'm willing to risk it.

I cross the distance with an explosive burst of speed. She's barely got time to cringe before I slam every bit of my 200-pound frame into her. She's maybe half my weight, and she flies back like she just got clipped by a semi on the highway. The loudest sound is that of her thin body slamming against the metal wall and rebounding off of it, limbs flailing, spaghetti-limp.

The radio sails out of her hand to points unknown.

I catch her body on the rebound and plant her face-down on the dirt floor of the garage. Drive one knee between her shoulder blades to a sad little wheeze of emptied lungs. Support hand on the nape of her neck, holding her down, her skin slick and hot.

"*Manos en la cabeza*!" I snarl at the back of her head.

She gags and coughs. Her body goes from limp to stiff beneath me, but I can tell she's not fighting me. She's just panicking, trying to get air. I pull some of my weight off her back and feel her chest reinflate.

"*Muchacha*," I say, bringing my voice down from smiting-god to stern command. "*Muchacha*."

I get something like, "Ungh?" from her, high-pitched and terrified.

"*Manos en la cabeza*."

She blubbers. Sobs. Chest hitching.

Then she obeys, slapping both hands to the back of her head. Hands with sparkly, pink, acrylic nails tipping the fingers. Entirely unsuited for farm work. What the hell is going on with this chick?

I clamp a hand over hers, then take stock.

Alright. Situation paused. Threat handled. Target compliant—at least for the moment.

Breathe. Get some oxygen in my brain. In through the nose, out through the mouth. Violence to circumspection.

Where'd that radio go?

With her pinned beneath me, I take a quick look around the floor of the garage, and spot the big, gray handheld radio laying just out of reach. I stare at it, listening. Wondering if I'm going to hear a transmission come through. Had she keyed it? Had her father? Had they gotten word out?

Who was on the other end of that radio?

The girl starts squealing something in Spanish. I have no idea what she's trying to say. Could've been begging for mercy, or maybe she was cursing me for what we'd done to her father. I realize her head is facing the open man-door in the back of the shop, and through that door, she can see the body of her father, curled up and dead.

"Ssh! *Cállate*!"

She doesn't quite *cállate*, because she's sobbing uncontrollably, but she stops talking.

I need to know if a transmission got out, because that is going to dictate my team's next actions. If there's a contingent of cartel soldiers rolling our way in some machine gun technical, then we need to make ourselves scarce.

I give her head a firm shake under my grip, trying to stifle her mewling.

"Hey. Hey!"

She splutters, but fear of me overrides her grief and she goes quiet.

"You speak English?"

Silence.

Then, in a tiny, strained voice: "Yes."

Marty's voice in my earpiece makes me jump. "Abe, where you at? We're comin' up on Structure E—you inside?"

Using the thumb of my gun-hand, I touch off my comms. "Yeah, I'm just inside the man-door. Got one female occupant, alive and compliant."

I hear footfalls outside the door. EZ's voice hollers out, "Coming in! Hold fire!"

"Come on!" I call back, then turn my attention to the girl again. "The radio—you understand? Did you call anyone on the radio?"

EZ comes in first, sweeping the room with his rifle as he moves towards me. Marty follows on his heels, armed with an M249 Squad Automatic Weapon. He posts up on the door, facing out.

The girl is starting to hyperventilate. Somewhere in all the gasping, I think she says "No."

"Did you press that button?" I demand. "Did you talk to anyone?"

"No!"

EZ slings his rifle and comes to a knee beside us.

"Restraints," I say, but he's already pulling a heavy zip-tie from his plate carrier.

"*Manos atras,*" EZ says, as I pull my weight off of her. EZ yanks her hands down to the small of her back.

"She speaks English," I tell him. "Girl, what's your name?"

Through a shuddering moan, she says "Isabella."

EZ loops the zip-tie around her wrists and tightens it until the girl gasps, her flesh pinched.

"Isabella, who's on the other end of that radio?"

"I...I don't know."

"Take a fucking guess, then."

Her head turns slightly, face all coated in dirt, mascara running. Little inky tears drop from the bridge of her nose. Her eyes meet mine, as though she is just now taking me in, actually looking at me. Seeing me. Seeing who I am.

Whatever she sees in me only terrifies her more.

Her mouth shudders open, and she speaks in Spanish, but these are words I know: "*Nuevas Fronteras.*"

It's a tumult of activity.

The radio and the girl come with me. EZ and Marty split off to nab the kids still hiding in the barn. Isabella goes ape shit about that and I have to stick an arm through her restraints and jack her bound hands up, bending her over double.

"You are not helping them," I snap, pulling her along past our vehicle, towards the corner of the main house. "My guys aren't gonna hurt them."

"Fuck you!" she groans.

I stop at the corner of the house, knowing Menendez is inside. "Yo! Dez! It's—"

Isabella stamps a heel down on my instep, yowling like a bobcat.

I'm not gonna lie and tell you it didn't hurt, but I'm more irritated than anything. I kick her feet out from under her. It's almost shameful how easy it is. She slams down on her belly, her arms stretched behind her, with me holding her bound wrists like a leash. I put a boot on the small of her back to keep her pinned down.

"Quit fuckin' around," I say to her, then raise my voice to holler back at Menendez. "It's Abe! I got one coming in!"

"Come on!" he calls back, his voice clear through the grated security door.

I heave the girl up to her feet again. She's young and flexible, and her torqued up shoulders don't seem to bother her at all. Pretty sure mine would've popped out of socket.

I pull her along, moving quick so she can barely keep up. We pass by the two front windows. Inside, I see the dim shape of Menendez, still hovering over the woman on the couch.

Mother and daughter catch sight of each other and start screaming in Spanish.

I wrestle her through the front door, drag her into the living room, and sling her onto the couch with her mother. They immediately huddle together, mewling unintelligible words to each other.

Childish cries come from behind me, and I turn to see EZ and Marty pulling the two younger kids towards the house. They have their weapons raised in high-readies, each towing a kid by the arm. These kids are younger, and more scared, and they're not fighting back, but they sure are raising a ruckus.

I key my comms. "Abe to Branch—we've secured the settlement."

"Roger 'at. You want us to come to you?"

"Negative. You and Lucky hold your position. Keep your eyes peeled. We might have company inbound."

"Copy. We'll hold."

EZ and Marty come in through the front door. The kids are straining against the grip of the two men, trying to get to their mother. I give Marty and EZ a jerk of my head to let them know it's okay, and they let the kids go. They bolt across the room and practically tackle their mother.

"What's the word, Abe?" Menendez presses, reminding me that he's been in the dark without a radio.

I bring him up to speed. Dead dad. Radio. Unknown if a transmission got out. Unknown if hostile forces are on their way to us.

Menendez blinks a few times, his brows beetled in ferocious thought. But I can see his temper rising because of the non-stop keening of the family.

I need to get them to calm down and shut up.

I snap my fingers at Marty. "Hey. Gimme your daypack."

Marty gives me the briefest look of consternation, but complies, slinging the pack off and tossing it to me. Opening the main compartment, I move around to the front of the couch. I move calm and slow, and I don't speak. My quiet becomes a curiosity to the children, and their crying goes down a notch or two.

Towards the bottom of Marty's daypack, I find his prized stash of MRE Pop-Tarts. I snag one and then squat down in front of the family. I put the daypack down between my feet, then tuck my pistol in the back of my waistband. Both hands free, I open the package to expose the bright, sugary pastry.

I hear a heavy sigh of loss come from Marty.

I'm focused on the two younger kids. Isabella and her mother are caught in a feedback loop of panic. The more the kids freak out, the more Isabella and her mom are going to freak out, which, in turn, only makes the kids freak out more. If I can get the younger kids focused on something else, I can break that loop.

And what kid doesn't like a mouthful of sugar?

The children have gone to sniffles and whimpers now.

Moving slow, as though to get a wild animal to eat from my hand, I hold the Pop-Tart out, first towards the boy—the youngest—and then towards the girl—the middle child. Isabella seems like she doesn't know whether to glare at me, or stare at the pastry. Her mother has gone quiet, rocking back and forth with her two kids huddled against her.

"Go ahead," I say, to whichever kid is the bravest.

The boy breaks first, but the middle girl jolts forward with a hissed remonstration. She takes the pastry instead. Gives it a cautious sniff.

I wait patiently, keeping all expression off my face.

The girl takes a cautious nibble, and I disengage, letting them know that the Pop-Tart doesn't come with any price besides being quiet.

I put Marty's daypack back together and hand it over to the mildly-disgruntled soldier.

I look to Menendez. "The older girl is Isabella. She speaks English. I'll use her to translate, but monitor and make sure she's not bullshitting me."

He nods.

"Isabella."

She's watching her younger sister pass the Pop-Tart to her brother, who takes a greedy mouthful. He chews. Then his eyes go comically wide as the sugar hits his tongue. His mind has been blown. There's something charming and sad about that.

Isabella tears her eyes off her sibling and looks at me with tousled hair hanging in front of her face. Oddly enough, that small bit of kindness has put her off-balance. She seems more nervous about me than before.

"Did your father get a transmission out?"

Her body suddenly shivers, like she'd just remembered that her father was dead. Her eyes water and her lips tremble. "I don't know."

"Ask your mother if she knows."

Isabella doesn't translate my question. She gives me a hooded look.

Her mother glances back and forth, not understanding anything we've said.

"Ask her," I say, more firmly.

Isabella seems to gird herself up, then speaks in Spanish to her mother. Her mother gawps a bit, and then her face contorts and she yammers something out, voice cracking. Isabella winces and turns accusatory, tear-bright eyes on me.

"She wants to know if that's why you killed him," Isabella gnashes out. "For using the radio."

I glance at the woman, and see confusion somewhere in all that grief and anger. It, in turn, confuses me. I give Menendez a questioning look, but he nods, confirming that everything was translated correctly.

"Alright," I grunt, chopping a hand through the air. "Let's cut the bullshit, Isabella. You and I both know who that radio contacts, and if there are *Nuevas Fronteras* goons on the way, I need to know about it."

The mother picks two words out of all I said and starts repeating them with rising alarm: "*Nuevas Fronteras? Nuevas Fronteras?!*"

I scowl at the girl. "What are you not telling me, Isabella?"

She clenches her jaw several times, not meeting my gaze. Still shuddering.

"Hey!" I snap. "What are you not telling me?"

"She doesn't know!" Isabella suddenly yells at me. "She thinks..." she glances rapidly between me and her mother. Then she shakes her head violently and stands up. "No." She faces me. "Take me outside."

"What?"

"Take me outside and I'll tell you what you want to know. But leave her out of it. She doesn't know."

I realize for the first time that Isabella's English is nearly flawless. Almost no perceptible accent. And I wonder if she grew up in the States.

I consider her proposition for a moment. Then nod and turn to my guys. "Marty. EZ. Watch these folks. Dez, you're with me."

CHAPTER 4

Out of the house and into bright sunshine.

I keep my hand on Isabella's restraints, though it seems the fight has gone out of her. At least she's not stomping on my feet.

We take a few strides out into the middle of the dusty yard. Then I stop and turn Isabella around, instructing her to sit cross-legged on the ground. She looks like she's considering giving me some lip about it, but then folds and lowers herself to the ground.

Me and Menendez squat down in front of her.

"So..." I begin, scratching my beard. "Your dad is in with the *Nuevas Fronteras* cartel, but your mom doesn't know about it?"

More tears come to her eyes, but she doesn't sob or blubber. They drip down and leave more inky streaks down her face.

I shift my weight. "Isabella, if you're trying to stall for time—"

She shoots me a look. "He wasn't my dad."

I blink. Okay. "Who was he to you?"

She scrunches her face, as though the question is hard to answer. "My uncle. And…I guess…step-dad, or something?"

I frown, not entirely understanding.

"My real dad died. Then we came to live with my uncle. And my mom and him…I think they started sleeping together, so…he was kind of my step-dad too."

I shake my head as though to clear it. This is a rabbit trail I don't really give a shit about. "Let's get back on track. Who's coming?"

"No one's coming. And yes, my uncle worked for *Nuevas Fronteras*, and my mom doesn't know about it."

"How do you know that no one's coming?"

Her eyes go far away again. "Because I reached him right after you…you…" she seemed unable to finish the thought. "And then I had the radio in my hands for the next few minutes. No one ever said anything over the radio." Her eyes flick to me, but still have a hollowness to them. "If he'd been talking with someone…they would've tried to talk back. Right? They would've said something while I was holding the radio. Right?"

I exchange a look with Menendez. We both stand up and take a step away from the girl. I keep an eye on her, but lean into Menendez and whisper: "Branch said he took the shot right when the guy brought the radio up to his mouth. He may have touched off the PTT, but he didn't get to say much, if anything."

"She could be lying," Menendez whispers back.

That's a distinct possibility. And it brings to mind another question.

"Isabella," I ask her. "How do you know that your uncle worked for the cartel, but your mom has no idea about it?"

She lets out a bitter scoff. "He thought he was keeping it a secret from all of us. But I pay attention."

"What does he do for the cartel?"

She bobs her shoulders. "Fixes their vehicles. Sometimes they take their vehicles here, and he fixes them in his shop. Sometimes he goes to them."

"So, cartel guys regularly come around here to have their vehicles fixed, and your mom never put two and two together?"

Isabella's eyes narrow. "She doesn't pay attention like I do. It's not like they wear a uniform, you know. But I know who they are." Again, her eyes get distant. "The way they walk. The way they talk. They way they get whatever they want. And the way my uncle was obviously scared of them. Definitely cartel."

"Alright." I allow her logic with a nod. "You say he went to them sometimes. They have a compound near here or something?"

"There's a big settlement," she answers. "Maybe fifteen or twenty miles south of here. It's not all cartel, but they run the place."

"Is that who he tried to reach on the radio?"

She nods.

I do the math in my head and turn to look at Menendez. "Fifteen miles away. If they sent a QRF, it'd take 'em as many minutes to get here."

Menendez squints towards the south. "Should've already been here, then."

"I told you," Isabella interjects. "No one's coming."

Menendez jabbers something irritable-sounding in Spanish, and then reverts to English. "They show up, how's about I cap you first for lying? That sound fair to you?"

She blanches a bit, and swallows hard. Then she juts her chin up at us. "Well, that's fair. 'Cause I already told you no one's coming."

Menendez glares at her for another beat, then smiles, though it's not particularly kind. "Where'd you learn to speak English so well?"

She sucks her teeth—a thoroughly teenager-ish sound. "Same place as you—America."

"You grew up there?"

"Yeah. And then we got deported. About a year before the plague and everything."

I refocus us on the matter at hand. "And you're willing to risk your life, and the life of your mom, and your brother and your sister, on the fact that the cartel ain't gonna show up here?"

Her head sags. "Yes. For God's sake. No one. Is coming."

I chew on that for a second. I think she's telling the truth.

Me and Menendez huddle again.

"You wanna pull Branch and Lucky in?" he asks.

I shake my head. "Not yet. But even if she's telling the truth..." I bare my teeth. "We got bigger issues."

Menendez picks up on my vibe and heaves a breath, shaking his head at the ground. "Shit, Abe. It's not like I wanted it to go this way, but..." he drops to a whisper. "Our team and that family can't *both* walk away from this. You know that, right?"

I can't help but grimace. "Now, hang on there, Dez. I understand what you're saying, but can we give this a few minutes of thought before we up and cut their throats?"

Despite our voices being lowered, Isabella overhears.

"Wait! Are you talking about killing all of us?" She sounds more offended than frightened. But that changes quick. "You can't do that! You told us you wouldn't! You said—"

Menendez points his pistol at her. "Don't make a handful of yourself, *muchacha*. It'll just make the decision that much easier for us."

She winces and quiets, but her breathing has gotten quick now, and I can hear little words on the exhales: "Please. Don't."

I don't *want* to. But we are in a mighty shit sandwich right now.

"Alright," Menendez says to me. "Go ahead. You got some great solution I can't see? Lay it on me. Because all I see from where I'm standing is this: The second we leave, they're gonna tell the cartel we're out here and the whole mission is boned."

"We won't!" Isabella hisses. "I swear it! We won't tell anyone!"

"Yeah, well, obviously we can't take your word on that," Menendez snaps.

"Destroy the radio, then!" she says. "Blow it up or something, I don't care. Or take it with you. It doesn't matter. But how else are we gonna tell them anything?"

"How about when they show up to get their oil changed or some shit?" I point out. "Isabella, I know you're scared, but you're talking out of your ass. Ain't no way in hell we're just gonna take y'all's word for something like this, and you know that. Now, you got a reasonable solution for us, I'm all ears, but I promise you, if you open your mouth with some dumb shit again, I'm gonna gag you and put you inside and have this conversation anyways."

That's probably what I should've done from the start. Not sure why I decided to have this conversation in front of her.

Maybe because I know it would've been easier for me to cave to Menendez's recommendation if I didn't have her sitting there in the corner of my vision.

Menendez gives me an expectant look. "I'm all ears too, Boss. But while you were out tidying up this mess, I already went down every possibility, and they all loop back to the same fact: We let these folks go, you might as well scrub the whole mission. It's simple math, Abe: One family, or seven. Sucks balls, but there it is. We knew this was a risk. You already know what we gotta do. Now you're just wasting time."

I swear, smearing a sweaty palm over my face. "Alright. I hear you, Dez. But at least gimme a minute to think about it."

Menendez huffs impatiently. "Fine."

I glower. "Hey! If I need to take an extra minute to make sure we're not leaving a viable option on the table before we go off and do some shit like this, then I'll take that time, Dez!"

"I said 'fine'!" he snaps back.

"You that eager to get their blood on your hands?"

"I said 'fine'!" he repeats, raising hands in surrender, one still holding his pistol. "Christ. You want me to smile and give you a back rub or something?"

"I want you to act like it's a little more serious than swatting a fly."

He glares back at me. "I'm sorry. Next time I come to an inevitable conclusion, I'll make sure to wring my hands and look real sad about it so we can all feel better about ourselves."

"Alright, just shut up. Now you're being petulant."

Menendez squints off to the south again, shaking his head. "Right," he mutters. "I'm the petulant one."

"What about a hostage?" the girl suddenly asks.

Menendez immediately whirls on her. "That's it. You're going inside."

I put a hand on his arm to halt him as the girl thrashes desperately to her knees, begging. "Please! Listen to me! I'm serious!"

"We can't take a hostage with us," Menendez growls, then looks at me, and realizes I'm considering the proposition. "Abe! We can't take a hostage with us!"

The girl rises to her feet. "Just listen! You can take me with you. I'll be your hostage. And—and I'm not just a hostage. I can pull my own weight. I know the people my uncle talked to. I can point them out to you." Her eyes jag between me and Menendez, but seem to focus more on me, probably because she knows I'm more on the fence than he is. "That's what you're here for right? You're fighting the cartel?"

I narrow my eyes at her. "What makes you think we're after the cartel?"

She blinks a few times. "You're, like, special ops, right? And you're American. And you know about *Nuevas Fronteras*. American special ops are always screwing around with the cartel and shit. Aren't they?"

"There is no 'American special ops' anymore," Menendez gripes, and he's right about that, but Isabella's definitely got our number. She's a quick thinker. I like that about her. Makes me want to kill her even less.

"You know them by sight?" I ask her. "You know their names?"

She nods. "Yes. Well...some of them."

Menendez looks at me, aghast. "You're not seriously considering this..."

"Would you let me do my due diligence?"

"We can't take a teenage girl on a fucking op with us!"

"Come on, Dez—you never had some local teenage kid embed with your team?"

He huffs again, not exactly conceding the point, but he knows I'm right. We all had combat time under our belts before the world went to shit, and the US military loves using the locals. We've all had some wide-eyed villager go on patrol with us to interpret and provide intel.

I look back to the girl. "This settlement that you were talking about—the one south of here that the cartel runs—you know who's in charge down there?"

I watch her face for signs of deception or hesitation, but I get nothing. She immediately nods in response to my question, and she seems sure of herself.

"Yes. His name's Angel. I can point him out to you."

I give Menendez an appraising look. To his credit, he's not so stubborn that he can't see the gift that's been plopped in our laps. It is, admittedly, not ideal. But nothing about this operation was ever going to be ideal. We hadn't anticipated dragging a teenage girl along with us, but then we also hadn't anticipated getting a shot at the cartel chain of command so quickly.

He's weighing her with fresh eyes now, running through the pros and cons of having her attached to us.

“There’s plenty of negatives to consider,” I say to him. “But here’s one big plus: We won’t have to merc an innocent family.”

He sighs, and in it, I can hear him giving way. He looks skyward. “Alright, Abe. Fine.” He looks at me. “But this is *your* decision. And when shit goes bad—which it will—it’ll be on *you*.”

I give him a look like he’s said something stupid. “It’s always been on me.”

I sit Isabella down at the kitchen table. We’ve switched out her restraints, so her hands are bound in front now.

“Marty,” I call into the living room. “Bring the mother in here. Leave the kids.”

Both the woman and her younger children whimper a bit when Marty pulls her off the couch and escorts her into the kitchen. Isabella looks ashen and nervous, and for just a moment, I almost feel bad for her. What a shitty day this has turned out to be for her.

Then I stop thinking about it.

Marty gets the woman to the table and pushes her down into a chair. She sits, stiff-backed, staring at her eldest daughter with tear-stained eyes.

Menendez stands between kitchen and living room, pistol tucked away, arms crossed over his chest. He made his reservations clear to me, but now that we’ve made a decision, he’s locked on and focused.

EZ's in the living room, leaning against a wall and making goofy faces at the young boy, trying to keep him distracted. His sister is not amused, but the boy just kind of stares with the ghost of a confused smile on his lips. Like he wants to laugh, but something in him hasn't lost sight of the danger he's in.

Mother and daughter at the kitchen table, neither speaking.

I flick a finger—daughter to mother. "Isabella, tell your mother you're going to be coming with us. Explain to her that if she betrays us to the cartel, she'll get you back in pieces. But if she keeps her mouth shut, we'll return you, unharmed."

Isabella swallows hard and starts translating in halting bursts of Spanish.

Marty slowly turns his head to look at me, eyes widening under beetled brows.

I meet his gaze, unflinching. "She's got intel on the cartel," I explain. "And we need a hostage."

Over in the living room, EZ is no longer making faces. Or at least, not making them at the young boy anymore. Now he's making one at me, and it seems to say, *you're fucking with me, right?*

Neither Marty nor EZ offer protest outside of their expressions.

Isabella finishes explaining things to her mother, which has gotten the woman all worked up again. They jabber back and forth a few times, then Isabella looks up at me.

"She wants to know...what does she tell them about my uncle, if the cartel comes asking for him?"

The woman sags in her chair, face wilting into the tabletop, sobbing and shuddering.

"You got infected around here, right?" I ask Isabella.

She looks briefly confused, until Menendez clarifies in Spanish: "*Los locos*."

Comprehension comes to Isabella. Then she nods.

I'd been wondering about that, as we hadn't seen any packs of primals since we left the refinery. But then, we are in a very warm region, in the middle of summer. The primals are probably smart enough to stay out of the sun during the heat of the day.

I wonder if primals in this region are more nocturnal than their northern relatives.

To Isabella, I say, "If the cartel comes sniffing around, she can tell them that he got taken by a pack of...*los locos*."

Isabella translates this.

The woman drags her head off the table and sits mute for a long time. Then she sniffles wetly and nods. Whispers something that sounds like a prayer.

"Does she understand everything she needs to do?" I ask, directing this question at both Isabella and Menendez. I get nods from both, then move around the table to Isabella. "Come with me. Where's your bedroom?"

Too stricken and numb now to do much but obey, Isabella just rises, hands still bound, and leads me off into the back of the house, by way of the single hallway. There are two bedrooms. Her parent's, and the one she shares with her two siblings.

Two twin mattresses, pressed together on the floor, blankets rumpled and tossed. I have an image in my mind of Isabella and her sister and her brother, all sleeping snugly together at night.

Isabella just stands in the middle of the room, not sure why we're there.

"You got a backpack? Or some sort of bag?"

She gives me an odd look. "No."

I sigh. Point to one of the smaller, thinner blankets on the mattresses. "Alright. Grab that blanket and lay it out. Where are your clothes?"

She lays the blanket out, then moves to a battered old dresser. I stop her before she can open a drawer. I yank each drawer open and riffle through the meager contents. Satisfied that there are no surprises, I step back.

"Don't worry about pants and shirts," I say. "Grab underwear and socks."

Slowly, almost embarrassed, she opens one of the drawers and begins grabbing panties, which she wads up tightly in her hands, as though she doesn't want me to see the form or fabric of them.

"How long will I be gone?" she asks, her voice hollow.

"Don't know. Just pack what you got. Throw it all in the blanket."

She clears out one whole drawer, which isn't all that much. These people don't have much. Best I can tell, she's got three pairs of underwear and as many socks. All of them look old and worse for wear. Holes in the toes of socks. Elastic underwear bands barely hanging on by a thread.

Once she's got it all piled in the blanket, I have her roll the thing up and knot the corners like a hobo's sack.

"This would be easier if I wasn't cuffed," she says as she works.

I ignore her. My attention has been drawn to a splash of color near the bedroom's single window. A rusted coat-hanger is perched on the sill, holding a hot-pink dress. The thing looks like it got taken out of a dumpster, or maybe liberated from a dead body, and then cleaned and patched up. There are torn sections that look inexpertly sewed. The hem of the dress is dark, as though soiled. There's a discolored patch on the hip that looks like it'd been some sort of stain that'd taken some elbow grease to get out.

Isabella stands there, looking at me, then looking at the dress.

"How old are you, Isabella?"

She hesitates, as though this is valuable information she's unsure about revealing. Then she averts her gaze. "Fifteen. Today."

I feel a tiny little note of sadness, somewhere in the center of me. I'd wondered why Isabella was wearing mascara. Now, with the dress hanging there, and the realization of her true age, I put the pieces together.

Isabella was turning fifteen today. Her *quinceañera.* She should've had a big party, family and friends celebrating her transition into womanhood. But none of that could happen nowadays, and so I see it all in flashes: One, dirt-poor family at the end of the world, trying to do the best they could. I see her mother, bartering who-knew-what to get her hands on a dress that wouldn't even have been fit for a second-hand store only a handful of years earlier. Then I imagine that woman unearthing the remnants of her own makeup, and some old acrylic nails, and dolling Isabella up for her big day.

And then we came along.

That's about the time I stop thinking about it.

"Well," I gruff, clearing my throat. "Happy birthday, then." I turn away from the dress that she would never wear. "Come on."

CHAPTER 5

WE'RE HEADING THROUGH A region of Mexico that seems dominated by abandoned ranchland. At the moment, we're trying to find some place to hole up for the night, but pickings are slim. We passed a small city a ways back, but abandoned urban areas are favorite nesting grounds for primals, so we decided to skip it and keep going.

When we spot the little defunct gas station, sitting on the side of a highway, all by itself, we can't pass it up.

"Hold up," I say, leaning forward to peer at the structure.

Menendez pulls the 4Runner to a stop. We've been threading our way along dirt roads that crisscross the flat landscape, not wanting to be on well-traveled roads where cartel patrols might spot us. We're now looking at a strip of blacktop, shimmering in the afternoon heat. The highway on which the gas station sits is cracked, and weeds have grown up between the pavement. There are clear tire tracks, though, where the weeds have been crushed by occasional passing vehicles.

But I wouldn't call it *well-traveled*.

And this gas station is probably the best we're going to get.

We're maybe four hundred yards from the gas station, and it *looks* abandoned, but there's no way to be sure until we get closer. It's a risk we're all willing to take. No one relishes the idea of sleeping in the 4Runner. There's barely enough room for us all to sit.

I turn to look into the back.

Isabella is squashed in the center of the back seat, between Lucky and Branch. She's still got her hands restrained and has been huffing and puffing about it for the last hour.

Marty and EZ are in the far back, sitting on our bundles of gear so that they have to hunch low, their heads touching the ceiling. Neither looks happy about their current circumstances.

"You recognize where we are?" I ask Isabella.

She seems surprised by the question, then furrows her brows and leans forward, peering around the landscape. Finally, she says, "I think so."

She doesn't sound too sure of herself.

I squint at her. "How far is this settlement you mentioned?"

She winces, as though the effort of recall is painful to her. "If this is the road I think it is, then...should just be a couple more miles south. I think this road leads straight into it. I think."

"She thinks," Marty grumbles from the back.

"Alright." I turn my attention to Menendez. "That gas station might be our best option for tonight. We can settle in and send a recon south to put eyes on the settlement."

Menendez glances at the dashboard clock, but it's wrong, so he checks his wristwatch instead. Frowns. "It's only fourteen-hundred."

"Yeah, and I'd like to get a full day's reconnaissance on the settlement before we attempt anything."

Menendez concedes with a nod.

"Branch and Lucky," I say, turning again to the back. "Go check out that gas station and radio us if it's all clear. We'll hold tight here."

"Got it," Branch says, and the two get out. Branch has stowed his big sniper rifle and is now armed with his short-barreled carbine. They close the doors behind them and head off towards the gas station at a trot.

"Isabella," I say, twisting to look at her again. "You've been to the settlement, right?"

She nods. "A couple of times."

"Most recently?"

She thinks about it for a second. "Earlier this year. Maybe a few months ago?"

That's good. Hopefully she'll remember some details.

"Place got a name?" I ask.

"They call it Pancho," she says. "It was a town called *General Francisco Villa*. I guess that's what it's still called, but everyone just calls it Pancho now."

Marty leans an elbow on the backrest behind Isabella. "Why they call it Pancho?"

Menendez turns to give his squadmate a sour glance. "Jesus, you hick. You live your whole life in Texas, and don't know shit about Mexicans?"

Marty looks put-upon. "Uh, yeah. Because I lived my whole life in *Texas*. Which is not Mexico."

Menendez sighs. "You ever heard of a guy named Pancho Villa?"

"Well…" Marty gazes thoughtfully at the ceiling. "I once ate at a Mexican restaurant called Pancho Villa's." He pronounces it like the [illegible]

"You're a paragon of multi-culturalism."

"I know. They had giant, fishbowl margaritas. They were really good."

"Yeah, well, Pancho Villa was a general in the Mexican Revolution. Real name Francisco Villa. Hence, a town named after him: *General Francisco Villa.*"

Marty and EZ exchange a bemused glance and titter quietly, as though to an inside joke.

Menendez frowns. "Tryna teach you some fucking history here. What's funny?"

"Say 'taco.'"

"Why?"

"Just say 'taco.'"

"*Taco*," Menendez says, but while Marty had said it like an American, Menendez says it like a native Spanish-speaker.

Marty and EZ giggle amongst themselves.

"Say 'enchilada,'" EZ puts in.

"*Enchilada*," Menendez snaps, again pronouncing it...well, I guess *correctly*. "What? What's so funny?"

"Now say 'hot dog,'" Marty says, barely restraining his mirth.

"Hot dog," Menendez says, sounding every bit the American.

Marty and EZ devolve into outright laughter.

Menendez looks stymied. "The fuck are you two on about?"

Getting ahold of himself, Marty explains: "Whenever you're talking normal, you sound like every other American. But as soon as you say some Mexican shit, you go full native."

"*Taco*," EZ says, over-affecting a Mexican accent. "*Enchilada*."

"You mean I pronounce shit *correctly*?" Menendez demands.

"No, it's cool," Marty laughs. "You're just trying to connect with your roots."

Menendez shakes his head and looks forward again. "You probably pronounce *pollo* like 'polo,' don't you, you ignorant fuck?"

"It's like how Italian-Americans can't just call it 'mozzarella' like everyone else. They gotta say it like *mootzarell*, to show off how Italian they are, even though they've never been to Italy."

Menendez spins back around. “Motherfucker, I was *born* in Mexico!”

Marty looks shocked. “What? You were born in Mexico?”

“Yes, shithead!”

“You’ve never mentioned that before.”

“Yes, I have!”

Marty gives him a suspicious squint. “Are you sure?”

Menendez gawks at him. “Am I…? Yeah, I’m pretty fuckin’ sure where I was born, you idiot.”

“Then why don’t you have a Mexican accent?”

“Because my family immigrated when I was six years old and I lost the accent.”

Marty and EZ give each other another sly look.

“Except when you wanna sound extra-Mexican,” EZ titters.

Menendez gives up. “Yeah, fuck me.” Then he puts on a thick, southern accent. “We’ll go eat at Pan-cho Vih-luz, and order the polo bur-eye-toe and say ‘grassy-ass’. You ignorant twats.”

The gas station is declared clear, and we move in, Menendez driving us up to the front, where Branch lurks in the dim interior, and Lucky stands outside, his boonie hat pulled low to shade his face.

“Valet service?” Lucky offers.

Menendez waves him off. "I'll have Marty do it. He's a racist asshole."

Lucky nods as though this is expected.

We unload our gear and our prisoner, and then Marty takes the keys and drives the Toyota around the back of the gas station and hides it in some brush there. Me and EZ maintain control of Isabella, though she's pretty cooperative at this point, and we take her into the abandoned convenience store.

It would've been a hole in the wall even before the world ended. Cramped aisles and a certain patina of dirt that's so ingrained, I know it was there even before all the windows got broken and everything inside looted through. There's literally nothing left on the shelves anymore. Not a stick of gum, nor a pint of motor oil.

Around the side of the front counter, there's a door that leads into a backroom. The latch is bent and twisted—looks like someone jacked the door open with a crowbar or something, and now the door won't stay closed. The backroom is a combination office and storage, with another door exiting out the back—this one still working, and latched.

It's a good place to bed down. Sheltered, out of the way, and with a back exit that gives us a straight shot to where the 4Runner is hidden. We deposit Isabella on one side of the room, and drop our gear bags on the other, as though the three strides of space will keep her from messing with our shit.

I stand over her and give her a stern look. “Tell me, Isabella. Do I need to zip-tie you to that pipe there, or can I trust you to be smart and not fuck around?”

She stares up at me from under her eyebrows. “I told you that I’d help you if you left my family alone. You left them alone. Now I’m going to help you.”

“So, you promise not to mess with our shit?”

Isabella tilts her head. “You promise to get me back to my family—alive?”

I can promise her no such thing. I know that, and I think she knows that too.

But I nod anyway. “I’ll do my absolute best.”

The half-promise only half-mollifies her. “Then I guess I’ll do my absolute best not to mess with your shit.”

I smile. “I guess that’s fair.”

Still, I leave EZ posted in the door to the backroom while I make the rest of our arrangements.

I send Lucky and Branch to scout south and see if they can put eyes on the settlement of Pancho and set up a hide from which we can recon the objective. I post Marty on the roof with his M249, then me and Menendez make our way back to the combination office and storeroom.

On the wall, there’s an old whiteboard, maybe three feet by three feet. It’s filled with blue writing in Spanish, and the smudgy ghosts of previous notes inadequately erased. The ink is dry-erase, but it’s been sitting there so long it takes a bit of spit-polishing to clear off, and even then, the board is smeared in blue.

One blue marker. A bit dried out, but still usable. I take the whiteboard off the wall, clear the surface of the small desk, and set it down. Then I turn and motion for Isabella to join me and Menendez.

She seems puzzled, but rises from the floor and comes hesitantly to stand between me and Menendez. She draws back a bit when I unsheathe my fixed-blade knife. I take her wrist. Her arms are tense and rigid.

"Relax," I tell her, then slide the blade between her skin and the plastic band. She hisses when I apply pressure, the knife's point digging into her flesh a bit. But then the zip-cuff pops and her hands are free.

I sheath my knife, put the marker in her fingers, then point to the whiteboard.

"I want you to draw out a map of Pancho, as best you can recall. Doesn't have to be perfectly detailed, but I want to know entrances, exits, main roads, anywhere there's guards or watchtowers, and where the cartel congregate. Can you do that?"

She twiddles the marker in her hands for a moment, biting her lower lip. Then she uncaps it. Leans over the whiteboard. And begins to draw.

"This is the main road in," she says. "Main gate. It's guarded—usually two guys on either side of the gate with machine guns..."

CHAPTER 6

Isabella let's out an irritable huff as she pulls away from the spotting scope and stretches a kink out of her neck. "It's getting dark."

"Yup," Branch says, not looking up from his scope. "So you best keep looking before we lose the light."

She glares at him and, somewhat theatrically, massages her neck. "I been staring through this thing for three hours."

Branch doesn't deign to respond.

I'm sitting cross-legged, just to Isabella's left. We're in the hide that Branch and Lucky set up for us. It's a cozy little lookout in a stand of brush, maybe a mile out from the front gates of Pancho. Unfortunately, the terrain is so flat that the front gates are about all that we can see from here.

"This is stupid," Isabella continues. "Angel's not going to randomly come to the front gate. We're wasting time."

"No, we're not," I say.

She turns to face me, all teenage irritation.

Branch stays in his riflescope. On the other side of him, Lucky is also seated cross-legged, watching me with a bemused look. Like he's thinking I'm getting what I deserve for pulling a fifteen-year-old girl into our op.

I refocus on Isabella. "We only got about forty-five minutes until full dark. Can you just stick it out for another forty-five minutes?"

"My neck hurts."

I nod. "Can you handle it for another forty-five minutes?"

She rolls her eyes and huffs again, but settles back into the spotting scope.

After about ten seconds, she grumbles, "And he's still not there."

"Keep looking."

"I *am* looking."

"Ssh."

We're trying to get a positive ID on this Angel guy that Isabella claims runs the cartel out of Pancho. She gave me and Menendez a physical description back at the convenience store, but it was pretty generic: Medium height, medium build, mid-thirties-ish. Shaved head. Goatee.

That describes about half of the people we've seen milling around the front of Pancho. All of which Branch pointed out to Isabella, only to be told, "That's not him."

She's probably right—if Angel is the man in charge, he likely won't be hanging around the front gate with his foot soldiers. He'll be holding court back in his clubhouse, which Isabella claims is situated right smack dab in the middle of the settlement.

I'd really hoped that Branch and Lucky would be able to find some random hill to give us some elevation and a better view into the settlement, but it simply was not to be. We're in the coastal plains, and it's flat as fuck around here. Pancho is a grid of houses and businesses that's just plopped down in the middle of those flatlands, with nothing else around it. No water towers. No cell towers. No other nearby structures where we could've spied on them from the roof. In fact, every structure inside Pancho is single-story, and save for the handful of them visible just behind the gates, the rest are hidden by trees.

I don't know whether the cartel intended for Pancho to be impossible to recon, but it's definitely working in their favor.

We endure the last forty-five minutes of failing daylight in silence.

No joy. No pronouncement of "There he is!" from Isabella.

Eventually she pulls back from the spotting scope and hangs her head so it's practically touching the ground. "It's too dark. I can't see anymore."

I let out a small, disappointed sigh. "Alright. Let's call it. Branch, do me a favor and leave the rifle."

He finally turns away from his riflescope and gives me a look like I just asked to fuck his wife.

"I'll take care of her," I say, defensively. Then grin. "I'll treat her real nice. Promise."

"The right of *prima nocte*," Lucky says, in a passable imitation of Longshanks from the movie *Braveheart*. "'Tis a lord's privilege."

"Cheekrest better not smell like your face," Branch gripes as he sits back on his haunches and grabs his daypack and carbine.

I open my mouth to tell him it'll smell like my balls—the comment is almost reflexive—but then I remember Isabella crouching right there next to me, and close my mouth again. This strikes me as odd. I'm not accustomed to the feeling of impropriety.

Instead, I keep it professional: "Branch, escort Isabella back to our hideout. Lucky, you'll stay with me. Branch, when you get back, send Dez up to relieve Lucky." I touch the side of my wristwatch to illuminate the face. It's 2050. "Dez and I will take first watch until midnight, and try to figure out how we're going to proceed."

Branch nods and he and Isabella move to exit our hidey hole.

I reach out and touch Isabella's ankle to stop her.

She turns and looks at me, her expression inscrutable in the dark.

"Don't try to run from Branch. He's fast. I guarantee you he'll catch you. And then things won't be so nice for you."

Hard to say, but I'm pretty sure I see the darkness around her eyes deepen as she frowns. "First of all, none of this has been *nice*," she spits. "Second of all, I already told you: I'm not gonna try anything. So you can stop threatening me."

I let go of her ankle. "Just making sure we're clear," I say, a bit lamely.

"Yeah, we're clear," she snarls, then turns and disappears into the gloom, Branch following close on her heels.

I stare into the darkness where they disappeared, listening to the quiet rustle of their movements as they fade into the night.

"Fuckin' teenagers," I grumble, shuffling about to orient myself with Branch's beloved rifle.

Taking advantage of the vacated space, Lucky stretches his legs out. "Yeah. So...I gotta ask, man...why'd you decide to bring her along with us?"

I settle in behind the rifle. "Come on, Lucky." I give him a side-eye. "I already told you why. What do you want from me?"

"Right," Lucky says. "She's got intel on the cartel and shit. I remember."

There's a long, pregnant silence.

"Or, you just didn't want to have to kill the family."

I shift, suddenly put off. "You tellin' me you would've been cool with that?"

"No, that's not what I'm saying," he replies, evenly. "I wouldn't have been *cool* with it."

"But you still think it was the better option?"

He doesn't respond, so I guess he's mulling that over. Frowning to myself, I smush my face down over the cheekrest and look through the scope. It's full dark, but the scope lets a lot of light in, and there's a decent moon tonight. I can't really make out faces, but I can at least see movement, and that's all I'm really concerned with at the moment—making sure Pancho doesn't send some random patrol right up our asses.

"I wouldn't have liked it if we had to merc that family," Lucky finally says. "But it would've been the smart thing to do."

"Then we wouldn't have the intel we have. We'd still be at square one, trying to find a cartel boss to snag. Now we have a target, and we have his location, and we have an asset that can positively ID him for us. So, no, it *wouldn't* have been the smartest thing."

"Come on, Abe," he says, like he's trying to get me to admit I'm lying.

I twist to look at him. "Why are you busting my balls right now?"

"I'm not busting your balls. I'm asking a legitimate question."

"You haven't asked a question. You just said a bunch of bullshit."

"Alright. Here's my question, then..." I hear Lucky shift, and his voice draws closer, leaning towards me. "You gone soft, Abe?"

It's the strangest thing. My face flushes and my scalp prickles and my heart starts thudding. I'm so surprised by this physiological reaction that I don't immediately answer. It takes me a second or two to realize that what I'm feeling is shame.

Shame...because I *didn't* execute an entire family.

Isn't that a bitch?

I don't know how else to defend myself except to go on the attack. "You wanna kill the bitch that bad, huh? Would that make you feel better? Is that what you want? You wanna cut her throat, backtrack to her ranch, and gun her family down? Would that make you feel all cozy and secure? What do you want right now, Lucky? Or are you just whining?"

"You know what I want?" Lucky says, his tone still level, not rising to match my anger. He speaks earnestly. "I want you to tell me this was a strategic decision, and not an emotional one. That's what I want. I want to know my team lead is still using his head, and not just putting us all at risk to assuage his own conscience."

Maybe it's the genuine pleading I hear in Lucky's voice, but I find my anger at the man fading rapidly. So when I speak again, I've matched his calmer tone.

"Yes, Lucky," I say. "I made the decision I made because it seemed like the option that would give this mission the best chance at success. Anyone can Monday-morning quarterback any decision that's ever been made, but those were the facts that I saw at the moment I made up my mind: I saw an opportunity for some real-time intel, in a country where we know jack-shit."

For a long moment, me and Lucky just stare at each other.

Then, finally, he nods. "Alright. Thanks. I feel better now."

I chuff disdainfully and shake my head. Then I get back behind the rifle, knowing full well that I just lied my ass off.

"Options are extremely limited," I tell Menendez.

It's almost 2200 hours now. Lucky has gone back to the gas station. It's just me and Menendez in the lookout now. And I'm trying to stay focused, but my mind keeps wandering, keeps doubting the wisdom of leaving Isabella at the convenience store with the others.

Maybe I should've stayed with her.

I don't think any of the guys would straight-up murder her in cold blood.

And since when did the life of one girl mean more to me than the mission?

Focus on the task at hand.

"We're not gonna get a good sense of the place from here, and Isabella was unable to identify this Angel character we're looking to nab." I sigh and rub my eyes, letting my head hang next to the rifle's buttstock to give my neck a rest for a moment. "Which means we got two options, as I see it. Option One—we infiltrate Pancho in the wee hours, find the cartel clubhouse, and try to snatch Angel and get him out of the settlement. Option Two—we wait for daylight and try to make contact using our cover stories, and hope they let us in."

Menendez looks grossed-out. "I don't like either of those options."

"Me neither," I admit.

"Option One is a definite no-go. We can't just infiltrate blind, with no idea of where guards and patrols are. There's zero chance of it not turning into a gunfight. I don't like it."

"Yeah," I concur.

"Option Two might work. But how long is it gonna take for us to ingratiate ourselves with the locals to the point that we get a shot at Angel? Days? Weeks? Lot can go wrong in that amount of time. Plus, it's time we can't afford to waste."

Yeah, he's pretty much reached all the same conclusions I came to.

I scratch vigorously at my beard, making a hesitant, thoughtful noise.

Menendez seems to perk up at literally any other option I might be thinking of. "What? You got something else?"

"Well..." I don't like it. In fact, I'd dismissed it out of hand earlier when I'd been racking my brain for the best way to go about this. "I'm reconsidering something. I didn't think it had much chance of success, but now that we've articulated the abject shittiness of our other options, it doesn't seem as bad as it did at first. Plus, it's much less risky for us."

"I already like it better. What is it?"

I look at the ink-blot of Menendez's shadowed face. "It's gonna require a lot of trust in Isabella."

CHAPTER 7

It's 0800 hours, and I'm groggy as hell. Didn't sleep much the night before. I don't feel great about what I've forced Isabella into. There's a lot of ways it could go wrong. If it does go wrong, me and the guys will probably be fine. We'll walk away.

Isabella won't. She'll be fucked.

If I were a normal person, I'd feel very guilty about that.

But...

But you're a black-hearted devil, remember?

And then I tell myself the oft-repeated refrain of the morally bankrupt: *Desperate times call for desperate measures.*

"Guards have clocked her," Branch says over the comms. He's over in the lookout with Lucky, watching as Isabella approaches the front gate of Pancho on foot. "They seem pretty relaxed about it. No obvious aggression."

Me, Menendez, Marty, and EZ are set up on the road, a few miles north of the gas station we slept in last night. We're hunkered down in a stand of trees, maybe fifty yards from the road.

All the guys have their earpieces in. They've been hearing Branch's updates.

I look, and see that their eyes are pinned on the horizon, in the direction of Pancho. Lips tight. Not nervous, per se, but...concerned.

I know that it has nothing to do with Isabella's safety.

We had a nice long conversation about it all last night. And when I say "nice" I mean "contentious," and when I say "conversation" I mean "argument."

One thing I miss about the old top-down military before the world ended? Being able to lay out a battle plan without every [illegible] feeling the need to voice their reservations. Nowadays, while I nominally outrank them, everyone knows that rank and chain of command is dead. Which leads to things like Marty and EZ—both corporals, officially—arguing with me—a fucking major—about my decision-making process.

"She's reached the front gate," Branch continues his narration. "Two of the guards are coming out to talk to her. No brandished weapons. Everything seems pretty calm and casual."

Finally, EZ breaks his silence and blows out a pent-up breath, giving me a severe look. "Man, I hope she don't bone us."

"Yeah," I grunt. "Me too."

Right about now, Isabella *should* be telling the guards at the front gate that she's the niece of the guy that fixes their vehicles, and that she desperately needs Angel's help, because her uncle is deathly ill.

Of course, she *could* just tell them that she's been taken hostage by a small group of Americans, and send the cartel after us. Because of this possibility—which was where all the contentious arguing came from—I was forced to tell Isabella that, if she betrayed us, we would go back and murder her family.

Given all the shaking and crying she did, I think she believed me.

"So far, everything looks good," Branch says, though his voice is still highly circumspect about the whole thing. "They're taking her in."

I key my comms. "We copy. Give it five minutes, and then move to your secondary position."

Branch acknowledges, and the comms go silent.

I figure if we don't see an aggressive response coming out of Pancho within five minutes, then Isabella *probably* hasn't screwed us over. Those five minutes pass in an agony of tension and impatience. Everything teetering on a knife edge, and none of us knowing which way it's going to fall.

That's what the guys are mainly concerned with, but that's the least of my worries. If Pancho suddenly erupts with vanloads of armed cartel soldiers, we'll be gone before they even get close. We'll disappear, and only suffer the minor setback of losing our source of local intel and having to find another lead.

But I don't think Isabella's going to do us like that. I watched her real hard when I explained what she needed to do. I trust my instincts with people. I'm not infallible, nor am I a mind-reader, but I'm right more often than I'm not. And my gut told me she was going to do what I asked of her.

What I *am* worried about is whether or not Angel will respond like I want him to. Will he come out himself? Or will he simply send someone else?

And even more than all that, I'm worried about the takedown itself.

Generally speaking, ambushing a vehicle is not a technique you use if you want to take someone alive. And, assuming Angel comes out personally, like I'm hoping, that means we'll have to avoid putting bullets in both him *and* Isabella.

So, yeah, there's about a dozen ways this could go horribly wrong.

The five minutes creep by so slow, I'm almost surprised when Branch transmits again: "All quiet at the front gate. We're moving to our secondary position."

"Copy," I say, then stand up and motion to the others. "Get in position."

The four of us spread out through the trees, keeping about twenty yards between us. Menendez is on the far left, closest to Pancho and the target vehicle we hope will be coming out soon. Next is Marty with his M249—our "most casualty-producing weapon"—followed by myself, and then EZ on the far right.

Then we settle in to wait some more. An empty spate of time that allows my brain to start picking at every loose thread in the plan. Will Angel come out? How many guys will he take with him? Will they be on high-alert, or will they be relaxed, allowing the ambush to take them by surprise?

Did I calculate the right amount of C4 necessary to crater the road? Will concrete shrapnel from the blast hit any of my guys? Will Branch's .338 Lapua Magnum round really be enough to disable an engine block? He assures me it will, but I've personally never used anything but a .50-cal to do that job.

Did I put us far enough away from Pancho that they won't hear the gunshots—or the explosion?

I do a lot of deep breathing as I wait. Run through every permutation of failure, wondering if I've done enough, and then, knowing I can't do anymore, I force myself just to think of the target. That's all that really matters. We just need Angel.

Get him, and get out. Everything else is just details.

Which, I'm told, is where the devil lives.

Almost forty-five minutes in, Branch sends out another transmission: "One vehicle spotted." By now, he's made it over to his secondary position, which covers our killbox, but also gives him a decent view of the road north of Pancho. "Faded blue panel-van."

"Fuck my life," I whisper. A panel van was possibly the worst vehicle our target could have chosen—with no windows in the back, we have no idea how many guys are packed in there.

The better part of a minute passes before the vehicle draws close enough for Branch to give us more details. "Two front-seat occupants. Both males. Neither matches the target description. No visual on the girl. They're about three minutes out from you."

"Copy—target's three minutes out," I reply, then clench my teeth, thinking furiously.

One hundred eighty seconds to make a life or death decision.

The plan had been for Isabella to get herself next to a window so we could ID her, and, if possible, open it and hang her arm out to signal whether Angel was in the vehicle or not.

Obviously, none of that's going to happen now. We don't know who's in the back of that van.

One of the hardest parts of being a successful operator is knowing when to be cautious, and when to dare greatly. Caution keeps you alive. But he who dares wins.

"We doing this thing, Boss?" Menendez hisses over the comms.

Fuck it. Fortune favors the bold.

"We're a go," I transmit. "Hose the driver and front passenger, but watch your angles—we do *not* want to penetrate into the back of the van. After the takedown, Marty and EZ will pull security. Dez, you and I will move to the rear of the vehicle and handle whoever's in the back. We do *not* have positive ID on the target, so keep your eyes open for anyone matching that description, and try not to put holes in them."

I get a series of affirmatives.

I squish myself up nice and tight with the trunk of a decent-sized tree. I've got a clear lane of fire into the killbox.

"Charge is primed and ready," Menendez transmits. "It's on you, Branch."

"Copy," Branch says, his voice blank with concentration. "Less than two minutes out. Standby for my shot."

The radio goes silent, as though all six of us have drawn a breath and held it. Around me, the sounds of birds twittering and flitting through the brush. Unseen insects keen and chitter. Mosquitos the size of wasps encircle me and start to encroach. One lands on my exposed wrist, nestles into my arm hair, and sticks its mouthpiece into me. I ignore it.

ID the target. Take him alive. Exfil the area.

Faintly, the growl of an approaching engine.

They probably have plenty of gas, don't they? They're *Nuevas Fronteras*, after all. Gas is kind of their thing. Will we have time to drain the van's tank?

Probably not.

ID the target. Take him—

"Visual," Menendez transmits.

I inhale, then press it out slow, settling in behind my rifle's optic.

The sound of the engine grows louder.

A glimmer of sunlight across a windshield.

There it is—old panel van with a faded blue paintjob.

The glare of sunlight clears from the windshield and I see the shadowy shapes of two figures in the front seats.

I click my select-fire over to semi-auto.

Everything happens in rapid succession.

Dust and spall erupts from the hood of the van, followed by the sound of a heavy projectile punching through sheet metal and gouging into the engine's internal workings.

The van swerves.

The road fifty yards ahead of it bursts like a volcano, blotting out my view of the van with a gray-black cloud of smoke and debris. I hear chunks of concrete pepper the woods like bullets, then the distinct *crunch* of the van slamming into the crater Menendez just blew in the road.

I still can't see shit, but apparently Marty does, because he opens up with his M249 in a long, sustained burst. Dimly, I see the glint of sparks as his automatic rounds rake the tires and wheels. Someone else is firing rapid semi-auto shots, but I can't tell who.

The dust clears enough that I see the shape of the van, askew and smoking in the crater. It feels really weird not to be shooting during a vehicle ambush, but I don't have a clear sight picture, and I'm not just going to spray when there are two people in the van that I don't want to kill.

I jolt to my feet, keeping my rifle trained on the van. The second the SAW goes quiet, I'm running. Marty transmits a heartbeat later: "Front occupants are down—move!"

I register the sound of EZ thrashing through the brush behind me, while Marty and Menendez burst out of the trees ahead, Marty angling for the front of the vehicle and Menendez heading for the back.

I close within ten yards of the van. The windshield is shockingly intact, but the doors are shredded—Marty was broadside to them and filled the cabin with nearly half a belt of ammunition. Still, as I reach the front passenger side of the vehicle, I take a quick check through the shattered window, ready to put anyone down that's still moving.

The front seat passenger and driver won't be getting up. Their bits are splattered all over the interior.

I catch a shadow of movement from the back of the van, but I'm already past the front door, heading for the rear. I slam my buttstock into the side of the van as a distraction and shout, "Hands up! Don't move!"

Then I'm next to the rear quarter panel, with Menendez to my left.

The rear door suddenly swings open. Someone shouts something in Spanish. Menendez leans for a sight picture. Then there's the snap of a supersonic round, and whoever was trying to get out of the van crumples to the concrete, their head hollowed out by Branch's shot.

Someone starts screaming, and it takes me half a second to realize it's a girl.

Menendez hits the rear of the van first, going wide around the open door.

Gunshots thump from inside the van and I see Menendez jerk.

I kick the rear door hard as I reach the back of the van, sending it swinging closed. I follow its arc, but it hits something before it can latch closed, and rebounds, swinging back open. I see two shapes crouching on the passenger-side wheel well. All I can tell is that they're both men, and neither has a shaved head. So I pump rounds into them as I cross to the rear-left side of the van, and I don't let up until I see them slump.

Out of the corner of my eye, I catch Menendez staggering sideways towards the rear-right, swearing up a storm, but he's got his rifle up and is clearly still in the fight. The van has double doors in the rear, and the right door is open, while the left one is still latched. I can't see what's beyond the latched door, but Menendez's angle lets him spot something and he shouts, "Don't you fucking—!"

Then he fires. Just once.

Another female shriek.

I lunge forward and rip the left door open.

The first thing I see is Isabella's face, speckled with blood, her eyes wide and mouth open, screaming.

Then I see the man directly behind her.

A man with a shaved head.

I jolt forward, using my support hand to hurl Isabella to the side. She goes sprawling into the two dead guys on the right side of the van.

I've got a clear shot on the guy that'd been behind her.

Shaved head. Goatee.

Our target—Angel.

I think he's grinning, but then realize it's a grimace of pain. He's got a bullet hole in his left shoulder, courtesy of Menendez. He's also got a black pistol in his right hand, and it's coming up, but it seems like he's momentarily stymied by whether to shoot at Menendez, or me.

That hesitation costs him.

I seize his gun hand by the wrist, torquing it violently to the side. In the same motion, I haul backwards, pivoting my hips with everything they have.

The pistol goes off, the bullet striking harmlessly into road, and the man comes flying out with a whoop. I don't let go of his wrist. He hits the concrete face-first, and I immediately drop my knee onto his gun arm. His hand spasms with the impact and I strip the pistol easily from his hand, then use it to clobber him in the side of the head—just to keep him from thinking too much. Then I hurl the thing into the brush on the side of the road.

Menendez slides in beside me, covering my exposed rear, still shouting in Spanish.

Angel—well, I've messed him up pretty good. The concrete took the skin off the left side of his face, along with a bit of his nose, and the pistol-whip opened a nice gash on his right temple. Blood rapidly begins sheeting into his dull, senseless eyes.

I clamp a hand on the back of his neck and smush his face into the road, then take that slim moment to glance behind me and see how much shit I'm in.

What I see is Menendez's ass, right in my face. Blood is seeping through his pants on the left side. Beyond him, I see Isabella thrashing as though in the middle of a seizure, trying to get out of the tangle of dead limbs I sprawled her in.

There's no one else in the vehicle.

"Isabella!" Menendez shouts at her. "Get out of the van!" Then he touches off his comms. "Van's clear! Get ready to exfil!"

I swing back to Angel. He's starting to come around a bit, and I feel his body stiffen beneath me. I sling my rifle and use both my hands to grapple his arms behind his back.

The guy lets out a slurry of loose syllables that I don't think would've made sense even if I spoke his language.

I keep his wrists pinned to the small of his back and growl down at him, "Hey, you ever been skull-fucked by a five-five-six?" I like to throw out random, insane-sounding threats. I've come to find that people are more compliant if they think you're mentally deranged.

I guess Angel speaks English because he goes limp.

"Menendez!" I call. "Restraints!"

Isabella finally manages to unlimber herself from the dead bodies and comes tumbling out of the van. The second she gets her feet on the pavement, she starts running.

"Isabella!" I yell at her, snatching her wrist as she passes.

She twirls like a sprinting dog hitting the end of its chain, then staggers and comes to a stop.

I let go of her wrist and hold eye contact with her. "It's over. Take a breath."

It's like she needed the reminder. I see her chest inflate. Her knees buckle and she drops into a tight, low squat, hands over her face.

"Hey. Hey, you with me?"

She blinks a few times. Then nods.

I jerk my head at the man I have pinned to the ground. "Is this the guy? Is this Angel?"

She nods again.

Well, halle-fuckin'-lujah.

"Alright, stay right there," I tell her, then swing back around to face the van.

Marty and EZ have reached the front doors now. They yank them open and drag the dead bodies out, then set to looting the corpses of anything of value. We need to make it look like raiders hit this van. Anything to obfuscate our trail.

Lucky's voice comes over the comms, breathless and shaking as he runs: "Lucky and Branch are on our way to the rally point."

"Copy that," I respond. "Give us two minutes, and we'll be enroute." I release the PTT and snap my fingers at Menendez. "Yo, I still need those zip-cuffs!"

"I know, I know," he says, finally managing to get the zip-cuff freed from where he had it threaded through the MOLLE straps of his armor. His hands are shaking bad. He starts to bend to put them on Angel's wrists, but then jerks upright again as a spasm of pain crosses his face. He hands the zip-cuff to me instead.

I loop it around Angel's wrists and cinch it tight—putting a little extra into it, because fuck this guy. Once I have him secure, I start patting him down for any other weapons, but my eyes stay on Menendez.

"How you doin' there, Buddy?" I ask him.

He bares his teeth and leans to one side, looking down at his left hip. Looks like the round hit him just beneath his armor. He makes a few pissed-off noises as he probes the area. "Just meat," he concludes. "Through and through. I'll live."

He totters backwards until his ass hits the bumper, then yanks his IFAK open and starts patching himself, muttering curses the whole time.

There are no more weapons on Angel's person. Still, I keep my knee in his back. Take a glance behind me to make sure Isabella hasn't run off on us. She's still squatting there, watching me work with eyes gone blank and glassy.

"You're a fucking dead man," a heavily-accented voice growls from beneath me.

In response, I reach around to the front of his face, hook my fingers into his nostrils, and yank his head back until he cries out. "Keep talkin' and I'll rip it off."

Marty and EZ have finished looting the driver and front seat passenger. They hustle to the back of the van and pull the two dead bodies out to flop on the concrete next to Angel.

"Marty," I call. "You good?"

He doesn't even look up from rifling through their pockets. "Ammo's good. I'm good."

"EZ?"

"Four mags and some change. Good to go."

I don't need to ask Dez. I can see his ammo situation is fine, and I already know he's got a hole in his side.

I hear a gagging noise and realize I've still got Angel's head all jacked up by the nostrils. I let him go. He doesn't speak.

To Menendez, I say, "You good to take point?"

Menendez finishes securing an Israeli bandage around his waist, then zips up his IFAK and stands, hefting his rifle and swapping out for a full mag. "Yeah, I got it."

I decide to refresh my own mag. "EZ, you're with me and the target. Marty, take rear guard. Isabella?"

She doesn't stir.

"Isabella."

Her eyes flick to mine.

"Stand up and come here."

She does so. Slowly. It makes me a little impatient, but I'm trying to cut her some slack. This might just be another day in the office for me, but for her, it's a waking nightmare.

"I want you to stay on Dez's ass. You got that?"

She nods.

"Can you talk to me, Isabella? Use your words?"

She seems to choke on them for a second or two. Then: "Yeah. I got it."

"Alright," Marty announces, zipping up the daypack where he's stowed whatever he looted. "We're done here."

I stand up, and EZ helps me pull Angel to his feet.

The guy immediately spits blood into my face.

My first instinct is to give him a strong right hook that he'll have no chance of blocking. But I don't want to knock him out. Then I'd have to carry him. So I just smile back in a way that I hope conveys the sentiment that there will be consequences—when it's convenient for me.

Instead of beating his head in, I key my comms. "Target is secure. Extracting to rally point." Then I nod at Menendez. "Let's move."

CHAPTER 8

"WHAT IS IT THAT you're hoping to accomplish here?" Angel asks me.

I'm using a roll of 100-mile-per-hour tape to secure his wrists and ankles to the legs and armrests of the chair I've seated him in. Lucky hovers behind me, his plate carrier doffed, leaving a sweaty imprint behind on his shirt. He's only got his holstered sidearm, staying hands-free for if Angel gets squirrelly.

I finish securing Angel's ankles to the chair and then smile up at him from my squatting position. He looks like death warmed over, and that gives me something like a feeling of satisfaction. Where the concrete had abraded the side of his face and the tip of his nose, it's all crusty and red-black, and weeping yellowish plasma. The gash in his temple has clotted up, but not before coating him in his own blood, down to the chest of the yellow shirt he's wearing.

The only one of Angel's wounds we bothered to do anything about was the bullet hole in his shoulder, and even that we did the bare minimum on. Usually, I cringe a bit when I have to stuff gauze into a wound channel—that gross tactile texture thing again. But in that particular instance, I'd somewhat enjoyed ramming the cloth into his flesh and hearing him caterwaul.

Okay. "Enjoy" is maybe too strong of a word. It's not an experience I'd pay for, and I won't be jacking off to it later. I just...

I got a lot of hate in my heart for these people. And I don't mind letting it out.

"Uh?" Angel's voice rises with the demanding syllable. He's trying to be powerful, but that's laughable in his current circumstance. "No, no. You didn't think this through, did you, *pendejo*!"

Still smiling, I stand up. "You cartel guys are all the same. So much machismo. Until I start pulling fingernails off. Then it's just a lot of crying and begging."

Predictably, Angel lets loose with a venomous diatribe, but I've already stopped listening. I bend down to where I deposited his boots and socks after I stripped his feet bare. I grab one of the socks. It's sweaty, and slightly crusty. "Lucky, you mind?"

Lucky moves in behind Angel and cuts off his runaway mouth by sinking him into a firm headlock. I move to stand in front, balling the sock in one hand.

"Open your mouth," Lucky commands. He gives Angel exactly two seconds to comply—which he doesn't—then rams his thumb firmly into the bundle of nerves just behind his jaw and beneath his ear. The "mandibular angle," it's called. Angel's eyes squinch shut against the pain, so Lucky pushes harder.

Angel gasps, mouth gaping.

I shove his own crusty sock into his mouth.

Lucky immediately clamps his hand over Angel's sock-stuffed hole to keep him from spitting it out, while I rip off a length of tape, then use it to seal his mouth shut.

Once that's done, Lucky releases the man and steps back.

Angel seethes through his nose, issuing a little snot-rocket that snags on the chin of his goatee and dangles there. He stares unholy daggers at me.

I pat him on the shoulder, my voice warm and friendly. "Don't worry Angel. You'll do plenty of talking later. When it's convenient for me."

He grunts and groans and thrashes ineffectually.

I look at Lucky. "You good to keep an eye on him?"

Lucky's nose curls like he just smelled shit, but he nods. "Yeah, I got you, Boss."

Then I leave Angel to Lucky's tender care.

Our current hideout is a little farmstead out in the middle of absolutely nothing. I guess the land around it was once cropland, but the fallow fields have turned into endless acres of brush, on its way towards being new-growth forest. It conceals the farmstead nicely, in case anyone from Pancho tries to mount a search for their beloved leader. But honestly, I'm not worried about them finding us.

We're roughly ten miles west of Pancho, and everything between is an expanse of featureless brush.

Where I've just left Lucky to guard Angel is what looks to me like an old tractor shed, without the tractor. Rusted, corrugated siding, surrounded by sapling trees. Stepping out of the shed, the farmstead is practically invisible to even me, and I'm standing in the middle of it. I can just barely make out the old house through the brush and brambles.

I push my way through the overgrowth, avoiding a spot where the biggest, evilest looking spider I've ever laid eyes on has parked its man-sized web. I'm not usually squeamish about spiders, but goddamn. Is there a nuclear power station that melted down somewhere around here?

Branch stands under the wilting awning of the house's front porch. His eyes are on the environment, and he only gives me the barest notice as I pass, his carbine slung casually on his armor-less chest.

The house hasn't endured the years of its disuse very well, and looks more like a shanty now. Sections of its wooden frame have rotted out and one entire side of the house is collapsed. The rest of the structure leans like a half-dead man about to pass out. The front door hangs off its hinges. Not a single window has glass in it. All that glass is inside, unrecognized until you hear it crunching beneath the layer of dead leaves that carpet the floors.

The interior doesn't even have the smell of human habitation anymore. Its scent is indistinguishable from that of the forest surrounding it.

Of course, *now* it smells a bit like sweaty, unwashed men—an odor that yours truly is strongly contributing to. I find it odd how I've gone pretty much nose-blind to that stink, and yet I can pick out the much lighter, almost delicate body odor of a young woman in all that.

It reminds me that we're all just animals when you get right down to it. It's just that so much of it lies beneath carefully-tended social constructs. A fragile mass-delusion that we've all agreed to believe in. Like the long-failed dollar, it is not based on anything real, but simply the faith we put in it. All it takes is a little shake-up, and the value of both the currency and our delusions of higher-mindedness plummet to zero.

Inside, we've made camp in what would've been the living room, as that's the only portion of the house that still has walls and a roof. It's a bit of a tight fit, which doesn't bother us, but I immediately notice that Isabella has staked out a place as far from everyone else as possible. She's sitting with her knees pulled up to her chest, her shoulders leaning against a moldering wall, not looking at anyone.

When I look away from her, I catch Marty watching me. He says nothing, but his eyes seem to communicate a concern for the girl's mental state.

I push past Marty, giving him a friendly shoulder-pat as I step over EZ's sprawled legs. He's sitting on the floor, itemizing what they looted after the takedown. Menendez is seated against another wall, bare-chested and working on his wound.

I pop a squat in front of Menendez. "You want a hand with that?"

He's currently debriding the wound with a little pair of stainless surgical scissors, and he does not look like he's having fun. He's pouring sweat and his face is all worked up and contorted. Every time he snips a little piece of dead flesh away from the wound, his mouth opens and closes with unsaid syllables.

He takes a break and breathes deep for a second, shaking his head. "Nah. Prefer to do my own cutting."

I glance down at the medical detritus scattered around his meager work area. I spot a used ampule of lidocaine and a spent syringe. Picking up the ampule, I read the expiration.

"Shit's two years out of date, man," I say. "Is it even doing anything for you?"

He seems to steel himself, and then gets back to gingerly snipping with shaking hands. "Not as much as I'd like."

"You could use one of the fentanyl lollipops and let me patch you up while you snooze."

He gives me an incredulous look. "I'm not wasting one of them on this piddly shit." He looks back down at his work. "I'll take a lollipop when my guts are hanging out."

I can appreciate that. We only have a few of the hard-core painkillers. Best to save them for something worse.

"You planning to stitch it or leave it open?" I ask.

He pauses again and considers this. "What do you think?"

I eyeball the wound. It's red and swollen, sure, but it's a small-diameter hole. Probably 9mm, and likely FMJ, as the exit doesn't look any bigger than the entry. There's maybe three inches of cavity between the two holes. That's not terrible, but you stitch it, you seal in any bacteria in the wound channel, and we don't have antibiotics with us.

"Leave it open," I decide. "Keep it clean and bandaged. We'll baby it and hope for the best."

He nods. "I'll be good. I'll punch bacteria in the face."

I give him an encouraging smile and a gentle squeeze on his calf, so as not to jostle his work. Then I stand up, and decide I can't pussy-foot around it any longer. I look at Isabella. She hasn't moved at all. I don't know what's rolling through her brain, but anytime someone draws inward like that, it's a bad sign. Particularly in the field.

She might not want to talk right now, but what she wants is immaterial in that moment. She *needs* to talk. Much like that wound channel, if you seal the bad shit in, it'll only fester and cause worse problems down the road.

So I'm told. I don't suffer from that type of thing. Black-hearted devil that I am.

I make my way over to her. EZ and Marty both stop what they're doing and watch me with tense interest, like I'm about to try to defuse a bomb.

I stand over her. She must know that I'm there, but she doesn't even twitch.

"Isabella."

Still nothing.

I give her hip a light nudge with the toe of my boot. "Hey."

She stirs as though woken from a dream. Or a nightmare. Looks down at my foot as though it has done something both confusing and deeply offensive. Then she raises her eyes to mine—but only for a flash. They seem to ricochet away from full eye contact.

"What?" She says it flat. Atonal.

I'm not known for being great with people's feelings. But then again, I am pretty good at reading them. It's just that I typically don't go in for pity-party type shit. I speak frankly, and people tend to get butthurt by that. But I think that's necessary sometimes. Maybe even most of the time.

Or maybe it's just that, when dealing with shit like this, I'm usually in a situation where I'm short on time. Fact is, we don't have days or weeks for her to work herself out of her funk and metabolize her trauma. So she's gonna have to muscle up and power through. She can make her peace with human cruelty later, when her life—and ours—isn't on the line.

So, to that end, I nudge her with my boot again. "Alright. Come on. Get up."

Her response is shockingly quick. She practically explodes off the ground, and then she's standing there, face all full of hate and discontent, with her hands balled at her side.

I only barely manage not to recoil. Instead, I make sure to look wholly unimpressed.

People, when they're pissed and hurt like this...man, they're like angry dogs. You show any weakness, and they'll just start going for the throat. They're hurting, and they want to make you hurt, either for revenge because they see you as the problem, or because misery loves company.

Best to nip that in the bud.

I roll my eyes and grab her upper arm. "Don't get froggy on me, girl." Then I start pulling her towards the door. "We're gonna talk."

"I don't wanna talk to you!"

"Yeah, well, sometimes you gotta do shit you don't wanna do. That's life." She's giving me some resistance, but I notice that it's not as furious as her tone implies. She *wants* to get shit off her chest, but she doesn't want to seem weak, so she's going to make me force her to say it.

That's fine. I can work with that.

We exit, and Branch watches us impassively from under arched eyebrows. He says nothing.

"Where are you taking me?" Isabella demands.

"Right over here," I say, motioning to our vehicle.

Her resistance, such as it was, gives out completely, so I decide to let go of her arm. She immediately hugs herself jealously and scowls at me. "Are you driving me somewhere?"

"No," I say, opening the passenger's door for her like a chauffeur.

She eyes me. Eyes the car seat.

I remember that I'm a large, threatening man. Oh yeah—and we killed her uncle. So, while I don't typically approach these things with a soft hand, I decide in that moment that perhaps I should put on the proverbial kid gloves. After all, I've got her up and moving and talking. So maybe I take my foot off the gas a bit here.

"If we're gonna talk," I say, softening both my tone and my expression. "It'll be easier with some privacy. Don't wanna walk out in the woods away from my armed friends, for obvious reasons. So..." I sweep a hand at the open door.

She considers me with slitted eyes for another long moment, then relents and gets in. I close her door, cross around, and get in the driver's seat. The 4Runner's been sitting in the shade, so it's not unbearable, but it's definitely stuffy. I get myself comfortable, elbows resting on the door panel and the center console, eyes straight ahead, where I can see the rusty siding of the tractor shed peeking through the greenery.

I wait her out.

Eventually, she says, in a quiet voice, "Is Angel in there?"

I glance over and see she is also staring at the tractor shed. "Yeah."

Her eyes remain fixed forward. "What are you going to do to him?"

"Don't worry about that."

"You're gonna torture him." It's a statement, not a question.

"So what if we do? He's cartel."

She finally looks at me. Well...*glares* at me. "You think you're so fucking righteous. But Angel's a better man than you'll ever be."

That raises my eyebrows. "Oh? You don't even know me."

She scoffs. "All you Americans are the same. You talk this big, cocky game, like the rest of the world desperately needs you, but all you do is make shit worse for everyone." She thrusts a finger towards the shed. "Angel was nice! You think everyone that works for the cartel is evil? My uncle worked for them—he wasn't evil." She thrashes around like she's about to hit me, but must've reconsidered. "Angel paid my uncle well for the work he did, and he was always nice! And then here you come, just killing everyone you come across like they don't even fucking matter, because if they're not American, then they're just trash, right?"

"No," I try to interject, but she runs over me.

"Did you even think about who you killed today? Did you even think about those men in the van that you just shot up like it was nothing?"

"We needed to get you and Angel out alive," I snap back. "I didn't have time to interview everyone in the van to see if they were nice guys. You telling me they wouldn't have fought back if they'd been given the chance? Bullshit. The only reason they're dead and I'm standing is because I was faster."

She's shaking her head as I finish, eyes wide as though mystified. "The two guys—the ones you shot, like, twenty times?" It wasn't that many times, but I don't bother correcting her. She leans in, hissing so a fine spray of spittle lands on my cheek. "They were *doctors*!"

I'm struck mute for a moment. My first thought is incredulity—why were there doctors in...

Ah. Right. The story about her uncle being deathly ill.

She takes advantage of my silence, and articulates the salient points, to really drive home the magnitude of my error. "Angel was worried about my uncle—he was *worried*—and so he took both of the doctors in Pancho to go see what they could do to help. Do you realize how fucked up that is? You made me lie about my uncle that *you* killed, and then you killed the only two doctors that Pancho had! Why? Because it was *easier*?"

I lean away from her, grimacing. I pinch the bridge of my nose, staring at the shed. All I can really muster from my brain's language centers is "Shit."

"Shit? That's all you can say?" This time she does hit me—more of a slap-shove to the shoulder, but it gets me riled nonetheless. "Do you even feel bad about it, or is this just another day of sweeping up the trash for you?" She tries to hit me again.

This time, I see it coming, so I deflect it down into the center console, maybe a bit harder than was necessary. She jerks back, holding her forearm.

I have the urge to shout in her face. Try to get her to back off.

Yeah, we're all just animals, and if you snap at me, I'll snap at you.

Except we can choose to deny those instincts.

My jaw clenches repeatedly, as though chewing on all the bitter things I want to say. Then, when I can fit them back down inside myself, I swallow.

I want to explain myself. But that kicks off a tug-of-war between my brain and my chest, which strains in my throat. Part of me wondering why I feel the need to explain myself to some fifteen-year-old girl—just an asset—when I've got a mission to worry about, and I don't have time for touchy feely, because the lives of seven families are hanging by a thread, and really, that should concern me way more than whether or not some chick I'll probably never see again in my life thinks I'm a monster.

But the other part of me...oh, that other damn part. It's the part that keeps whispering, *Maybe you are a monster, you sociopathic fuck. If you're not, then why can't you articulate yourself?*

Am I trying to explain myself to the girl?

Or am I trying to explain myself...to myself?

Perhaps both. Because I want to stop thinking that something human in me broke somewhere between the collapse of the social contract and me spending the last few months of my life hunting *Nuevas Fronteras* down and exterminating them. But I also see that Isabella's perspective on why we're down here in the first place is obviously a bit skewed.

I open my mouth to tell her all about the seven families that we're down here to rescue. So she knows I'm not an evil man. And so she sees that, despite her own limited reference point, the cartel is *full* of evil men.

Then I snap my mouth shut again.

She stares at me, eyebrows raised expectantly. Waiting for my explanation.

But I know how that conversation is going to go. If I tell her the truth about our mission, all she'll hear is a bunch of excuses. Even as I play the words over in my head, all I hear is a desperate attempt to sound righteous.

And I know that she'll mainly cue in on one point: Those seven families are all American. And then she'll ask me—probably shrilly, and with a metric fuckton of that disdain that only the youthfully ignorant can summon—if saving American lives justifies me murdering all the Mexicans I want.

The whole rabid, filthy conversation plays out in my head. And I have no desire to go down that road.

Sometimes—oftentimes—silence is the better option.

"Nothing, huh?" she says, managing to sound almost disappointed in me. Which is interesting. Because it smarts a bit.

The hell is wrong with me?

Isabella chuffs rudely. "You really got nothing—"

"Shut your mouth," I say—not loud, or commanding. That's not necessary right now. For all this girl's bluster, she's terrified of me. Her outburst was a desperate attempt to see how human I am. To see if I could be reasoned with, or cajoled, or manipulated by my emotions.

She's barking up the wrong tree.

I've got a job to do. And I don't need the girl to understand me in order to do that job. I'll settle for compliance out of fear. It's more expedient.

"I'm not a teenage girlfriend for you to blabber your hurt feelings to. I'm here to accomplish a mission. And I'll put a goddamn bullet in whoever gets in my way, whether they understood the consequences when they stepped in front of me or not. I don't have feelings. I don't have morals. I have an objective. And I strongly advise you not to be one of the people that stands in the way of that." I stare at her blankly, emotionlessly. No anger. No aggression. I'm not threatening her. I'm simply telling her the rules. How shit works in my world. "Nod your head 'yes' if you understand what I'm telling you."

Her chin quivers. She draws slowly back from me. Her eyes flitter in a sort of panic between mine, trying to find something she can recognize, and failing utterly.

She nods.

I look away from her. Back to the rusted shed. "Now get the fuck out of my car, go back inside the house, and stare at your fucking wall."

It's obvious she's taken my meaning quite well. She exits the vehicle, not in a huff, but as though she is trying to move without being seen or heard. Like she's tiptoeing around a sleeping bear.

She closes the door gently behind her, pressing it until it latches, rather than slamming it. Then she turns, shoulders cinched up and head hanging, and walks directly back into the house.

Branch watches her pass without comment.

Then he glances questioningly at me, but I look away.

I stare at the shed, where, apparently, I've got just the nicest guy that's ever worked for the cartel, waiting to be taken apart, so I can get the intel I need to complete my objective.

Way to go, Abe. You're so fucking good at this.

CHAPTER 9

ANGEL DOESN'T LAST AS long as I'm sure he thought he would.

It's about as long as I figured.

It's easy to talk a big game when you've still got all the parts of yourself. But, as they start getting taken away, men stop thinking about higher ideals like loyalty. The human being is, after all, an animal.

I'll give Angel credit, though: he held out through losing most of his fingers. But everyone's got their bugaboos. And his was a common one.

Do you know what the most commonly-shared dream is?

It's the one where all your teeth are falling out of your mouth.

Almost everyone has had that dream before. Experts say that it comes from a feeling of powerlessness. It's something almost every human shares, and it goes straight down into the core of who we are as animals.

You see, teeth are very important. We use them to talk. We use them to eat. And, going back to our primate ancestors, they're pretty much our primary weapon. That's three very important things to the human-animal: The ability to socialize, the ability to feed yourself, and the ability to defend yourself. Taking those away is deeply and instinctively disturbing to most.

As it was to Angel.

"Alright," I say, gently, giving Angel a little shoulder massage. "Calm down. I won't take any more as long as you keep talking, okay?"

Angel whimpers and coughs and spits blood. The sounds he makes seem morphed and hollow by the re-arranged structure of his mouth.

I swallow thickly and harden myself.

This is always the worst part. It's the part where you have to show a little compassion—a tiny reward to motivate them to keep talking. And it's a mindfuck for everyone involved. For them, because you don't really have compassion, do you? And for you because, even if your compassion is an act, it makes it oh-so-hard to keep seeing them as a puzzle box to be solved if only you can find the right buttons to push.

Even if your compassion is fraudulent, you still wind up seeing them as a person.

"How about some water?" I say, moving around to the side and grabbing the liter bottle off the floor. It's so scuffed up from years of reuse, it makes the water inside look dirty, though it's not.

I uncap the water and bring it over to Angel. I put it to his lips, but stop before I tilt it up. "It's warm, but that'll make it hurt less on your exposed roots. Still. Try to just swallow it and not let it touch anything but your tongue."

His bleary, tear-streaked eyes stare at the water bottle. Then he looks up at me, and there's no more defiance left in him. Just fear, which he no longer has the energy to hide anymore.

I put my hand gently to the back of his head, guiding it to an incline, almost baptismal. I hover the mouth of the bottle just over his cracked and swollen lips—it's my bottle, and I don't want him getting his blood on it. My movements are tender. Compassionate.

Angel winces and splutters, his throat working as he awkwardly tries to swallow without letting any of it touch the jagged remnants of his upper teeth.

"Okay," I say, tilting the bottle back to neutral. "Let's not overdo it."

He moans, as though something intrinsic to his being has been taken away from him.

I cap the bottle, glancing up at Lucky. His expression is hard to read. There's a flatness to his lips. A tightness to the corners of his eyes. A slight wrinkle to his flared nostrils. Pity, perhaps? Or disgust?

We've both seen enough not to be disgusted by gore. A ruined body that's dead is nothing to comment on. But that same body, alive and gibbering and screeching, sticks in your mind. Human suffering is off-putting in a way that inanimate viscera never can be.

I set the bottle down at my feet and regard the broken man before me. "The name you gave me—Diego Beltran. Who is he?"

Angel looks like a bloody rag that's been wrung out. His head lolls to one side, his eyelids fluttering as he looks at me. Then his head sags forward, chin to chest, and he spits again, but not to defy or insult. A gobbet of red, with a little white chunk of tooth in it, dribbles down his chest and disappears amidst the blood already soaking his shirt.

"Will you kill me?" he breathes.

"That's not the plan," I respond, truthfully. "If I kill you, I've got no way of knowing whether the information you're giving me is true. So, my plan is to leave you alive. Here. Chained up and secured. You'll die of dehydration in three days. If the information you give me is good, I'll be back before then to cut you loose. If not, then I'll just leave you to wither."

Angel shakes his head. "No."

I frown, and glance questioningly at Lucky. Should I get the hammer and flathead screwdriver again? Start working my way through his molars?

Lucky only shrugs.

"I wasn't asking if you *intend* to kill me," Angel says, raising his head just a bit to meet my eyes. His are hollowed out. Bereft of anything. "I was asking you *to* kill me."

Huh. Isn't that odd? You get a guy to start talking by tweaking his primordial instincts to survive, and when he finally decides to talk, he wants to die. People are strange beings. Beings constantly torn between their instincts and their conscious thoughts, be they rational or irrational.

I've taken nearly everything from him. You wouldn't think losing your thumbs and forefingers and a handful of your teeth would be *everything*, but in this new world we live in, that is what it represents.

How are you going to survive when you can't hold anything? When you can't eat solid food? No one is going to take care of you. There are no prosthetics. No dental reconstruction.

Besides that, he'll have lost all standing in the cartel.

I make an uncertain noise and cross my arms over my chest. "I dunno."

Weird to threaten someone with *not* killing them.

"I'll tell you the truth," Angel rasps. "I swear it on my mother. On the Virgin Mary. On—"

I wave that off. "Just shooting straight with you here, Angel: Your word doesn't carry much weight with me."

He stares at me for a long moment. I guess he's thinking, but I can't tell what's going on in his head. His face is blank. His eyes give away nothing. And I don't get the sense that it's a poker face. I get the sense that he's just...done. Drained. Empty.

The guy wants to die. He's got no fight left in him.

I glance at my watch. I've only been going at him for two hours now. And I think, *that's gotta be a record*, but the thought has no humor in it. It doesn't make me feel victorious. It just makes me tired.

I get that feeling a lot lately. And it always seems to come with an image: Me, sliding under some blankets, pulling them over my head, and passing the fuck out. Sure, I haven't slept much, but it's not just physical exhaustion that I'm feeling. It's a desire to unplug from this reality. Go somewhere else.

"Alright, Angel," I sigh. "You tell me what you know about Deigo Beltran. If it's good shit...I'll put you out of your misery."

Something like the scantest breath of life comes back into his eyes, which strikes me as ironic. He tilts his head back, as though basking in the sun, though there is none of that to be had in the dim confines of the shed.

"*La vida esta la miseria*," Angel mutters at the rafters. Then tilts his head to me. "You understand?"

"I don't habla."

Angel wheezes. Or maybe it was a chuckle. I can't really tell. "'I don't habla,' he says. Fucking Americans."

"Remember how we were just starting to play nice?" I ask. "Let's not ruin that."

Angel closes his eyes for a long moment. Then he takes a deep breath, opens them again, and begins to speak.

"Diego Beltran," I dub the little rock, and place it in the center of the area I've scuffed clear of leaves and debris. "That's our new target."

The rest of the team are squatting or down on one knee in a tight huddle-up surrounding my makeshift sand table. We're outside, in front of the house. I have myself positioned to keep an eye on the open front door. Isabella's still inside, and I don't want her making a run for it.

If we were making any progress in the trust-each-other-department, the conversation in the 4Runner put an end to it.

"According to Angel," I continue. "Diego was one of Mateo Ibarra's top guys, though there was apparently some tension there. Diego thought he shoulda been running shit, and would do little things to try to wrest power away from Mateo—I won't get into the boring details. In any case, when word got back to the cartel about us charbroiling Mateo, Diego was quick to take charge. So." I point at the rock. "He is now in charge of *Nuevas Fronteras.*"

"Uh..." EZ raises his hand, giving me an uncertain look. "Thought we were working our way up the food chain, Boss. Now we're gonna jump right to the top?"

I shrug. "If anybody knows where those families are being held, it's gonna be Diego Beltran."

EZ's face screws up. "Guy's gonna have an army around him."

I hold up an index finger. "Not necessarily. Angel says that the cartel's been a little fractious since word of Mateo's death hit. They're still reeling. Nominally, Diego has taken power, but that power isn't consolidated, and there are several others that are vying to oust Diego."

"Great." EZ wipes a hand across his face. "So he'll have an army *and* he'll be fucking paranoid."

"You know," I say, narrowing my eyes at EZ. "For once, I'd like to just get all the details out before you start jaw jacking. If you could listen for five fucking minutes, your concerns might be answered."

EZ pulls back, holding up both hands. "Alright. Damn, man. Just saying. Little critical thinking never hurt a plan, you know."

Menendez breaks in, looking like his wound has severely taxed his patience. "EZ, just let the guy get everything out first. Christ."

Marty pets his friend's shoulder. "Quiet now, my chocolate bunny."

"I'm quiet," EZ says in a sarcastically low tone. "I'm being quiet."

Menendez looks at my glowering visage. "You good? Need to take a walk?"

"No, I'm fine." I shake my head. "Like running a day-care, except all the toddlers have guns. Anyways. Diego hasn't consolidated power, and he's worried about a few key areas where he—" I look significantly at EZ "—being paranoid—thinks the others might make a push on him. Which actually gives us an advantage, because he's got his forces spread thin right now, trying to cover too many bases."

I grab a stick off the ground and draw a square in the dirt around the rock that represents Diego Beltran. "In addition to that, he's not far." I draw a line away from the square and rock, then draw a circle and point at it. "That's Pancho." I draw another circle off to the side. "We're somewhere roughly in here. And that line from Pancho to Diego's location is the main road heading south out of Pancho. Angel estimated it's maybe thirty miles. If we move around Pancho, and find this road heading south, we can follow it to this compound Diego's holed up in. Obviously, we're not gonna take the road itself. Angel says it's patrolled. But we can try to run parallel to it. It'll take us a little longer, but Diego's compound shouldn't be hard to find."

I scratch a jagged line near Diego's location. "Right around here, the land starts to get into the foothills of the Sierra Madres. Angel said there's one, kind of conspicuous mountain sticking out of the foothills, just to the east of the road. That's where Diego's compound is. It's an old vineyard, and it's supposed to be visible from the road."

I lean back on my haunches, tapping my stylus-stick against my knee. "Once we find it, we proceed like we did with Pancho—move in, recon the area, gather intel, and form a plan to infiltrate and get our hands on Diego. How we choose to proceed will be entirely based on what we find when we get there, *but*...we have an additional advantage in this situation." I glance about at the others, and I'm glad to see their faces are much less dubious than when

I started. Even EZ's. "Because *Nuevas Fronteras* has split into several bickering factions, we can misdirect attention onto one of Diego's in-house enemies. His people will be more likely to believe that it's one of the other cartel factions that took their boss down, because they're already primed to think that's where the threat is coming from. If we play our cards right, we can take down the new head of the cartel, find out where the families are being held, *and* make a clean break for Texas."

I then gird myself up to open the floor to questions, comments, and concerns. But in the quiet of my pause, we all hear something.

A clatter of wood.

Every single one of us whips around in the direction the noise came from: the house. Hands go to holstered sidearms.

I stand up, staring at the open front door of the house. "Isabella?" I call out.

Silence for a beat.

Then the sound of rapid footfalls.

I churn into a sprint, the others right on my heels. I knife-hand either side of the house and shout, "Go around the back!"

Along the front stoop of the house, our rifles are leaned up against a fallen timber, because we didn't want Isabella getting any ideas. I snatch up the nearest rifle—I don't know whose it is, and I don't really know why I think I need my rifle against an unarmed girl. I guess I just grab it out of instinct.

I burst into the dilapidated house, my eyes immediately whipping to the corner where I'd left Isabella.

She's not there.

I shout her name again as I tear to where she was, and the second I get there, I see the hole that hadn't been there before—debris from the fallen section of the house pushed out of the way to create a narrow space, leading out the back. Beyond that hole, I see the woods that surrounds the farmstead. The brush is still moving from someone's passing, and I get the barest glimpse of Isabella's white camisole.

"Son of a *bitch*!" I immediately ram my substantial bulk against the hole she's cleared, widening it. Rusty nails jab at me, but I'm all forward momentum now and plow heedlessly through them, thrusting and kicking fallen walls and rotting framework out of my way. "She's run out the back!" I yell to the others.

What the fuck is she thinking? Does she not remember what I said I was going to do to her family if she pulled some shit like this?

Or does she just not believe me?

I mean, sure, I wasn't *actually* going to do that, but I thought she believed me. Apparently not, if she's willing to call my bluff.

It takes me about five seconds to burst through the debris, and then I'm hauling ass through the woods. I catch sight of the others, running parallel to me. We don't need all of them chasing after this girl, and I don't want to leave our shit unguarded.

"Hold up!" I shout at them. "Go back to the house! Branch—stay with me!"

I choose him because he's out ahead of me already. Definitely the fastest guy in the group.

The others tromp to a stop and peel off. Branch slows by a small increment and I close the gap with him. We run abreast of each other in the last known direction of Isabella. Get about another fifty yards into the woods before I start to slow.

"Ease up," I huff. I'm not gassed, but I don't want to sprint past a whip-thin girl hiding under a tree stump or some shit. "She can't outpace us over distance. Let's make sure she's not bedded down."

We still keep a good pace, but we get more circumspect. Her white camisole won't do her any favors. She can't hide *that* well. Unless she burrows down into the leaves. But I don't think she had enough of a head start for that.

Another twenty yards into the woods, and it starts to thin out into the lower-lying brush that has overtaken the surrounding croplands.

Me and Branch stutter to a stop at the edge of the seemingly-endless expanse of chest-high weeds. Our eyes whip back and forth across the long-fallow fields. There's not even the hint of movement out there.

"Shit," Branch says, breathing hard and looking behind us, back into the woods. "Did we run by her?"

I keep eyeing the brush ahead. It's high, but if she was up and running, I'm almost positive we'd see the movement at the very least, if not her white camisole. She's gotta be bedded down somewhere—either ahead of us in the brush, or behind us in the woods.

"Hold what you got," I say to Branch. "Watch the woodline and make sure she doesn't slip out into the brush." Then I start working my way along the edge of the field, moving much slower now, looking for sign.

A background thought: Why am I even chasing after this bitch? We don't really need her anymore. And the chances of her actually finding her way all the way back to Pancho to dime us out is unlikely.

Unlikely. But not impossible.

If she's not useful, and she's a threat to the mission, why not just put her down when you catch sight of her next?

That's pragmatism. Plain. Simple. Black and white.

It's also sociopathic.

I stop after about thirty yards, feeling like I've gone too far. I double back towards where Branch is still keeping an eye on the woodline, his pistol in hand now, ported to his chest. I move past him at a jog, then slow again to search the other side of him.

Dammit. Shoulda gone this direction in the first place. Bad coin flip.

It's pretty damn obvious where she's gone: There's a section of brambles she's torn through, leaving the pale undersides of the leaves upturned as she exited the woods and plowed into the overgrown field. She left a clear path parted through the tall grass and shrubs.

"Branch, over here!"

He lopes over, sees what I've found, and nods.

"You any good at tracking?" I ask.

He quirks a brow. "Why? 'Cause I'm Cherokee?"

"Obviously."

He offers the barest of smirks, then steps ahead of me and starts moving into the path Isabella left behind. "Yeah, I'm actually pretty good," he admits in low tones. "Not that it'll be necessary. She left a fucking highway behind her. But I resent the stereotype."

I match his volume, almost whispering. "Yeah, well, you can call me a Hadji if it makes you feel better. I don't care."

He's moving through the brush at a walking pace, knees bent, shoulders hunched. A stalking posture. He glances over his shoulder at me. "Are you Muslim?"

"Parents were. I never took to it."

"Yeah? How'd they feel about that?"

"Extremely displeased," I answer, remembering back to them, and almost feeling something, but I put it away. "Cut me off when I joined the Army."

We go quiet, listening for any movement ahead of us. Another twenty yards or so into the weeds, and I pull us to a stop. She's gotta be close. No way she got that much of a head start on us.

"Isabella!" I shout into the field. "Don't be an idiot! You're not gonna make it out here on your own! I know you're scared, but you're not thinking straight! We are not your enemy!"

Surprisingly, she responds. What's most surprising about it, though, is that her response is the pop of a small caliber pistol, the projectile snapping wide of us through the brush.

Me and Branch both drop to a squat. He raises his pistol, and I raise my rifle, but right before I put my finger to the trigger, I stop myself. Then I lunge out and smack Branch's pistol down before he can start laying return fire.

He snaps accusatory eyes at me. "The fuck, man? She just shot at us!"

"I know she just shot at us!" I hiss back.

"Yeah, well, I don't wanna get shot!"

"Shut up a second!"

He complies.

We hold our breaths, eyeing the brush in the direction where the gunshot came from. It was pretty close. Maybe another thirty yards ahead, and a bit to the right. But the brush is way too thick to see that far.

"Where'd she get a fucking gun?" Branch demands.

"I told everyone to secure their shit," I growl back, finding my anger rising, and it has less to do with the fact that Isabella just winged a bullet at us, and a lot more to do with the question of which asshat left a loaded firearm unsecured in the house.

I raise my voice again. "Isabella! Not fucking cool! You shoot at us again, we're gonna start shooting back, and I think you know how that's gonna end! I am *trying* not to kill you, but you are making it *really* fucking difficult! Cut the shit!"

We wait, heads ducked, in case her response is the same as before.

Complete and utter silence. Even the birds and insects have gone quiet.

I take a breath to start in on some more dialogue, my brain trying to summon up some strategy for how to build rapport and negotiate with an armed teenager. Before I can say anything, the sound of crashing brush erupts from ahead of us.

"She's moving!" I snap, coming upright, my rifle shouldered—just in case.

I catch sight of her—head and shoulders clearly visible, hauling ass away from us in a bounding, almost gazelle-like stride as she hurdles thick grasses. Her black hair whips behind her, and her head turns, taking a single glance over her shoulder. Her eyes are wide, mouth hanging open. She's scared shitless.

I start to sprint after her, but only get about two strides before Branch seizes my arm.

"Abe! Wait!"

I turn to look at him, incredulous, but he's not looking at me. His eyes are fixed far ahead, and slightly left of where Isabella is still careening through the brush, racking up distance.

He points. "Look."

I follow his gesture, and immediately see what he's spotted.

Maybe two hundred yards out, something else is moving through the brush, on an intercept course with Isabella. Several somethings, actually. And they're moving fast.

Inhumanly fast.

"Oh, *shit*!" I break into a sprint again, Branch right on my ass. "Isabella! Stop! Primals!" In the moment, I can't remember what she said they were known as around here, so I just start yelling out everything I've heard them called, hoping one of those words will get through to her. "Infected! Crazies! Hunters! Teepios!" Can she not hear me? Does she think I'm lying? I don't know which is the problem, but she's clearly not getting the message, because she hasn't stopped running.

Branch hollers, but it's not at me or Isabella. "Lucky! Dez! We need backup!"

I catch a flash of deeply-brown skin through the overgrowth. There's at least four of them. And there's no way the rest of the team is gonna get here in time.

We get this deep into Mexico without seeing a trace of them, and they pick this precise moment to jump us. Un-fucking-believable.

They're closing within fifty yards of Isabella, but I'm right on her tail. I can see the movement of the primals surging towards us on the left. I can see the gun in her grip—a pocket pistol that looks small even in her hands.

I've gotta get her to stop running.

"Isabella! They're coming!" I don't know if that foreboding wording will be enough to get through to her, but I don't wait to find out. She glances back again. Sees how close I am. And I see her gun hand coming up.

But my rifle is already shouldered.

Still at a dead sprint, I fire a string on full-auto—not at Isabella, but at the encroaching pack of primals. The rounds pepper the brush to the left, but I know my chances of actually hitting something are minimal. I can only hope that Isabella has enough sense to see that I'm *clearly* not firing at her.

She raises the gun anyway.

But I haven't stopped running, and she's slowed drastically in her spin to take aim at me. I'm almost offended that she'd still point the thing at me. Has she *still* not realized what's happening?

Doesn't matter. She doesn't get the shot off.

Right as the pistol comes level, I swing my rifle like baton, cracking her in the wrist and sending the pistol twirling off into the brush. My forward momentum is too much to arrest. I bowl into her, both of our bodies going horizontal, then tumbling end-over-end.

Branch slides into place over top of us, his pistol barking a steady rhythm—trying to conserve his single magazine. I swirl to my feet and reach down, seizing Isabella's arm with my support hand while I level my rifle, pinning it under my armpit.

She's almost upright when I see it coming: Wide open mouth full of too-long teeth, black hair dreadlocked and swinging as the creature tears around a bush on all fours. I jerk my rifle over and squeeze the trigger on full-auto. Firing a rifle one-handed is possibly the most inaccurate way to engage a target, but the bastard is close, and it catches everything I send it, right to the head and shoulders.

Even with half its head gone, I swear to God, it still leaps. Maybe its brain had already sent that signal to its muscles by the time my rounds shut it off, but it slams into Isabella, tearing her arm out of my grip.

She squeals, full-moon eyes locking with mine.

I'm pretty sure the thing's dead, but I find myself unable to turn my back on her. I lunge into the tiny space between their bodies, planting a knee there and ramming the dead thing off to the side, giving the remnants of its head a quick burst at point-blank.

Then I whip my rifle up to the incoming threats, shouldering it again with both hands. Branch is dead ahead and backing up while firing.

"Last rounds!" he shouts as he comes abreast of me.

Isabella hasn't stopped screaming.

Another one bursts through the foliage, several strides to my right. As I'm swinging my sights to bear on it, it does something odd: It skids to a stop, and starts backpedaling.

Primals—infected, crazies, whatever you want to call them—are not mindless. They're predators, and they're nasty, but what makes them the worst is that they're cunning. Smart enough to know when prey isn't worth the fight.

This one has seen its dead packmate, and decided that this particular dinner menu is a bit too costly.

It howls as it turns, warning the rest of the pack off.

I see no reason to disengage. There's no ROE's when it comes to primals. We're not at war. We're just trying to make each other extinct.

I flick my select fire to semi-auto and sight square on its back, then send three rounds into it, the first snapping its spine, the next two impacting somewhere in the top of its shoulders as it collapses. Paralyzed or dead. I don't care which, and I'm not sticking around to find out.

I push to my feet, grabbing Isabella by the arm again and yanking her up. She wails, and for a moment, I think I've pulled her arm out of socket.

Another shape skitters just on the other side of a skein of weeds. I get the slightest flash of feral eyes through the greenery. Branch pivots deftly and fires three rounds at it, sending his pistol into lockback. He's empty, and I don't know whether he hit the beast, but I can hear it crashing away through the brush now.

Branch ducks around me as I start pulling Isabella back towards the farmstead. I know what he wants, so I jut my right hip out to him and feel my sidearm jerked out of my holster.

I get two steps before Isabella's wailing registers with me again.

I whirl on her, still pulling. "The fuck is your problem?"

The words are already out of my mouth by the time I see what her problem is.

She's holding one leg off the ground. The ankle is clearly bent in an unnatural way.

Shit. Not good.

"I can't!" she sobs. "I can't!"

I swear and dip into a half-crouch, yanking her across my shoulders in a fireman's carry. She's tiny, and I've trained to do this with two-hundred-pound men in full kit, so the motion is breezy-easy. She splutters and gags in my ear, my shoulders gouging her belly as I take off running again.

"Branch! Swap!"

I slow my pace just enough to let Branch come around, unclip my rifle from its sling, and put the pistol he'd liberated from me back in my hands.

"About a half a mag left in that!" I snap at him as I accelerate again. "Keep those fuckers off my back!"

Then I hoof it.

Okay. So, yes, highly-trained operative, pulled many a full-grown man to safety in a firefight, and I was always a PT stud. Or at least I was in my twenties. Now, pushing forty…well, I've already mentioned the hazards of being an aging operator.

All the strength is still there. But the endurance? Yeah, not so much anymore. Nonstop punishment, no rest, and bad nutrition don't help.

As light as she is compared to a man in kit, it's still a hundred pounds on my shoulders, and I'm pushing my legs as hard as I can, after taking them to the limit just to get to her. I can feel that dreaded "wall" looming up in front of me, lactic acid boiling through my quads, and my lungs suddenly start to feel like they've been scrubbed with a wire brush.

I hit the edge of where the fields of brush meet the forest around the farmstead, and it's the simple act of trying to duck under a low-hanging tree limb so Isabella doesn't get a branch to the face that does it.

I feel my left oblique tear. I know it's my oblique, because I've torn it before doing basically this same thing, except it was with a seabag with rocks in it that I'd had slung over my shoulders, and I'd just been trying to get some conditioning in.

It doesn't stop me, but I'm already swearing inwardly, knowing that the initial tearing sensation is nothing compared to how it's going to feel once I stop moving.

I blame Isabella for this shit, and I don't think I'm being a dick to say that.

Gritting my teeth and pushing through the woods, my pace begins to falter enough that Branch is just trotting along beside me, like an indomitable drill instructor beside a fat recruit on a ten-mile run.

"I can take her!" Branch says, but at that point, I can see the house peeking through the trees, maybe thirty yards ahead. There's no point in stopping to do a switch now.

"I got it!" I snarl back, then wonder how much of that is just stubborn pride.

By the time we reach the house, I've gone to my dark place.

Fuck this shit. Fuck Mexico. And fuck me for getting old.

CHAPTER 10

Despite my piss-off-edness, I do try to put Isabella down easy. Branch and the others help unload her, clearly seeing that I'm not bending naturally, and they get her to the ground without too much tumbling and jostling of her busted ankle.

She still mewls and immediately pulls the leg up, clutching the swelling extremity.

I'm on one knee at that point, and I stay there, trying to make it look like I'm just catching my breath, but really, I think it's going to be a minute before I can go upright again. The torn oblique is seizing up pretty hard, the pain of it similar to a broken rib.

I also don't think it'd be wise to bend over to check on her ankle at this point, so, down on one knee, with my hands braced on my hips and gasping for air, I wheeze out, "Check her ankle. She got tackled by a primal."

At least, I hope that's what it was. Coulda been me tackling her that did it.

Hopefully she doesn't know which it was.

"You were the one that broke my ankle!" she squeals at me, red-faced and pouring tears from the pain.

Figures.

"You were the one that ran away like a fucking idiot!" I snap. "And you don't know that it's broken—could just be sprained."

"You threatened to kill me!" she spits back.

"I threatened to kill you if..." You know what? I don't even know why I'm arguing with this twat. "Just shut up. Shut your mouth or I'll gag you, how's that?"

Branch is kneeling on the other side of her now, lifting her leg and gently brushing her clawing hands away from her ankle. One glance tells me that it's bad. She might be right. It might actually be broken. It's swelled to twice its normal size, and already a purplish hue is tinting her skin.

She does shut up, but mostly because Branch starts speaking softly to her, with the bedside manner of a kind old pediatrician. "Can you move it? Try to move it."

I can't tell if she actually tries, but she yowls.

"Okay, let's get this shoe off," Branch says, cradling her foot in his lap and gingerly undoing the laces.

I find something else to be pissed about, and pivot slightly to glare at the others that are hovering around us. "And who in the fuck left their goddamn pea-shooter in the house?"

I'm all prepared to light into Marty or EZ for being dumbfucks, but then I notice Menendez with a stricken look on his face, patting his pockets like he's misplaced his wallet.

"Oh, shit," he murmurs, then starts looking around as though he'll find what's missing laying around at his feet.

"Jesus Christ, Dez," I breathe. "Really?"

He makes eye contact with me, his face slack. "I keep a little Ruger LCP in my pocket. It musta fallen out when I was patching myself up. I didn't even notice it was gone. Shit. *Shit.*"

I stare at him, trying to bridle my fury, but it's a wild horse that doesn't want to stop bucking and kicking. I manage to lasso it by reminding myself that Menendez is the leader of this team, and it wouldn't do to bust his balls in front of his men.

I hang my head instead. "Alright. Get her inside the house. Branch, see what you can do for that ankle."

Lucky assists Branch in hoisting the girl up and navigating her inside. Marty and EZ hover close behind, like they want to be helpful, but don't know how.

Menendez stands over me, still looking shamefaced. "I'm sorry, man. Massive oversight. Did she shoot at you guys?"

"Yeah," I grumble, wanting nothing more than to get horizontal and give my seizing oblique a rest. It feels like it's ratcheting tighter by the second. "She shot at us. Didn't hit us though. All's well that ends well."

Menendez looks concerned. "You alright, Abe?"

"Uh-huh. Just tweaked something. I'll be fine." I desperately need him to get lost. "Go in there and help them out."

"I don't think they need any help."

"Go on." I wave a hand at the door through which everyone has disappeared. I can still hear Branch's soft questions, and Isabella's whimpering answers.

Menendez seems to realize that I want privacy for a moment. And maybe that's stupid. Maybe that's just some macho bullshit. But I really need to lie down, and I really don't want my team seeing me gasping and cringing. I'm holding it together purely to save face at this point.

"Alright." Menendez turns for the house. Then stops. Looks back at me. "You didn't happen to grab that Ruger, did you?"

"No, motherfucker!" I gnash out. "You're never getting that piece of shit back! Go inside!"

"Alright!" Menendez backs away, then turns and heads for the house, grumbling, "Ornery old fuck."

I can't even deny it.

I wait until he's disappeared inside. I look at the door, and the glassless windows. Making sure that no one's peeking out at me. Then, groaning and cursing, I very slowly lower myself to my back in the dirt and leaves.

The pain lessens, and the endorphins rush in. But I don't think I'll be getting up in the next ten minutes or so.

So I lay there, staring up at the sky, and whisper to my body what a weak turd it is, and how it needs to unfuck itself.

"Ankle's definitely broken," Branch announces as he joins the group, perhaps a half-hour later.

"Ah, shit," I mutter, rubbing my face. This just keeps getting better.

I'm upright, at least. There's something positive. I'm standing pretty near to where I laid in gasping, pathetic agony for a solid fifteen minutes. I feel like I'm doing a good job of hiding my discomfort. My abs have to take on the load of holding me erect, so it's a bit of a challenge to speak in an un-strained manner, but I think I'm pulling it off. No one has asked me what's wrong, so that's good.

Branch fidgets and exchanges a look with Lucky, then with Menendez. Finally, he looks pointedly at me and speaks in a low tone that's obviously trying not to be heard by the girl, ten yards away in the house. "What're we doing here, Abe?"

To give myself a moment to think, I decide to be obtuse. "What do you mean?"

Branch glances over his shoulder at the house, where Marty and EZ are keeping a watch on Isabella, though she's definitely not going to be running anywhere now. "I mean..." he sighs and looks at the ground between our feet. "Look, man. I'm not trying to be a heartless asshole, but we've got a job to do, and she's outlived her usefulness. The fuck do you think we're going to do with a lame teenage girl?"

I raise my eyebrows. "The fuck do *you* think we're going to do?"

He meets my gaze. "Definitely not take her with us."

I look to Menendez, then Lucky, hoping for some support, but they both seem to agree with Branch's assessment. "Whaddaya wanna do? Just leave her?"

Branch's expression remains level. "Yeah. Pretty much."

I huff and puff and glance around again, though it's pretty obvious I'm alone in how I see things. "So, you wanna just leave a lame, teenage girl to die in the middle of nowhere?"

Judging by how he steps in and rolls his eyes, Menendez has clearly had enough. "No, Abe. No one *wants* to leave a teenage girl to die. No one *wanted* to take her with us in the first fucking place. But here she is, and here we are, and you can't honestly look me in the eye and tell me that a lame-ass adolescent that hates our guts is a wise thing to keep around when we're about to try to sneak into the belly of the beast." He's getting flustered with anger, gesticulating madly. "What is she gonna do? We can't take her with us on foot. She gonna sit in the fucking car? Take up room we don't have? Eat rations we can't spare? Bitch at us?" He puts his hands on his hips and narrows his eyes at me. "I'm tryna make sense of this, Abe, but I just can't figure why in the fuck you insist on keeping her around."

Branch steps up, putting a hand on both me and Menendez's shoulders. "Look. I get it. You didn't want to kill her family. And yeah, she was useful in getting our hands on Angel. But, as harsh as it is, we need to look at reality here. We're already up against it, man. And she's just dead weight."

"Yeah," Menendez says, contributing nothing but his agreement.

I nod. "Okay. Alright." I hang my head. "You guys are right. Go put her down."

The ensuing silence is exactly what I expected. I glance up at them from beneath my brows. All three of them look taken aback. Then they start to look, each to the other, like they're trying to see if anyone else has the balls to take on that task.

It seems no one does.

"Go ahead," I say, motioning to the house. "It's fine. It'll be quick. Just—" I mime pointing a pistol and firing. "Bang—two seconds of terror, and then it's lights out. She won't know any better. In fact, you could probably do it in the back of her head, and she wouldn't even know. Then there wouldn't even be the two seconds of terror. And that would make it okay, right?" I look at each of them, but no one's meeting my gaze at that point. "Right? Huh?"

Successfully making my point doesn't cool my heels at all. I get even more pissed.

It's weird. Sometimes I feel like I live my life, always just one degree away from being in a shitty mood.

I throw my arms wide, and stifle the wince from the pain it causes in my side. "Whaaaaaat?" I gasp, in mock surprise. "No one wants to cap a fifteen-year-old in the back of the head? No one wants to commit cold-blooded murder? Oh, but it's for the mission, guys. Right? Just think about all those families we're going to save, and, really, compared to them, what's one Mexican chick? The ends justify the means. Right? Right?" I spit in the dirt, because I still can't get any eye contact. "Oh, okay. So you figured, hey, tell Abe to off the bitch, because he doesn't have a soul, but God forbid you be the one to do the deed. That about the size of it?"

Menendez pats a hand in the air. "Alright. Cool your jets."

"Cool *my* jets?" I ask, though I do bring my tone down a good bit. "Y'all are the ones begging for me to kill the girl. Whose jets need to be cooled?"

"We're not asking you to kill her," Menendez seethes, also trying to keep his volume down.

"Oh? Then what are you asking?"

"You know." Menendez shrugs. "Just...Leave her behind."

"Leave her behind?"

"Yeah. We can leave some water and rations and shit. Tell her to stay put. All goes well, we can come back through this way and drop her off with her mom on the way out."

I pull my head back. "Drop her off with her mom? What the fuck are you talking about, Dez? This isn't a carpool for kids' soccer. We're in the middle of nowhere, and now we know for certain that there's a pack of primals in this area. It'd be *more* merciful just to shoot her in the back of the head."

Menendez arches his eyebrows. "Well. Then..." he sweeps an inviting hand towards the house.

I glare. "Fuck you, Dez. I'm not capping her. And I'm not leaving her behind."

"So..." Menendez looks skyward. "Your plan is to just let her run amok and possibly get us killed?"

"I don't think she's running anywhere."

Menendez closes his eyes, pinching the bridge of his nose. "Abe. I want you to take a minute and really think about what you're saying here. Actually imagine how this is going to work out, and then explain it to me." He opens his eyes, blinks, and crosses his arms over his chest. "Go ahead. Paint me a picture of how we all don't die in Mexico because of her."

Unfortunately, I've spent *hours* doing that ever since I chose not to kill the family and to take her with us. And no, I don't have an answer. Everything is fantasy. I've been crushed between the proverbial rock and hard place, and there's not a reasonable conclusion in which everyone walks away with a happy ending.

Someone's getting fucked. Either us, or Isabella, or the families we're here to save.

"Look," I sigh, easing my torso back and forth to forestall an impending cramp in my oblique. "You want me to admit that it's shitty? Alright. It's shitty. It's a giant load of shit. But we're in it. And I'm not gonna kill the girl, and

I'm not gonna leave her behind, because that's basically killing her, and it doesn't seem like any of you are going to kill her, so we're stuck with her. It's not ideal, and I'm not trying to tell you that it is. I'm just telling you where we're at. This is where we're at. You want me to tell you the future? Sorry. No can do. I'm not clairvoyant. So...what's left?" I raise my hands in a shrug. "Keep pushing forward. Adapt and overcome. Hope for the best. Mitigate our weaknesses, and maximize our strengths. That's all there is. That's all we can do."

"We could ask EZ and Marty if either of them will do it," Lucky suggests.

I shake my head, giving him an *are you stupid* look. "I think you're missing the point I was making. If I'm not willing to do it, I'm damn sure not gonna look the other way and let someone else do it. She stays alive. And she comes with us."

All three of them look briefly defeated, but they don't push the issue.

I wonder if they really *want* to push the issue. I wonder why they even brought it up in the first place. Did they really think I was gonna be on board with it? And what does that say about who they think I am?

"Alright," Menendez says in a relenting tone. "Just promise me this..." He leans forward and puts a fist to my chest—not threatening, but pleading. "If it becomes clear that it's either her or the mission, you'll do what needs to be done to make sure my team and those families get out alive."

I chew on that for a moment, but there's no way I can deny Menendez. In a way, when you take out all the morality and emotion of it, it's a reasonable request.

If you look at it pragmatically.

You know...like a sociopath.

I nod. "You got my word, Dez. If it comes to that, team and mission come first."

The others look mollified.

I feel like I've only put off the inevitable.

That night, we eat well.

Which is odd to say, remembering back to being active duty in the US military, back when there was one, and it was the military of the richest, most well-supplied country in the world. Back then, I would've considered it unfortunate to have to eat an MRE, thinking of all those preservatives I was putting in my system, and whether or not this particular "entrée" would stop me up or give me the runs.

After months of living on whatever scraps could be stolen from whatever cartel outpost I had just raided, an actual MRE is a luxury. Even if it is vegetarian lasagna.

Prior to all this shit, Menendez and his crew had been with another Project Hometown Coordinator—the one from Texas, who, very appropriately, was called "Tex."

Unfortunately, Tex didn't make it. But we still had access to one of his bunkers, and managed to use it to resupply the refineries, some of which we took with us when we left on this mission.

The mood is oddly lighthearted, as we all eat our preservative-filled mush in the dim glow of a rechargeable solar lantern. Packets are traded: Skittles and jalapeno cheese spread seem to be a one-to-one exchange, while apparently two packs of crackers is worth one pack of peanut butter.

Even Isabella gets in on the action.

Hoping to make some peace, I approach her with my dessert pack. She's sitting with her leg propped up on Branch's daypack, her ankle in a splint. Between her broken bone, Menendez's gunshot wound, and my torn oblique, we've dipped into our supply of ibuprofen pretty hard. Or "Ranger Candy," as Menendez insists on calling it.

The strain on her face when she looks up at me tells me it's not quite enough to block all her pain. Welcome to military life. Shot? Stabbed? Blown up? Take some ibuprofen and make sure you hydrate.

I show her my peace offering. "I have in my possession one packet of vanilla pound cake. Three hundred calories of straight fat and carbs. What'll you give me for it?"

She blinks. Looks at the pound cake. Looks at the various packets from her own MRE, strewn between her legs. Is that the barest hint of a smile I detect?

It seems strange, but then, coming that close to death and surviving can do different things to different people. Some people quake and obsess about it and go quiet and stare into the middle distance. Others get a rush of appreciation for another day.

I'm pleased to see she's the latter sort. Proves she's got some resilience.

Makes me wonder if I can actually keep my promise to Menendez.

I see a glint of spiteful glee in her eyes as she comes up with a packet of grape-flavored drink mix. Which, I should point out, I abhor. She holds it up, raising a single eyebrow.

"Oh, damn," EZ remarks, everyone watching the exchange. "Señorita's pushing a hard bargain."

I make an unconvinced sound and lean over to inspect the rest of what she's got. Frankly, I'd've just given her the pound cake. It is a peace offering, after all. But I don't want to make her think that I consider an MRE pound cake to be appropriate restitution for trauma, death threats, a broken ankle, and a dead uncle.

What I'm *trying* to do is make her feel like she's a part of us. Build some rapport. I don't know if it'll work, and I highly doubt it'll be enough, but it's worth a shot, and you gotta start somewhere.

"The drink mix *and* the crackers," I say. "Come on. That's more than fair."

She shrugs. "Sorry. I need my crackers. I'm a growing girl. And I'm injured. Grape drink. Take it or leave it."

EZ whistles.

"Bro," Marty puts in. "Take the drink mix. EZ'll give you almost anything for some more grape drink. You know he loves that grape drink."

Lucky coughs. "Goddamn."

EZ glowers at Marty. "Motherfucker, we don't call it grape drink. We don't call it by the flavor, we call it by the color. Purple drink, red drink, etcetera. I've explained this before."

"So, if it's orange-flavored, what do you call it?"

"Orange drink," EZ says, with a scoff. "Obviously."

Lucky shakes his head, peering at EZ. "Why you let him get away with that shit? I'm offended *for* you."

EZ looks sidelong at Marty, then loops an arm around his shoulder. "Look, guys. I don't know if you've figured it out yet, but..." he lowers his voice to a whisper. "Marty here's got a touch of the 'tism."

Branch points a spork at the two men. "You know what? That actually makes a lot of sense."

"Explains a lot," Lucky agrees.

EZ ruffles Marty's hair. "Tardy Marty here was a Make-A-Wish kid. Right before the world ended, they granted his one wish to be an 'army man.' Let him put on the BDU's and hang out with some soldiers, but right then, the plague came stateside, and Marty's Make-A-Wish handler got ate, and by then, everything was chaos, and so Marty, well, he just blended into the rest of the inbred cow-fuckers from Texas." EZ sighs. "So, you see, it'd be wrong for me to react badly to an autistic kid. He doesn't know what he's saying. He just repeats what he read on some far-right online chat board while he was living in his mother-sister-wife's basement." EZ pinches Marty's cheek fiercely, then gives it a light slap.

Marty grins and takes it.

"Wow," is about all I can say, then turn back to Isabella, who seems singularly confused by the whole exchange. "Alright, hardball. It's a deal."

We make the swap. I take the grape drink mix back to my area, having no intention of drinking it. Isabella pockets the pound cake, saving it for later.

I settle myself down into my spot and finish off my vegetarian lasagna, while the others chatter, and Isabella listens with an expression like she doesn't quite know how to take these guys. I don't blame her. It'd be culture shock for anyone, let alone for a person who doesn't necessarily see us as the good guys.

Once or twice she smiles at a joke, but never outright laughs.

Once or twice she glances at me, but her eyes never stay for long.

Right as everyone is finishing up and consolidating their trash, a howl shudders through the night outside.

As one, everybody freezes. I'm the first to move, grabbing my rifle from the floor beside me. Then everyone grabs theirs.

Any semblance of friendliness has been ripped out of Isabella's face. Now it is only pure terror. She looks like she wants to get to her feet, but can't.

I rise to mine and pat a hand at her. "Take it easy," I say in a low, calm tone, but my eyes are scouring the open windows. "I don't think they'll give us any more trouble tonight."

The others are on their feet as well, spreading out in the dim hovel to cover any openings—Branch squatting to point his rifle through the hole Isabella made through the wrecked half of the house, and which I widened a good bit when I went after her.

"That was close by," EZ observes in a hushed voice.

Isabella is shaking her head. "How do you know they won't mess with us again? If they're that close..."

She trails off, staring at me. She seems to know I'm not saying something.

I don't want to tell her that I left the primals an offering of sorts. I dragged Angel's body out to the edge of the woods. An attempt to distract them for the night, since we'll be gone in the morning.

"Just...trust me," I murmur.

For a long moment, we're all silent. Waiting. Listening.

"I don't think they'll be coming around again tonight," I announce, with more confidence than is probably justified. Maybe the guys know it's fake, but I'm doing it for Isabella.

She, however, doesn't seem to really hear me. She still looks scared, but I notice that she doesn't look at me. Or anyone else for that matter. She's hunched over, with someone's poncho liner pulled up to her chest. Her eyes glimmer wetly.

I think she knows.

And she probably hates me for it.

Sucks. Thought I'd made a little headway with the pound cake.

Irritated, though unsure who I'm irritated with, I assign EZ the first watch, and settle in to get snuggly with my own poncho liner, using my daypack as a pillow. EZ settles in just outside the door, where he can keep an eye on both our environs and Isabella. The lantern is doused, and the house falls into darkness.

No one talks anymore.

I lay with my rifle on my chest and stare at the blackness overhead, which seems to be an endless void, beckoning me into it.

CHAPTER 11

I'VE HEARD IT SAID that the devil roams about like a lion, seeking souls to devour.

But I think, if there is a devil at all, it's the wrinkly gray one inside your skull.

Let me explain.

I was surprised when I woke up. Surprised, because I remember staring into the darkness...and then I was awake. Which means I slept through the whole night. After everything that'd happened the day before, I figured my sleep would be fitful and shallow.

And I think, *Man, I must've really needed sleep.*

But then my devil-brain challenges me, *What kind of man sleeps soundly after all that?*

Oh. Right. A sociopath.

God in heaven, my brain just won't let this idea go. And I'm getting sick of it. The taste of it is stale and nauseous in my mind. I can't keep obsessing over this. It's going to make me stop and think in a moment when action is required to save my life, or the lives of others.

I make the decision, right then and there, as I lean up and scrape the crust out of the corners of my eyes: No more of this shit. Introspection is a luxury that only a man at peace can afford. When, and if, I ever get to that point, I can torture myself with regrets for all the live-long day. But right now, I need to stay focused on what matters—not some whimpering, existential anxieties.

Pragmatism is what I need. Fuck the internal consequences. Those are problems for future me. Right now, my only problem is finding those families, and getting them and my team back to Texas. All other considerations can fuck right off.

So I take Isabella, and her dead uncle, and the doctors I shot, and Angel, and I cram them all into the mass grave of my mind, where lies the rotting remnants of so many other questionable decisions that I don't have the time or the energy to address. Then I cover them up with my stubborn will, like pouring a truckload of concrete over it all, sealing it for future me to unearth, if I ever get the hankering for masochistic self-flagellation.

Me. Five guys. Seven families.

Anyone that gets in the way, will get put down.

It's nice and simple.

I'll be honest, I feel relief, cool and numb, flow over me.

I don't even bother looking over at Isabella in the blueish dawn light, save to make sure she's still there. I glance at the door, and find Lucky stretching languidly and yawning.

"Morning, Sunshine," he murmurs.

"Yup," I say, testing the integrity of my torso as I give it a slight twist and bend. No, sleep, as solid as it apparently was, did not magically knit the torn muscle fibers back together. Of course not. I'm almost forty, so, naturally, that'll take about six months.

Whatever.

"You doin' alright?" Lucky asks, with a note of downplayed concern.

"Peachy," I say, cheerier than is warranted, then rise to my feet, clenching my jaw so the pain doesn't show on my face. "Life is pain. If anyone tells you different, they're selling you something."

"Mm. I like that. You come up with that on your own?"

I smirk at him as I stuff my sleeping accoutrements—such as they are—into my daypack. "*The Princess Bride*, Lucky. Get cultured."

By then, everyone is stirring. Grumbling. Groaning. Farting.

Isabella sits up, glowering, bleary-eyed. "I…uh…"

I take my rifle and sling into it. "Gotta piss?"

She nods, vigorously.

I sigh, looking around at the wreckage on her side of the house. There's not a whole lot to work with over there, but it'll have to be enough. I approach the fallen timbers of the house, and select a length of wood that I estimate is about chest-height on Isabella, and not too thick, and not too rotted out. I yank it out of the pile of detritus and bring it over to her.

"What am I supposed to do with this?" she asks.

"Crutch," I say. "Unless you want me to escort you and hold your hand while you piss."

She nods with some consternation, then struggles her way to her feet. I watch her, but don't lend a hand. She's gonna be busted long after we're gone from her country. She'll need to figure out how to move around on her own. No time like the present.

She gets herself upright, her broken ankle hovering over the ground as she balances on one foot and gets the makeshift crutch under her armpit, which can't be too comfortable, since there's no cross-piece. But we can handle that later.

She hesitates, avoiding eye-contact. "Um. It's not just piss."

"Okay," I say, frowning. "Do what you gotta do, Isabella. I'm not keeping a record of your shits and pisses."

She flushes and glares at me. "I don't have...how do I...clean myself up?"

I roll my eyes, then search the ground around her bed area until I find the thin bit of napkin that came with her MRE. I bend—slowly and painfully—and pluck it up.

I dangle it in front of Isabella's face, pinched between two fingers. "Here you go."

She snatches it, looking horrified. "That's it?"

"Such is life."

"It's not enough!" she protests.

"Lemme show you a trick," I say, holding up my hands to demonstrate. I stick out my index finger, then make a hook with it. "One finger to scoop your asshole clean." Then I make a ring with my thumb and forefinger on my other hand, and swipe the imaginarily-shitty index finger through it. "Get the shit off your finger. Use the napkin to clean your hands. Boom. Done."

She stares at me, agog.

I frown. "Whaddaya want, princess? A fucking bidet? Go handle your shit. Literally."

I ignore the hurt look she casts me as she hobbles towards the door.

"Don't go running off," I snipe at her back.

Briefly, I start to feel bad, then remember that I don't give a fuck.

I turn to where Marty and EZ are getting mobile, watching me like I've kicked a kitten. "EZ. Go keep an eye on her."

EZ throws his hands out. "Why me?"

I give him an innocent look. "Well, I'd send Marty, but he'll get turned on."

EZ huffs, but takes up his rifle and heads out.

Marty's face is all pinched up. "That's gross, man."

"You're gross."

"I mean, sure, but not *that* gross."

"Oh, quit whining and come gimme a hand."

"I'm not wiping your ass."

"Color me heartbroken."

We exit out into the early-morning light. The birds are in a riot of activity, chittering and flitting through the trees. The air is heavy and humid, and oddly cool, I think, though I know it won't last long.

We move to the 4Runner, and I motion towards the brush all around us. "I wanna camouflage it a bit. If we're gonna be running parallel to a road that's got patrols on it, I wanna be able to hide in the brush."

Marty puts his hands on his hips and inspects the brush, then tilts his head at the vehicle like a dog that's heard a weird noise. "How we gonna affix the brush to it?"

I open the driver's door and grab the roll of OD green tape from the side pocket of the door. "Hundred mile-per-hour tape, naturally."

He nods, approvingly. "Naturally."

By the time the sun breaches the trees, everyone's up and about. Isabella returns, holding her hands like she's got nuclear waste on them. EZ pours some water over them, and she scrubs vigorously, looking disgusted and ashamed.

Lucky appropriates a length of 100-mph tape from me and works on making a padded brace for her armpit. He uses all our MRE trash from the previous night to make the pad, stuffing it all into one of the mylar bags the meals come in. I appreciate the resourcefulness.

Me and Marty continue to work on making our vehicle look like a bush.

"You could be a little nicer to the chick," Marty observes, quietly.

I frown at him as I tape a bundle of grass to the A-frame, hoping to hide our vehicle's silhouette. "This, coming from you?"

Marty pulls his head back as he holds a chunk of bush in place for me to tape. "The fuck's that supposed to mean? I'm nice."

"No, you're not," I say, flatly. Tape the bush down in two places.

He squints at me. "I feel like you're projecting."

I shrug. "You're right. I'm not nice. But I'm not projecting." I pause, looking at him. "You're not nice. EZ's not nice. None of us are nice. If we were nice, we wouldn't be doing this job. Nice people die. Mean people get shit done." I lean into him, lowering my voice, because I can feel myself getting irritated. "I get it, Marty. I brought a fifteen-year-old girl along with us, and now everyone thinks they have to be nice for her sake. But the sooner everyone can realize that she's just an asset—an asset that may or may not be useful in the future, and nothing more—the sooner everyone can get back to being who they need to be."

Marty considers this, not looking terribly convinced. "I feel like you just woke up grumpy."

"No. I woke up right as rain." I draw a circle in the air with my hand, indicating the squad. "We're all here for one reason, and one reason only. To extract as many families as we can, so the refinery workers will stop sabotaging our shit up and keep pumping the fuel that we need. That's it.

There's nothing else to it." I look sternly at Marty. "And the second anyone gets in the way of that, you put them down, you understand me? I don't care who they are. We can't mess around here, Marty. You wanna feel bad about it later, when we get back to civilization? Whatever. But right now, we're behind enemy lines, and there just ain't time for feeling bad. Just do what you need to do to get the job done."

Marty blinks a few times, then looks away from me, lips pursing in thought.

I knuckle him in the shoulder. "You picking up what I'm laying down?"

"Yeah," he says, a little quietly. "I got it. Mission first."

We finish camouflaging the 4Runner in silence.

Thank God for the clarity of a good night's sleep. I feel like the last few sleepless nights have clouded my judgement. Made me drunk on sleep deprivation. Now I'm seeing clearly again, and I regard my efforts to play nice with Isabella like you might recall some dumb shit you pulled while in a drunken stupor. The hell was I thinking?

Ah well. Sleep deprivation's a bitch, but I'm back to being me now.

I do consider the possibility that I may have set the wrong tone with the squad. Maybe that's why Marty was being all bleeding-heart earlier. It might be Menendez's squad, but I'm the one in charge of the operation, and, as loose as authority is with us these days, I know that the others look up to me, and might be taking their cues from me.

Best to nip this in the bud before we go further.

Once we get everything packed up, and all semblance of our being here erased as best we can, I put Isabella in the backseat and close the door behind her, cutting her off from the rest of the team. I pull them away from the Toyota a few strides, and speak to them in a lower tone, though, if I'm being honest, I don't *really* care if Isabella overhears us.

I'm not saying anything to them that I didn't make clear to her yesterday.

"Gents, we're about to head into it," I begin. "I realize I've been a little distracted with Tiny Tim in the back, there, and I don't want to send the wrong message, so let me be ultra clear with you guys: She is an asset. Her only value is in what she can do to help us accomplish what we came here to do. That's it. I'm gonna keep her around because she might still prove useful. But, in your minds, I want you to put her into the mental category of a tool. Everyone around us is an enemy that wants to kill us, and she's no different, even if we've managed to pacify her for now. So, let's reset our heads good and proper. We're going after these families. That's all that matters. Everything else is distraction." I raise my eyebrows. "We all on the same page?"

I scan their faces. Marty and EZ seem a little reticent, but they nod. Branch seems not to care either way. Lucky shrugs like I've said something obvious.

Menendez gives me a searching look, but then nods approvingly.

Great. Super. I'm glad to be myself again.

Life is so much simpler when you don't give a shit.

I smile at them. "Alright. Let's go ruin someone's day."

CHAPTER 12

MENENDEZ'S VOICE IS A whisper in my ear: "Either the Universe is really smiling down on us right now...or your boy Angel misled us."

Call me a pessimist if you will, but I immediately put more weight on the latter.

Frowning, I wait for Menendez to continue his transmission, but he doesn't. I key my comms. "Care to elaborate on that, Dez?"

As I say it, my eyes slip to the mountaintop a few miles away. As though I could spot where Menendez and Branch have made their hide, right over top of the vineyard. Obviously, I can't, or they wouldn't be very good at their job.

The twelve hours since we left the farmstead passed with shocking uneventfulness. We traveled the overgrown dirt paths in a southerly direction until we started to get into the foothills of the Sierra Madres, as Angel had promised. We spotted one vehicle moving on the far-off road—what might've been a patrol—but it sped on, never stopping, and certainly not giving us any attention. That was as action-packed as the day got.

Also, just as Angel had promised, the vineyard where he claimed Diego Beltran had made his new home was not hard to find. Right around midday, we spotted it in the distance: A conspicuous mountain jutting out from around the rolling foothills. Working our way around that mountain, we found the vineyard itself, positioned about midway up the southern slope.

It was done up in Spanish style, or at least that's my take on it, not being an architecture whiz. White stone walls—or maybe it was adobe—with red clay tile rooves. I don't think it was making wine anymore, though the acres upon acres of grape trellises were still visible as evenly-spaced lines of overgrown green that dominated the slopes just below the house itself.

Not really a house. It was a fucking mansion.

The rest of the day was spent setting up our little base camp, roughly three miles southwest of the mountain, and then inching closer, probing for sentries and fortifications. So far, it'd been a breeze. Menendez and Branch had set up an overwatch position near the peak of the mountain, with what they said was a great view of the entire compound. Then Marty, EZ, and Lucky had worked their way around the mountain to get a better idea of the security measures closer in to our objective.

So far, reports are making it seem like this is going to be a walk in the park.

In response to my request to elaborate, Menendez transmits a small, almost bewildered chuckle, and explains:

"Welp. I've got a grand total of seven guards spotted. Three teams of two on roving patrol, and one guy with a two-forty-bravo in a machine gun nest in the bell tower. You see the bell tower, right?"

I squint at the structure in the distance, its white walls ablaze with pinkish light from the setting sun. Right smack dab in the center of it all, a tower juts up, presumably with a bell in it, though I can't see that with my naked eye.

"Yeah, I can see the bell tower. What else?"

"Oh, let's see. Four kids—three boys and a girl—ranging from what looks like five or six years of age, to maybe ten. They're out playing soccer right now, with an adult female. She's maybe in her twenties or thirties."

How serene. "Any sign of the target?"

"Possibly. Branch spotted a dude that matches the description—longer, salt-and-pepper hair, pulled back in a pony tail, clean shaven, tall and lean. He was standing in a doorway, watching the kids play soccer and smoking a cigar. He never came out, though."

"Goddamn. That does seem...suspiciously light."

"You're telling me," Menendez comments.

"Alright. Keep an eye on things. I need to know where Diego Beltran sleeps, and where the non-combatants are going to be when things go lights-out."

"We copy."

"Marty, EZ, and Lucky. Can you talk?"

I wait for a few seconds, then receive two clicks back.

"Alright, I copy. As soon as you can talk, give me a sitrep."

I settle back in the driver's seat of the 4Runner, grimacing and shifting about. I need to get up and move. I hate it with a passion, but I had to nut up and admit to the guys that I tweaked my old man body in the kerfuffle yesterday. I elected to stay behind and babysit, to give it a bit more rest.

I glance sourly at the rearview mirror. Isabella sits sullenly in the backseat, staring out the window.

I grab the bottle of ibuprofen from the cupholder in the center console. Shake out four pills and swallow them dry. Then I hold the bottle up. "How's your ankle? You need some?"

She drags her gaze from the distance and skewers me with it in the rearview. Then she leans forward and opens her hand. I twist, shaking four out for her. She pops them in her mouth and tries to swallow them dry like I did, but splutters and gags and looks panicked for a moment.

Muttering, I proffer my bottle of water to her, which she sucks at greedily, all while glaring at me over the top of it. I decide to let her keep the bottle for now.

I open my door and slide out. Step away from the vehicle a single pace. The windows are all down and the engine's off—keys in my pocket—so I'm not worried about her locking me out if she got such an idea in her head.

I do some slow stretches and a few calisthenic movements.

"What's wrong with you?" Isabella asks, with a bit of snark in her voice.

"Nothing," I grunt.

She quirks an eyebrow. "Thought you said you pulled something."

"Well, then why'd you ask?"

"Why are you such an asshole?" she suddenly demands.

I pause in the process of easing my torso into a side-bend. "Maybe because you shot at me."

She bristles. "I thought you were going to shoot me!"

"I should have. Woulda simplified things."

Her eyes turn to venomous slits. "Why didn't you then?"

I stand upright and stare back at her, thinking, *Because I've never shot a kid before.*

What I actually say is, "Momentary lapse of judgment. Are you trying to give me an excuse to rectify it?"

She considers me with those slit eyes for a moment. Then she juts her chin out. "I'm not afraid of you."

I step up to the side of the vehicle and lean my elbows in the open window. "Honeybuns, I don't need you to be afraid of me. You can listen to your own survival instinct as much or as little as you want. Won't cost me nothing but a bullet."

She wags a finger at me and speaks as though she's a detective solving a mystery. "See, I don't think you'll actually kill me. I don't think you have it in you."

I look at her with bland, half-lidded eyes. "You have remarkably little evidence to base that on."

"Uh, you didn't shoot me," she says. "After I shot at you. And then, again, you didn't shoot me *when I was pointing the gun right at you*. I think that's evidence enough."

"I had bigger problems."

"Bigger problems than me pointing a gun at your head?"

"You couldn't hit the broad side of a barn, little girl."

"I think you know that's bullshit."

"I think I'm glad I broke your ankle. You deserve it."

"I think I'm glad you strained your back. Asshole."

"It's my oblique." I know—that was lame.

"Whatever."

"So, yesterday, I'm a heartless American that doesn't care who he kills, and today I've got a warm caramel center and I could never bring myself to hurt you?"

She raises her hands in a shrug. "You had every reason to. And you didn't. I rest my case."

The radio chirps in my ear. "EZ to Abe, you ready to copy?"

I retreat from the vehicle, waving a hand at Isabella. "Just shut the fuck up." She says something snappy, but I don't catch it. "Go ahead with it, EZ."

EZ's voice is slow and deliberate, carefully articulating his whispered words. "We are at the northwestern corner of the compound. There's a wall around the compound, roughly eight feet high. No guards posted outside of it. No security measures in the woods around it. And...I think we've marked a good entrance point."

Menendez was right. This feels too easy.

"Good work. Hold what you got." I release my PTT and stand there, considering what I know to this point.

So far, we've got a walled compound, with minimal security inside, and nonexistent security around it. By all appearances, this place has the look of a juicy peach, ripe for the picking.

Now, I know what you're thinking: If it's too good to be true, it usually is. And you're right. But here's another adage for you: Don't look a gift horse in the mouth.

We're all indoctrinated by movies and TV, where the steely-eyed hero looks to his buxom female companion—who of course, just can't wait to jump his bones—and says, "It's quiet. Maybe a little *too* quiet." From which we are all deeply influenced to believe that an easy op is a trap.

But sometimes shit is just easy. And anyone who's actually been in combat will tell you, there's rarely a Bond villain masterminding some byzantine plan to draw you in unawares. When you get right down to it, if shit looks easy, that's called an opportunity, and if you pass it up because you're paranoid that it's some carefully-laid trap, you're an idiot that watches too much TV.

When the enemy gives you an opening, you take advantage of it.

Chances are, this is just what Angel said it would be: Diego Beltran is spread thin, trying to make his new position as head of the *Nuevas Fronteras* cartel official. He's got the manpower to guard his compound, but not enough to secure the whole mountain.

I'm also not going to up and assume he's an idiot, or inept. If he's left himself this exposed, it'd be smarter to assume he's got a good goddamn reason for it. He took a risk, perceiving that the most likely threat would come from other quarters. It doesn't make him dumb that he didn't realize a small American strike team would try to infiltrate his mountain compound.

Okay. So we have what looks like a golden opportunity to A) take the newly-sprouted head off the snake, and B) find out where the seven families of the refinery workers are being held.

I know that time is not on our side. For all I know, whoever's holding those families could be executing wives and kids every hour on the hour. And that makes me want to have my guys hold position, and infiltrate tonight, as soon as they identify where Diego lays his head.

And this is where I encounter the dilemma of hesitation versus patience.

Hesitation is bad. You don't know what the future holds. We wait, and for all I know, a busload of fresh cartel soldiers could arrive, and the mountain could be crawling with foot patrols by dawn. Or maybe Diego up and decides to go somewhere, and we don't have time to set up an ambush, or Diego takes too many soldiers with him to make a takedown practical.

On the other hand, patience is a virtue, and has won many a battle. Waiting and watching can only provide us with more data, and the more data we have, the better prepared we will be to take on the threats arrayed against us.

Fools rush in where angels fear to tread.

Yeah, I've got about ten different axioms rolling through my head, and they all contradict each other.

I hate dilemmas.

Here's another factor I have to consider: I have full faith in the guys' ability to hold their positions and infiltrate the compound tonight—or more accurately, very early next morning. They're all tough as nails, and, despite how they talk, they are professionals. No one will fall asleep on the job, or fail to identify a threat because their blood sugar was low.

But having your team rested and fed is always an advantage.

I rub my face and scratch vigorously at my beard.

You can worry over something forever, but eventually, you gotta make a decision. I've considered the facts at hand, and run down the most likely permutations of what we've observed. Now I gotta make the call.

I press the PTT again. "Alright, gents. EZ, I want your team to pull back and return to base camp. You copy?"

EZ acknowledges with a whispered "We copy."

"Menendez, I want you to hold tight with Branch and keep an eye on the compound. I'm gonna let Lucky grab some food and some sleep, and then send him up to relieve you. Branch, you got enough food and water to maintain overwatch for the next twenty-four hours?"

After a second, Menendez responds for him: "He says he's got seventy-two hours in his daypack."

"Tonight, I wanna know where everyone sleeps, if and when there's guard changes—all that good shit. As of right now, we'll plan to go hot in..." I check my wristwatch and do some quick math. "...thirty-three hours. Between now and then, Branch, I need you to keep a special eye out for anything suspicious, any changes—anything not consistent with what you've seen so far. You know what to look for. Everyone copy?"

"Five by five, Boss," Menendez sighs into the radio.

I feel his pain.

I hate waiting.

CHAPTER 13

Time gets wonky as hell when you're waiting to do violence.

Sometimes you look at your watch, thinking hours have gone by, only to discover it's been a paltry thirty minutes since you last checked. At other times, you check your watch and your stomach knots up at how much time you've already lost, and you wish you had more of it to prepare.

This can be mentally fatiguing, and for the man patiently—or impatiently—waiting for a green light, mental fatigue is just as much an enemy as the guy that wants to kill you.

I set my watch to vibrate an alarm every three hours, so that I'm not constantly checking it. I take naps between the alarms. Hydrate. Get some calories in me. In between those things, I keep myself busy.

I dig us in a little better, pulling the 4Runner back behind a knoll, to keep it hidden from the vineyard, then refresh the brushy camouflage over it. We're in a decently-dense forest, and the nearby road is about a mile away, but I still chop some extra brush down and make a sort of privacy screen with it, so we can at least use our red-light filters without that scant illumination being spotted by prying eyes.

I take a lot of yoga breaks, doing my best to rehab my oblique as much as possible. I hold no illusions—I'm not gonna be a hundred percent by the time we move. I'm just keeping it loose and warm.

We have 27 hours left by the time EZ, Marty, and Lucky return to base camp.

With them there, I keep one of us on watch at all times, rotating every three hours. I'm less concerned with roving cartel finding us than I am with another pack of primals sniffing us out.

After letting Lucky sleep for six hours, I send him back up to relieve Menendez, carrying a spare radio battery for Branch.

Twenty-one hours to go.

During all this, Isabella is absolutely useless. Every time I see her sitting up against the rear tire of the Toyota, eating our food and drinking our water and contributing jack-shit to our efforts, I have to remind myself that she didn't have a choice—I forced her to be here.

Still. I'm gonna have to figure out what to do with her. Because we can't afford to leave someone behind to babysit. We need everyone on this op. Which leaves me with yet another dilemma—what to do with her while we're gone.

Menendez makes it back right before the sun comes up on our second day reconning the vineyard. He's sweaty, and haggard, and tired. I want to pick his brain, but I can see the exhaustion all over him, so I mother him instead, making him eat, hydrate, take a handful of ibuprofen, and then send him to bed for three hours.

In a monumental demonstration of patience, I even let him stretch and take a shit after he wakes up. We're down to twelve hours.

"First thing's first," I say, keeping my voice down. "We need to figure out what we're gonna do with Isabella."

He's munching on one of Marty's MRE Pop Tarts, and washing it down with water. He glances over his shoulder at her. "Yeah. I think you know my position on that."

I scrape my teeth over my bottom lip. "Dez. You can be a part of the solution, or I can just ignore your ass and make the call on my own."

He harrumphs. "I guess that means you won't be showing her the pretty flowers."

That's not even worth responding to, so I don't. "I don't wanna leave anyone behind to babysit. And obviously we can't take her with us."

Menendez shrugs, shoving the last third of his pastry in his mouth. "Then tie her to a tree," he says, dribbling crumbs.

Honestly, I'd considered that. Still am. It is an option. Just...not ideal.

"Can you think of a way we can make her work for us?" I ask. "Get some use out of her?"

Menendez shakes his head. "She is currently three miles from our objective, and I don't even like her being *that* close."

"She did good back in Pancho."

"Yeah, I think that was the last use we're gonna get out of her, Abe. Case in point—she tried to shoot you." He gives me a suspicious look. "Also, I feel like you're trying to work me around to an idea."

I decide to give up on subtlety. I was never good at it anyways.

"I was thinking about having her drive the 4Runner. You know. As an extract vehicle."

Menendez's water bottle is almost to his lips, and it halts there. Then lowers. "Abe. No offense and all that. But that's fucking dumb."

"Yeah, I know it's fucking dumb," I gripe. "Which is why I'm asking you for better ideas, but you're not exactly helping me out in that regard."

Menendez smacks his lips. Holds up two fingers, and ticks them off. "Two options, as I see it: Slit her throat and be done with the whole thing; or tie her to a tree." He shrugs. "Those are my ideas. I got nothing else for you."

I'd like to say that I take umbrage to those suggestions. But I don't.

Sure, I'm still not giving a fuck. But not giving a fuck doesn't mean I'm gonna slit her throat.

"Not gonna kill her," I reiterate for the umpteenth time. "And while tying her to a tree is a viable option...I'm not a fan."

"I didn't say you had to like it. I just said those were the options as I see them."

"I tie her to a tree, she might get eaten."

"We haven't seen any primal activity in this area."

"Yeah, we didn't see any primal activity over at the farmstead either. Until we did."

Menendez huffs and throws his hands out. "What do you want me to tell you, Abe?"

I sigh. "Just hoping you had some genius idea I hadn't thought of."

"Nope. I'm thinking about the op. Which is what you should be thinking about."

"I *am* thinking about the op."

"No, you're distracted by what to do with a little girl before you *go* on the op."

"Alright, okay," I say, waving irritably. "We'll table it." I switch topics. "You made a good sketch of the compound?"

He smiles wryly and pulls a sheet of paper from his sleeve-pocket. "I made *a* sketch. Don't expect artistry. But it's accurate. Ish." He unfolds the paper and inspects it with a clinical eye. "For a kindergartener."

Using his sketch and his memory, we construct as detailed a model of the compound as we can from sticks and rocks. By that afternoon we have a pretty decent miniature of the compound we intend to infiltrate. It measures roughly six feet by four, laid out on the flattest section of ground we could find near our base camp.

The others join us and look on appreciatively.

"Now, *that's* a fucking sand table," Marty quips.

"Top grade," EZ says, giving us a golf clap. "Gold star for both of you. You've got a good chance of winning the junior high science fair."

"But where's the volcano?" Marty asks, as though disappointed.

I glance over at Isabella, who's now standing on one leg, peering over at the model with mild curiosity. And then looking at Marty and EZ with a confusion that borders on distaste.

I know what she's thinking in that moment, but that's because she can't see what I see. She doesn't know about guys like this, and what happens in their brains when they know they're heading into the thick of it.

They know that tonight could be their last. There's no last hurrah party. No way to celebrate what might be their final hours on earth. They'll wait in the woods, dirty and grimy, until it's go time, and then they'll do their jobs, and in the doing, they might get killed.

She sees a bunch of cocky assholes, bloodthirsty and war-hardened, who think they're invincible.

I see a group of guys pretending to be something they wished they never had to be, in the hopes that it'll keep the fear from addling their minds. A silently-agreed-upon collective delusion of fearlessness. And woe to the dipshit that mentions mortality and shatters that fragile illusion.

I turn back to the model, sweeping all of my misgivings under a mental rug.

What we have represented here is a walled compound, with five structures inside of it. The wall is roughly rectangular, with the long sides facing north and south, and the short sides facing east and west. The north side butts up against the mountain, while the south side looks out over the descending hills.

Inside, the main residence is pushed back against the northern wall. There's a pool behind it, and a pool house off to the side. Directly in front of the house is an open parking area with a defunct fountain. Then, along the southern wall, there are the last three structures. The winery, which sits in the center, across from the house. Then there's some sort of equipment shed or warehouse on the east side of the winery, and a big, five-car garage on the west side.

Menendez takes a long, straight stick, and starts identifying things. "This here's the main house. Roughly six thousand square feet. Two stories. Seven bedrooms, five bathrooms." Menendez taps one side of the house and then the other. "There's three bedrooms on the west side, and four on the east side." He taps the center. "Kitchen and living areas seem to be in the middle. We're not quite sure which side the master bedroom is on, which is likely where Diego Beltran rests his head, but my guess is that it's on the west side."

"Check that," I put in. "Branch ID'd our target last night, retiring to a bedroom on the west side. You must've missed it while you were hiking back."

Menendez nods. "Alright. So. Target will likely be in a bedroom on the west side." He looks at me. "Branch ID which bedroom?"

I squat down behind the model of the house, and use my own stick to point. "There's a window on the northeastern corner. Branch said that's where he saw Diego settle in for the night. The thirty-year-old female was with him. This was around midnight. Prior to that, our target was drinking at a firepit near the pool area."

Menendez seems pleased by this. "Hopefully, that's a regular occurrence, and he's drunk every night. The pool, as you see denoted by these artfully placed leaves and pebbles here—I did that, isn't it nice?—is pretty big, but it's mostly drained. Also, the compound does *not* have electricity, so it's gonna be dark when we go in. So. You know. Don't fall in and break your neck." Menendez shifts his pointer to another structure. "This is the pool house, which is now housing ten of the fourteen guards—"

"Whoa!" I stand up from my squat. "Where'd fourteen come from? I thought there were seven."

"Seven on duty," Menendez amends. "Branch is still working out their schedules, but what we saw when we first reported in was just one shift."

I let out a disgruntled growl, but acquiesce, because…well, there really ain't shit I can do about it. The op is still achievable. Just a little more dangerous.

"Alright," I say. "Ten live in the pool house. Continue."

"Yeah, we think those are the foot soldier types," Menendez continues. "The other four are possibly Diego's personal bodyguards, as they stay in the house with him at night. Now…" Menendez gestures to the open area directly in front of the house. "This is a big parking pad. No cover, except for a gaudy-ass fountain right smack dab in the middle, and I don't think anyone wants to get pinned down there, so…let's avoid that. Across from the house is what we believe to be the winery—that's the one with the belltower and the machine gun nest in it."

Menendez retracts his pointer stick, then passes it to EZ. "You wanna tell us what you found?"

EZ accepts the stick, then points to the western end of the compound. "Yeah. So, either through a complete lack of foresight, or maybe they just haven't gotten around to it since Diego took the place over, but they've let the brush grow in pretty close to the walls. Best spot is right in here, where we can literally walk right up to the wall and be concealed the whole way. There's an entry point right there in the wall. A wooden man-door, currently padlocked, but it's nothing our bolt-cutters can't handle. We'll want to come in around the west side of the mountain to stay concealed, but we should be able to get to that door without being detected."

"Nice work, EZ," Menendez says, then turns to me. "On you, Boss."

I cross my arms over my chest, stroking my beard as I examine what lays before me. The only real hiccup was the increased number of guards from what I'd originally planned for. I inspect my reasoning carefully, but I don't think it really changes how we're going to do this.

"Alright, gentlemen," I proceed. "I'll save the nitty-gritty for our final brief in..." I check my watch. "Three hours. Still need the guard scheduling from Branch. But here are the basics. First and foremost, me and Dez have combined our incredible strategic minds and decided that we are *not* going to attempt to extract Diego Beltran."

EZ and Marty raise eyebrows at this.

I continue: "Instead, our objective will be to secure the target first, and then secure the compound. So, stealthy infiltration, then we'll get loud and spicy. To that end, we're going to split into two teams. Team One will be me, Marty, and EZ, and we'll be making entry at that man door on the western end of the compound. Team Two will be Dez and Lucky. Lucky will pull down from Branch's overwatch position while we're on approach, and meet us on the north side of the mountain. Once we go around the western side and reach the compound wall, Team Two will split off for the central section of the wall, near the pool house. They will scale the wall and plant charges on the pool house. Once that's done, Team One will perform a stealthy breach on the man-door and enter the compound, sticking to the back wall, and making our way over to the rear of the house. If all goes well, we'll breach the target's bedroom window. The second we're inside, Team Two will blow the pool house. Branch will take out the guard in the bell tower, and then assist Team Two in eliminating the rest of the patrols.

"While they're doing that, Team One will secure the target and his lady friend in the master bedroom, then take over the west end of the house. Once Team Two is done mopping up the exterior guards, they're going to come right in the front door and meet up with us. Once combined, we'll eliminate any other guards inside the house, secure all noncombatants, then we're going to take our foot off the gas, do a slow and deliberate sweep of the rest of the compound, and once we're all clear, we will reconvene at the house and get what we need from Diego Beltran."

"Blue on blue?" Menendez reminds me.

"Right. Friendly fire will be an issue. I'd love it if we had NODs and IR patches, but we don't, so we're going to do it old school. Verbal identifier will be 'Alamo,' and I want you guys all screaming that shit the second we go hot until both teams are recombined in the house." I arch my brows. "Any questions?"

Marty twiddles his fingers in the air. "Yeah. One small issue."

"Oh?"

He jags his eyes meaningfully towards Isabella. “It’s about a hundred pounds and sassy.”

I glance at the girl. She’s still watching us, but I don’t think she got the reference, because nothing in her face changes.

I nod to Marty and the others. “I’ll handle that.”

It’s 2200 hours. Six hours until go time at 0400.

Impatient to get going, I stand at the back of the Toyota with the lift gate open and zip-ties in hand.

Isabella balances on one foot, looking at me like I’m two hundred pounds of shit.

“Are you fucking serious?” she hisses at me.

Beleaguered, I look to the rest of the team, who are all kitted up and ready to roll. They’ve very deliberately positioned themselves away from me and Isabella, and are doing a good job pretending they don’t know what’s going on.

“I’m doing this for you,” I say, as evenly as I’m able. “And yes, I’m fucking serious.”

“Oh, for *me*? Why don’t I get to decide what’s best for me?”

“Because this isn’t a discussion.”

“And what if I say no?”

“You can say whatever you want. But I’m going to restrain you and put you in the back of the vehicle. You can fight me if you want, but you know how that’s going to go.

So how about you save yourself some missing teeth, and just go with it."

"And you're just going to leave me here?" she continues to protest.

"Unless you wanna hike up a mountain on a crutch."

She seems to consider this, and I realize my error: I made it sound like a choice.

"Okay. I'll hike with the crutch."

"I was being sarcastic. You're not coming with us."

"But—"

"Sit. Down."

She seems to register the change in my tone and body language, and I think she knows I'm about two seconds away from getting rough with her. She makes a bitter face, and spits out, "This is bullshit," and then sits on the rear bumper.

I zip-tie her wrists, and then her ankles—to which she theatrically hisses, though I was very gentle with her broken ankle. As I work, I explain. "This will be safer for you. You'll be in the car, so if any primals come sniffing around, you'll be protected."

I don't point out that primals could easily punch through the glass if they got worked up enough. She'll just have to be quiet and not draw their attention.

She doesn't speak as I link her wrists to her ankles.

When I finish, she looks up at me, and all the fire's gone out of her. She looks scared. "You're gonna come back, right?"

"Of course we're coming back." I nod to the supplies which we've removed from the rear of the 4Runner to make room for her. "At the very least, we gotta come back for our shit, right? But it's gonna be a while."

"How long?"

"Depends. But I wouldn't expect us until tomorrow. Maybe around midday, if all goes well."

She looks horrified. "That's a long fucking time!"

I sigh and, since I've already got her restrained, I allow myself the luxury of looking apologetic. "I know. But it's the best we could come up with to do what we need to do, and keep you safe at the same time."

"Take the zip-ties off," she pleads. "I won't do anything stupid. I promise."

"Sorry, Hon," I say, pushing her into the back. "After what you pulled, I can't really trust you."

"I'm sorry! I swear I won't—"

I slam the tailgate closed.

I fully expect her to scream and thrash.

She is surprisingly quiet. That's good.

I lean into the window, not looking at her, because I don't want to see the accusation in her eyes. "It'll be best if you stay quiet. Don't want to attract primals."

She doesn't respond.

I grab my rifle from where it's leaning against the rear wheel and sling into it. Then I step over to my team. "You guys ready?"

Menendez turns his back and keys the comms. "Comm check. Comm check."

Everyone hears him and gives a thumbs up.

Branch comes over the line: "I got you, Dez. Y'all getting ready to head our way?"

"We're enroute," Menendez confirms. "ETA about four hours."

Single file, with Marty and his SAW on point, we head out into the gathering gloom.

CHAPTER 14

CROUCHED AT THE BASE of a tree, with my rifle braced against its trunk, I hold my reticle on the man in the bell tower. It's hard to tell in the darkness, with a hundred yards between us, but it seems like the guy is looking right at me.

My team is utterly still.

I breathe very slowly, but my mind races—is he actually looking at me? At us? Or is he just looking in our direction?

No. His body language isn't alerted. He's just staring off into the dark. He has no idea that four rifles are staring right back at him.

At least, that's what I tell myself to keep my heartrate from bumping my reticle too much.

Ten, long seconds pass.

Shit. People don't usually stare at one point for that long...

Then he pivots and looks off to my left. His posture is loose and bored.

"Get ready," I breathe out, quieter than the gentle breeze that cools my sweat-soaked skin.

Another few seconds, and then the guy in the bell tower turns and faces away from us, looking out over the declining slope of the mountain and the dark vineyards beneath.

"Move," I whisper.

With barely more than a rustle of fabric and leaves, Lucky and Menendez ease out of position behind me and slip quietly down the side of the mountain. There's a half-moon tonight, and mostly clear skies, and I see their shadowy shapes snaking through the trees. Then they're swallowed up in black as they slide into the shadows at the base of the compound's wall.

It's 0330 hours, and according to Branch, we're gonna hit the sweet spot between the guard shifts. Apparently, they swap out at midday and midnight. Which means we're heading in on their fourth hour of pacing the darkness in agonizing boredom. They'll be as complacent as we'll ever catch them.

I wait for the guy in the bell tower to make another full turn, which takes about five minutes. The next time he faces away, the rest of us move, taking the same path that Lucky and Menendez took, down to the base of the wall.

I'm keeping my sights on the bell tower the whole time, ready to tell everyone to freeze if he happens to turn around again. He doesn't.

At the wall, we hang a right where Lucky and Menendez had gone left. EZ leads us. Our progress is slow and methodical to keep the noise down. We halt often to look, listen, and smell.

"Team One," Branch's voice shushes in our earpieces. "You're twenty yards from your entry point. No hostiles nearby."

We stay quiet, but pick up the pace.

"Team Two," Branch says to Lucky and Menendez. "Go quiet. Two guards on the other side of the wall from you. Otherwise, you're right where you need to be, so hold there."

Our team reaches a section of thick brush, and EZ goes onto his belly, squirming through a narrow opening beneath the branches. I let Marty go through after him, but hold my position outside.

"Alright, Team Two. Guards have passed. Abe, I'm gonna need your eyes on the bell tower, you copy?"

I give him two clicks to acknowledge, then slowly ease myself away from the wall, until I can just see the top of the bell tower and the man inside. I slide behind an overhanging tree limb, so I'm peering through the foliage.

This is going to take some coordination. We need to get Lucky and Menendez over the wall, but we have to do it when there are no guards in sight, and the guy in the bell tower is facing away. Branch is keeping track of the guards, but the bell tower is my responsibility.

"Team Two is clear of guards for about two minutes." Branch says. "Abe, it's on you."

The guy in the tower is already facing away, but I don't know how long he's been doing that. I decide to wait it out. Menendez and Lucky's window closes—there's guards patrolling the wall nearby their location.

Another minute goes by.

"Alright," Branch says. "Got another opening for you, Team Two. Again, wait for Abe's mark."

The guard in the tower faces away again.

There's the window we've been waiting for—no guards nearby, and the guy in the bell tower is facing away.

"Mark," I whisper into my comms.

I hold on the bell tower, my oblique beginning to ache.

Who am I kidding? It's been aching the whole time. I'm just now noticing it because I've been motionless for a long stretch.

"Team Two is in the compound," Branch says. "Moving to concealment. Lucky, you gotta get smaller than that. Squish in. There you go. Hold what you got."

Over the next ten minutes, Branch and I continue to coordinate with Lucky and Menendez, so they can get their explosives placed on the pool house and get back into hiding.

Only then do I relinquish my watch on the bell tower and crawl into the bushes with EZ and Marty. On the other side of the brush, there's an open space overrun with brambles, in which EZ and Marty are standing beside a heavy-looking wooden door, mortared into the side of the wall.

Marty has a smallish pair of bolt cutters in his hand, and has positioned himself next to the door's latch. The latch is secured with a rusted padlock that looks like it was made in the time of blacksmiths.

I key my comms twice again.

"That you, Abe?" Branch asks.

I key twice again.

"You got about fifteen seconds to talk."

"Lemme know when we're clear to cut the padlock."

"Roger. Standby. Two guards coming up on your location. Hold quiet."

We remain motionless. On the other side of the wall, the faint sound of footfalls reaches my ears. Someone murmurs something in Spanish. Someone else responds in kind. The footfalls draw closer to the door in the wall.

Then they stop.

Ear-ringing silence.

There is the temptation to click to Branch for an update, but if it was anything important, he would've let me know. And a second later, I hear the distinct sound of piss splashing on the ground.

The guy's stream is uneven. Trickling. Then pouring. Then trickling again.

One of the guards says something, snickering. I imagine it's a jibe about urinary health. The guy that's pissing gives his compatriot a gruff response, which is followed by another spurt of hard pissing. Then a few dribbles. Then a muttered curse and the sound of a zipper.

The footfalls continue. Then begin to recede.

"Standby another twenty seconds or so," Branch says. "Oh, and, friendly heads up: the piss puddle's directly to the left of the door."

I appreciate that.

After about twenty seconds he says, "Okay, go ahead and pop the padlock, but don't make entry."

I nod to Marty, but he's already got the mouth of the bolt cutter around the padlock. He squeezes, silently straining to get the under-sized tool to cut through the thick, rusty hasp.

When it happens, it is loud. But we anticipated that.

A sharp *ping!*

We all go still.

"It's cut," I transmit to Branch.

"Roger that. Not seeing any reaction from the guards. I don't think anyone heard it. But hold what you got. Piss-patrol's around the back of the garage now, but the second patrol is just passing Team Two's location, moving around the back of the main house. They'll be in sight of you in a few seconds. Once they pass—and if I can get the guy in the bell tower to cooperate—you'll have about two minutes to get to the target's window and breach it. How copy?"

"I copy—on your mark, two minutes to get in position and breach the window."

I turn and nod to EZ. He slings his daypack off, goes into the front compartment, and comes out with two small explosive charges—neither bigger than a wad of chewed bubble gum. Detcord connects them, along with a spool of it leading to the detonator itself.

He holds the explosives and detonator gingerly in one hand, while he uses the other to sling back into his pack. His hands will be tied up, his rifle dangling from its sling.

Marty hefts his M249, and puts his back to the wall, just to the left of the door where the latch is. His stance is ready, but relaxed. I move to the right side of the door where the hinges are. Take a moment to double-check that the door swings outward.

EZ and his little breaching charge settle in behind Marty.

I cup my hand over my watch and illuminate the face.

It's 0350. We're right on time.

By 0352, we hear the treads of the second roving patrol moving past the door.

Thirty seconds after that, Branch speaks in our ears, his voice showing the first hints of strain. "Standby for entry. Just waiting on the guy in the bell tower to look away. And...Move. Move now."

There is the urge to burst through like a race-horse from the starter, but I keep my movement slow and deliberate, easing the rusting latch clear of the doorframe, trying to minimize the squeak of metal-on-metal. I feel the door come ajar in my hand, then pull it open. It catches on the brambles that have grown up at the base, but I'm able to tug it open enough for Marty to squirt through. EZ goes next, and I flow through right on his ass.

We're out in the open, exposed.

About fifty yards to the back of the main house.

Marty's making a B-line for it, his light machine gun shouldered as his long strides eat up the distance—not quite running, but definitely not taking his time.

Our boots swish through tall grass. It is the only sound we make.

We approach the western side of the house. There are windows all across that side on both levels. Their glass is as dark as the night without. No curtains or blinds. Marty keeps his SAW on the ground floor, and I scan the second level. No shapes in the windows. Everyone's snuggled in for the night.

Marty reaches the side of the house and posts up, his weapon still on the windows. There's just enough space between the windows and the back corner of the house for all three of us to squish in. I move around Marty and take the point position, nearest the corner.

"One minute, thirty seconds," Branch updates us.

From my position I can see some outdoor furniture and the beginnings of the expansive concrete patio that surrounds the pool. I catch the swampy scent of the leftover pool water. Just above eye-level, I can see an overhanging shade awning, and an open umbrella.

EZ's hand squeezes my shoulder, letting me know they're ready to proceed.

I ease cautiously around the corner.

And then I freeze.

What in the actual fuck?

My mind is suddenly blaring out all kinds of alarm signals. Because right there, two steps away from me under the shade awning, there's a little boy.

How in the hell is this happening? Why didn't Branch...

Then I realize Branch can't see the kid, because he's underneath the damn awning. Little bastard must've slipped out while Branch was focused on the guards. Why the kid is there, and why the guards didn't make a fuss about it and escort him back inside, are mysteries that I rapidly realize are immaterial.

The kid *is* there.

And then he turns and looks right at me.

Not seeing what I'm seeing, EZ jostles into my back.

I am supremely aware that the kid might up and scream, and I don't want to make that happen by charging up on him, so I hold my ground. For an instant, he looks at me like perhaps he figures I'm one of the guards. That doesn't last long, and his eyes begin to widen, and his body stiffens, and his mouth shudders open.

I step towards him, lowering my rifle and raising my support hand, fingers to my lips in the universal gesture for *stay quiet*.

The boy's panic-response falters. He just can't seem to connect the dots. He doesn't know what is actually happening. But I can see his chest starting to heave with hyperventilation.

I take another step, and the kid's within arm's reach of me.

He's frozen. Paralyzed by terror. Confused by my presence, and my motion for silence. Just old enough to understand the threat, but still too young to realize that not every adult should be trusted.

Letting my rifle hang, I resist the urge to lunge, and ease my hands forward, putting one hand over his mouth, and the other around his chest. I can feel the tremors in him, and I know that any sudden movement on my part will overwhelm him with fear. As gently as I'm able, I pull him out of the patio chair he's sitting in.

What the hell am I gonna do with him?

Distantly, I hear Branch's voice: "Lucky. Dez. Team One's hung up on something. Be ready for shit to go south."

Clock's ticking, Abe.

I need to get my rifle back up. I need to cover the target's window. We need to install the breaching charges and make entry. And we've only got a minute left to do it.

"Ssh," I whisper into the kid's ear, trying to imbue my tone with as much comfort as I can, given the circumstances. I turn to find EZ and Marty, squashed against the corner of the house, both looking shell-shocked.

I need to cover the window. And I need EZ to place the charges.

So I ease the kid into Marty's arms. For a moment, Marty doesn't seem to understand, then he slings his M249 to the side and accepts the kid, who's now gone as stiff as a board. Marty's hand replaces mine over the kid's mouth.

"Ssh," I repeat, looking right into the boy's eyes, and putting a finger to my lips again. Then I catch Marty's look, and it very clearly communicates what he can't verbalize: *What am I supposed to do with this?*

I give Marty a nod, then turn back around and shoulder my rifle.

I get two steps before a series of tiny noises halts me once more.

A muted moan.

The scuff of a foot.

A gurgle.

I glance over my shoulder just in time to see Marty pulling his knife out from where he'd buried it to the hilt under the boy's chin.

CHAPTER 15

I AM STARING AT Marty. He is staring back at me.

The boy is staring at nothing.

His shuddering feet go limp. The terror goes out of his eyes and they droop, half-lidded.

I feel like my brain is filled with screeching feedback. The edges of my vision sparkle, and everything I see is only the two degrees of focus that tunnel vision allows. At the end of that tunnel, there is only Marty's face, and the face of the boy, now gone slack in death, blood as black as night dribbling down his chest and over Marty's bare arm.

Marty eases the boy down to the ground. Swipes his knife clean on his pant leg. Sheaths it.

Then he comes upright again and shoulders his M249.

He nods forward, as though I need to get back on track.

Branch's voice again, piqued with urgency: "Forty-five seconds, Abe. You gotta move."

My throat constricts as guilt and anger surge up inside of me. But the swell never breaks. I can't let it break. Not now.

"Abe!" EZ hisses—the first verbalization since we made entry. And that, of all things, is what gets me to realize how much I need to refocus myself: The fact that my teammate had to actually speak to me during a stealthy entry.

I whip around. The target's window is straight ahead. Thirty yards across the back of the house. My feet start moving like they have a mind of their own. A strange calm blankets me, as though nothing I do from here on out has any real import. Like this is just an inconsequential dream.

"Alright," Branch says, sounding relieved. "Team One is back on track. Approaching the target's window. Team Two, standby for go."

Does he even know what happened?

Nope. Don't think about that. *Can't* think about that.

My whole world is this window and the target inside. Everything else is a problem for future me.

"Twenty seconds, guys," Branch says as I take a knee, five yards from the window, and EZ moves around me, a wad of explosive in each hand.

EZ slides in low at the base of the window. It's about one foot off the ground—floor to ceiling windows. He presses both charges to the glass at once, then rapidly begins to unspool the detcord, moving backward to my position. He crouches, facing me, detonator in hand. His eyes have an eerie, unreadable quality to them.

I feel Marty's hand on my shoulder.

"Breach is set," Branch says, and we all lower our heads, as though in prayer. "On my go. Three. Two. One. Go."

A thunderclap.

The smack of a pressure wave hitting my body, buffeting my sinuses.

I'm up. Moving.

Smoke swirls. Glass tinkles like chimes. The window is a gaping, empty frame.

Shouts in the distance.

I hit the window and step through, activating my weaponlight. The bright beam skewers a man and a woman in their bed, dazed and shocked and thrashing beneath the covers. They both squint into my weaponlight. Then they both start screaming.

"*No te muevas*!" I bellow. "*No te muevas*!"

Big room. Ornate bed. Glass crunches beneath my feet as I charge to the nearest side of the bed, where the man—the target—is reaching for something on his nightstand. I spear him hard in the face with the muzzle of my rifle, rocking his head back and spraying the upholstered headboard with blood. I ram my left hip against his reaching arm, pinning it to the wall. I feel the nightstand—and presumably the weapon upon it—against my ass, and kick backward, sending it crashing behind me.

EZ leaps across the bed and tackles the shrieking woman.

Then there is a bone-jarring explosion that makes our little breaching charge sound like a party popper. The whole house trembles, and I hear shrapnel peppering the exterior wall.

That would be the pool house, being reduced to splinters.

Gunfire erupts from everywhere at once.

I snag the target by his long hair and rip him out of bed, dragging his half-conscious form to the floor where I drive my knee into his back. I'm facing the breached window, with my back to the master bedroom door.

Marty is posted just inside the shattered window, his SAW chattering away at things outside. Return fire slaps the side of the house, sending stone dust and wooden splinters scattering. Marty ducks further inside, swearing.

I've got the window, but I need Marty on the door.

"Door!" I shout at him.

He pivots at the same instant that I hear the bedroom door slamming open. Someone shouts, and starts firing what sounds like a pistol. Marty drops to a knee, the rounds going just over his shoulders to impact the wall behind him, then spits out a burst from the M249 that causes someone to screech and tumble to the floor.

Out of my peripheral, I see a guy sprawl at the foot of the bed, writhing.

Marty fires another burst into him, killing him instantly, then slides into position at the corner of the bed, using the dead body as a sandbag.

I'm still covering the blasted window. A dark shape looms, backlit by firelight from the burning pool house. All I know is that it doesn't yell "Alamo" and it's not wearing armor like the rest of my team, so I put three rounds in it, spilling it backwards and out of sight.

A yowl that sounds like nothing so much as an enraged puma peals from the other side of the bed. I turn reflexively, and see a naked woman all over EZ's back, trying to claw at his face.

EZ roars, lets his rifle hang, then grabs one of the woman's arms with both of his, and slings her into a catastrophically-violent body slam. The floorboards rattle as she hits the ground.

I feel the guy under my knee start to move. Shit—I'd almost forgotten about him.

There is *way* too much going on at this precise moment to reason with this fucker, so I rear back and drive a fist into his temple, hoping to knock him senseless for a few more seconds until I can get control of the situation in the bedroom. His head bounces off the ground and he makes an insensate croaking noise and goes limp again.

I get both hands back on my rifle and sweep it up to cover the window again.

Marty's got the bedroom door covered, but I can still hear thrashing from the other side of the bed—EZ grunting and growling, and the woman screaming and snarling.

"EZ!" I holler. "You alright?"

I hazard a glance over my shoulder and catch EZ reeling backward, a hand to his face, swearing up a storm.

Then I hear Branch shouting in my ear: "Abe! Watch your six!"

I spin back to the window just in time to catch another guard leaning cautiously out from the broken window frame, an AK already leveled. I fire without thought, and he fires back. My rounds shatter the window frame next to him, and his rounds slap the mattress between me and Marty, sending out little bursts of fluff.

Both of us just keep shooting.

I am faster, and a better shot.

His head snaps back and he's out.

Marty starts firing at the bedroom door—another guard trying to make it inside. They quickly realize it's a bad idea, and I hear them squeal like a stuck pig.

Then I hear EZ shout "Mother*fuck*!" and there's another brief moment of scrambling, followed by the woman screaming, and then three sharp pistol shots.

That's concerning. But I stay focused on the window until Branch transmits, "Abe, you're clear!"

I whirl back around, still very conscious of the fact that I've been straddling the target for ten or fifteen seconds now, and I can't just keep knocking him senseless or I'll give him brain damage or something, and he won't be able to answer my questions.

On the other side of the bed, I see EZ, pointing his pistol at the ground, and by the diffuse glow of our weaponlights, I see an expression on his face that's something like shock. Like he is surprised at something he did.

I hear a croaking gurgle from the woman.

EZ fires one more round. Then his expression flattens out and he holsters his pistol and snatches up his rifle again, addressing it to the bedroom door.

What the fuck has just happened?

I swallow. My spit tastes like gunsmoke.

I breathe, widening my focus.

I hear the crackle of gunfire from outside, and the muted pops of Lucky and Menendez's suppressed rifles. Good—they're still in the fight.

I also hear Branch, calling targets and locations for them, and doubtless harvesting a few souls of his own.

"Marty!" I snap. "Talk to me!"

"One hostile just outside the door," he calls out. "I think I hit him, but he's still in the fight."

"EZ—what's going on?"

He falters for a moment. "Shit...uh...female's down. She grabbed my rifle."

I immediately understand what he's trying to say. When someone grabs your rifle, you can get in a tugging match with them, or you can simply let go of the rifle—it's on a sling, so it's not like they'll be able to do much with it—and transition to your pistol.

The woman must've grabbed his rifle, and by the tone of EZ's voice it sounds like his reaction to that was more instinctive than conscious. It sounds like he maybe regrets that. But what's done is done. Can't take the bullet back once you send it.

"Alright, we're good." I call, dropping my voice to an almost conversational tone. "Marty, keep cover on that door. EZ, help me with the target."

As though hearing me, the man I'm still pinning to the ground begins to groan and stir again. I give him a light thump with my muzzle against the side of his face, just to remind him that I'm there, and repeat my earlier exhortation: "*No te muevas.*"

EZ scrambles over the bed and lands beside me, slinging his rifle and producing zip-ties. I keep my knee on the target's back, dividing my attention between him and the exterior window. Outside, the night has turned into smoky, flickering umber, as the pool house burns.

Someone shouts in Spanish from outside the bedroom door.

The target tries to respond as EZ secures his hands behind his back, but whatever he had to say is drowned out by another burst of fire from Marty.

We've killed two guards. There are two more in the house—that we know of. One of them is definitely in the hallway.

EZ binds the target's feet, then uses a third zip-tie to link his wrists to his ankles, hog-tying him. I nudge EZ with my elbow and jerk my head towards the bedding. "Pillow case." He leans over, swipes a pillow off the bed, shucks the cover off and holds it ready to hood the target.

I grab the man's hair again and tilt his face towards me so our eyes connect. "Are you Diego Beltran?"

He blinks, but I can see in his expression there is no confusion. That's confirmation enough for me.

"*Chinga tu madre, puto!*" he spits at me.

EZ hoods him, then produces the roll of 100 mile-per-hour tape from his cargo pocket and loops it rapidly around Diego's neck, cinching the pillow case tight so he can't worm out of it.

I key my comms. "Team One is inside. Target is secured. We're holding. Lucky and Dez, what's your status?"

They don't immediately respond, which makes my guts get all squirmy.

Distantly, I hear a pair of suppressed rifles yammering back and forth with some unsuppressed firearms. Good. They're still alive and in the fight.

"Abe to Team Two. Lucky and Dez, what's your status?"

This time Menendez responds: "At the front of the house, moving to make entry."

"Copy that. Branch, how we lookin'?"

"Bell tower's down. Both roving patrols are down. All hostiles in the pool house eliminated. Whatcha need, brother?"

"I need you to keep an eye on the target. Can you see him?"

"For now, yeah, but it'll be dark when y'all take your weaponlights out of there."

I snatch a flashlight from my plate carrier and click it on, then set it to the side so it splashes white light all over the hog-tied Diego Beltran. "How's that?"

"Yeah, I got you."

"Alright, keep him covered. We're moving to clear the rest of the house." I pull myself off of Diego Beltran, leaving him to squirm and moan. I move to Marty and seize ahold of the dragstrap on the back of his armor.

"Up," I say, as I help him to his feet, his M249 never leaving the shredded bedroom door.

Menendez transmits again. "We're holding at the front door."

I shuck a grenade from my rig and slip around the bed, to the left side of the door. "Roger that. Wait for the boom."

"Standing by."

Marty holds coverage on the door from the corner of the bed, while EZ stacks up behind me. I take a quick look at the guy. His right eye got clawed up pretty bad in that scuffle with the woman. He's squinting it closed, and there are scratch marks across it, seeping blood.

"You good?" I ask.

He nods. "I'm good."

"There's another door directly across from this one," I point out. "I'll cover the hall. EZ and Marty, you clear the room across."

They both acknowledge.

I pull the pin on the grenade, let the spoon fly off, and cook it down.

One. Two.

I toss it underhanded into the hall. Watch it skitter across the ground, rebound off the far wall, and then I duck for cover as I hear the guard out there yelp and start to scramble away—

BOOM

The floors and walls quake, and a gout of smoke, dust, and debris avalanches into the room.

My ears are ringing, but I feel EZ squeeze my shoulder and his muted voice say, "Move."

I clear the corner, rifle up. Plunge through the doorway and pivot right to address the hall.

There's a dismembered body scattered all over the place. I find what is left of the head and torso and put two rounds in it, just to be safe.

EZ and Marty jostle past behind me, and a half-second later I hear a door shatter as they kick it down.

I stay focused on the hallway, but I can't see shit through the smoke, my weaponlight reflecting off of it like high-beams in fog. I douse the light just as I detect the sound of the front door slamming open, someone shouting in Spanish, someone shouting in English, then two sharp pistol reports, followed by a dozen suppressed rifle shots.

Then a sound like a sack of potatoes hitting the ground.

A see a smudge of darkness through the smoke—someone at the end of the hall, crawling pathetically like a wounded animal. Then two more suppressed rifle shots and they go still.

"Alamo!" I call down the hall, my own voice dim in my ears.

"Alamo!" comes the response.

"Clear," I hear EZ call from behind me.

A hand lands on my shoulder, and the muzzle of Marty's M249 juts out in my left peripheral.

The smoke is clearing. Down the hall I see a shape peek out. I start to raise my rifle to it but it calls out "Alamo," and I realize it's Menendez.

"Hold there," I call down to him. "We're coming to you."

Menendez slips out of sight again.

I move down the hall, controlling the pace. We need to decelerate. It's slow and deliberate from here on out. There are two more doors before we reach the atrium and recombine with Lucky and Menendez. One's a bedroom, the other's a bath. I maintain coverage while Marty and EZ clear them—they're empty.

With the smoke cleared, my weaponlight reaches all the way across the house. The hall bisects the structure lengthwise, and I can see the far end where the other four bedrooms are at. No movement. But there should be four kids somewhere down there...

Check that. Three kids now.

We reach the middle of the house. It's a massive atrium with an unlit, crystal chandelier and a spiral staircase. Two rooms open to either side—living or lounge areas of some sort. Lucky is holding on the staircase, covering the upper level, and Menendez is close to the open front door, covering one of the rooms.

Menendez gestures with his rifle to the room he's holding. "Library." Then he nods to the other room across the atrium. "Sitting room. They're both clear."

Library *and* sitting room. Fancy-shmancy.

A large cased opening at the back of the atrium leads to a massive tiled kitchen and an attached dining room. Marty and EZ clear these without incident. Then me and EZ hold the hallway to the rest of the bedrooms, while Marty, Menendez, and Lucky clear the second story.

A sense of stillness hits me. I hear only the treads of my guys on the second level. They're not kicking doors anymore, but taking it slow and cautious.

In the quiet, a distant mewling reaches my ears, coming from behind us.

I quirk my head, but don't fully turn. Is that...?

"FYI, target's getting a little squirmy," Branch observes. "He's not going anywhere, but he's doing a good bit of thrashing."

The mewling crystallizes in my mind, and starts to form itself into language.

"Gabriella! Gabriella!"

I don't know why, but a part of me cringes.

He's yelling for the woman. And he just keeps on going. At first, it seems like he's trying to get her to respond, his voice stricken with worry. Then, he must've connected some dots, because the voice turns to agony and rage. Then he's just screaming her name, knowing she isn't going to respond.

I should've gagged the bastard.

I hazard a glance to my right, where EZ is stationed, his rifle pointing down the hall. I worry for a moment that he might be affected by the screaming, but if he is, he doesn't show it. He stays rock-steady, holding that hallway.

"How's that eye, EZ?" I ask, trying to distract him from the screaming.

"Probly lacerated my cornea," he answers, deadpan. "I'll live."

"Got any vision on that side?"

"Little foggy."

"You let me take point, then."

"Roger that."

Diego Beltran is no longer calling out for Gabriella. Now it's just anguished keening.

Hard to treat them like animals when they show human grief. I wish he'd shut up.

Out of my peripheral, EZ fidgets. "Sorry about the woman."

I don't respond because I'm not sure what to say back. No worries? Not a problem? It's all good, bro?

"I coulda just knocked her out," he continues, his voice hushed, but not betraying much emotion. "God, what a bitch. She just latched on, and I didn't even think about it. Just let her take the rifle, grabbed my secondary, and put three in her pelvis. Fuck." He lets out a long, heavy sigh. "That's my bad."

That's my bad. It suddenly strikes me as horrifically comical. *Oh, I just shot an unarmed woman that I probably should've just butt-stroked. My bad.*

"You reacted. It happens."

"Yeah. Well..."

"She played a stupid game and got a stupid prize."

Why do I keep saying that? What does it even mean?

"I'm just saying, I know I fucked up. I'm better than that."

Yeah, I think. *We're all better than that. Until we're not.*

CHAPTER 16

We find the three kids in a bedroom with a window that overlooks the pool area. They're not hard to find. The second our boots step into the room, it sounds like a litter of puppies have been stuffed under the bed—so much whimpering and sniffling.

I step to the side of the bedroom door, my weapon-light illuminating the bottom of the bed frame, where a tiny hand jerks back as though burned by the light. "Dez, you're up."

Menendez steps forward and eases into a squat, but doesn't approach the kids just yet. Me and EZ have our rifles covering the bed, while Lucky and Marty hold in the hall outside. I don't think the kids are armed, but you never know. Guard could've pushed a pistol into one of their hands and told them to fight back if they were found. It's happened before.

Menendez speaks to them in Spanish, his tone very calm and genial, belying literally everything we've done up to that point. Convincing them to come out on their own.

I think of the boy again, out by the pool. How he'd just accepted my motion for silence. Didn't struggle when I picked him up. Only made a noise as he was being killed. But up to that point, in a way, he'd trusted us. Unable to conceive that we might be the ones to end his life.

That seems so odd to me. After all the shit the world has been through in the last years, not to mention that these kids were presumably Diego's, and had grown up in a violent crime syndicate, I'd just expected them to be more...I don't know...jaded.

Had Diego managed what so few parents in the world had been able to do? Had he shielded his children from the worst of human nature that was now on full display, unfettered by law and order? Had he protected their innocence?

Menendez eventually gets a response from beneath the bed. I think it's the girl. The eldest of the bunch, according to Branch's observations. Just like Isabella. They exchange a few words, and it all seems so friendly. Like he's just a social worker, here to talk to them.

After a minute or two of this, three pairs of hands appear. Three different sizes. All of them empty.

Menendez sidles closer to the bed and gently begins helping the children squirm out from underneath. I lower my rifle, since it's become clear that none of them are armed. The beam of my weaponlight refracts off the floor, uplighting their faces. Branch was right—none of them are older than ten, at the most.

"Put 'em in the atrium," I say to Menendez. "Marty, you're with me. We're gonna go fetch Diego."

We lead the way out of the room, and I cast a glance over my shoulder to see Menendez escorting the kids in a trembling bunch, coaxing them with soft words.

Ahead, the hall to the master bedroom is quiet. Diego's given up on screaming out his grief. Does he know Gabriella's dead? Or does he just suspect?

One thing I'm sure he doesn't know: We killed one of his kids.

It's almost like Marty reads my mind. I'm halfway down the hall when he stops me with a quiet, "Hey."

I pause and look around at him. His eyes search my face.

"Did you *not* want me to...uh...eliminate the kid?"

The ringing in my ears has dulled a good bit, but now it comes back as though my eardrums have been freshly perforated. I feel my face heat up. I try hard not to let my complete shock at this question show on my face. I don't know how much I succeeded.

"No," I say, keeping my voice down. "I didn't want you to kill him."

Marty blinks, and for the barest of seconds, has the good grace to look down at his feet. But then he looks back up, defensive. "What the fuck was I *supposed* to do?"

I think about shooting him. But then, that's not an uncommon thought for me. It just kind of rises up when people piss me off—how easy it would be to snatch their life away, and then I wouldn't have to deal with them. Obviously, it's not something I indulge in. But it's always there, waiting for the smallest disturbance to jostle it and cause it to rise to the surface.

I take a deep breath and remind myself that, when the boy had been in my hands, I'd had the exact same thought that Marty had just verbalized: *What the fuck do I do now?* And then I'd simply passed the kid off. Passed off responsibility. And for that, I'm just as much to blame as Marty.

Hadn't I told Marty that if anyone got in the way of our objective, no matter who they were, to put them down?

It's my turn to look at the ground. Shame threatens to shake me.

Hey me, weren't we not giving a fuck?

Yeah. Not giving a fuck is what made me tell that shit to Marty. Which is probably why he thought I'd passed the kid to him to be dispatched.

Not giving a fuck is my armor.

It's just getting really goddamn heavy right about now.

"We don't have time for this shit," I growl, turning back for the master bedroom. "Get your head on straight," I say, and I'm really not sure whether that was directed at Marty or myself. "Branch, check fire, me and Marty are entering the master bedroom."

Diego starts up again as he hears us enter the room. At first, he speaks in Spanish, but then seems to remember that we spoke English, and switches to that. He's obviously fluent, and only has the slightest accent.

"Where's my wife?" he demands, as me and Marty step around the bed to his hog-tied form. "Where's my wife? What'd you do to my wife?"

Marty pulls out his knife—the very same one that he used to kill the kid—and cuts the zip-tie linking Diego's wrists to his ankles. The man gasps as his body loosens, but then gets right back into it.

"Where is she? You motherfuckers, I swear to God, if you did something..." His voice cracks as me and Marty each seize an arm and pull him up. "If you did something to my wife I'm going to—"

I punch him hard in the gut. Obviously, he can't see it coming with the hood over his head, and his belly is soft and unprepared for it. I knock the wind out of him.

He gags and wheezes as we drag him out of the room. His bound feet bump along behind him, tumbling over the remains of the guard I blew up.

"We have your children," I tell him. "That's who you should worry about. It is in your best interest—and theirs—to be completely cooperative."

To his credit, that shuts him up. When he's able to breathe again, he starts sobbing, and in those cries I know that he's realized the truth about his wife. He is as enraged as he is bereft.

In the atrium of the house, Menendez, EZ, and Lucky are standing over the three children, who are all sitting, cross-legged against one wall. Their faces are tear-streaked. The youngest of them is openly weeping. The others look on with that sort of emotional blankness you see in war orphans after their house and family just got bombed into particles.

We seat Diego on the atrium wall opposite them, near a large display case filled with decorative bric-a-brac that I don't pay much mind to. Marty uses his knife again to cut the duct tape holding the pillow case over Diego's head, then rips it off.

I watch the man's face carefully to see what unguarded truths this moment will reveal. Tears and snot wet his clean-shaven face. His dark eyes go wide at the sight of his children, then they squinch up, and fresh tears rise.

He jabbers to them in Spanish, something that I guess is meant to comfort them, but it only seems to work them up even worse. Then he cuts himself off, midsentence. I see the way his eyes bounce from child to child. One, two, three...

Then back again, like he doesn't want to believe his eyes.

One, two, three.

"*Donde esta Emil?*" he utters to the children. "*Donde esta su hermano?*"

The eldest girl's face collapses. She shakes her head. "*No se, papa!*"

Diego jerks his face to me, panic and impotent fury flushing his skin. "Where is my other son? What'd you do with my son? What'd you do to my Emil?"

Squatting down at Diego's side, I can see Marty looking at me out of my peripheral. I don't look back. I keep my face impassive. "I don't know anything about another kid." Then, before Diego can ask anything else about the fate of his third son, I seize his face and direct it at his surviving children. "Three children," I hiss into his ear. "Three children is what we have. Look at them. Focus on them. They are all that is left of your life. Keep them safe, Diego. Cooperate. Don't ask questions. Just tell me what I want to know."

He hyperventilates, looking at his kids. Then my words strike home. He realizes the need to control himself. He makes an animal noise and bares his teeth, and starts sucking in deep breaths and snorting them out his nose, causing more snot to rocket all over his upper lip. But he manages to slow his breathing. And after that, he is quiet.

I look at Lucky, Menendez, and EZ. "You guys start clearing the rest of the compound. Marty, handle the kids."

Marty moves across the atrium to stand guard over the three children, while the rest of our team moves out the front door. Did I choose Marty randomly? Or was it because I know he's okay with killing kids?

Would he do it again, in *these* circumstances?

Would I order him to do it?

They say that when you're about to die, your life flashes before your eyes. But I've never heard of that happening at the prospect of killing someone else. In that moment, though, that's what happens to me.

I see every line I've ever crossed. And I have crossed...so fucking many. So many times when I thought I was better than that. Until I wasn't.

But this?

This is death. The cold, calculated execution of innocents—it is not a threat to my life, but a threat to who I am. Who I *wish* I could've been, in another life, when the world hadn't gone so terribly wrong.

Maybe that's why my life flashes before my eyes. Because if I cross this last, final line, I'll not only be killing them. I'll be killing myself.

I try to tell myself that I am *not giving a fuck*.

It is a small and flimsy shelter against reality.

It is a pup-tent in the face of a hurricane.

But I can't allow any of this to show. I need to remember who Diego is.

Perhaps a loving father. Perhaps a loving husband.

But a monster. The leader of a cartel that has massacred more innocents with callous disregard than all the pieces of shit I've removed from existence in my entire life. He is reptilian. He is the true sociopath in this situation—not me. And if he detects my hesitation, if he gets even the barest whiff of it, he will push me across a line I never intended to cross. He will make me do things I never wanted to admit that I was even capable of doing.

But I need him to *believe* that I am capable of those things.

I need to act like the black-hearted devil I know I am.

"Diego," I say, my voice dead-level. I wait for him to look at me. "Your cartel is currently in possession of seven families. These families belong to seven workers in a refinery in Texas. I am here for those families. That's it. You're going to tell me where they are, and how I can get them safely back to Texas, or I am going to start taking your children apart right in front of you. One by one. These are the facts. This is the reality you now find yourself in. How honest and cooperative you are will dictate whether your children will know that their father loved them, or whether they will die in agony, knowing that their pain and death was because you never really gave a fuck. It's all up to you, Diego. Do you understand?"

He stares at me. In his eyes, I see what I had expected to see. And it disappoints me. It disappoints me that people are as shitty as I think they are.

He is not shocked by my threats. His eyes are shrewd. He is sniffing out my words, scenting for the hint of an empty threat. Trying to suss out whether I am the type of man to be able to do what I claim.

I stare back at him, unflinching.

What do you see in my eyes, Diego?

Which side of me do you see? The side that doesn't give a fuck, and will cross any line to complete a mission? Do you see a sociopath like yourself? Or do you see a desperate man, trying to bluff his way out of a massacre?

"Do you believe me?" I whisper.

His eyes don't change. He just keeps peering at me. Into me.

My earpiece crackles, and Menendez's voice comes over the line.

"Abe. We got a problem."

I don't break eye contact with Diego.

I can't look away. To look away would be to flinch. It would be a tell, right as I'm pushing all my chips into the pot.

I reach up to my PTT, but I don't press it yet. I think about what I've threatened to do. And I imagine myself as the type of man that is capable of doing it. I become that person. I become *worse* than that person. I think of what I promised him I'd do, and I imagine myself *wanting* to do it.

I hope he sees the devil in me.

I smirk at him as I key the comms. "Go ahead, Dez."

"Checking bodies," Dez says, his words rapid and succinct. "One of the guards had a satphone. Line was still open when I picked it up. I heard voices in the background. And..." the barest hint of hesitation. "I think I heard engines."

I still haven't looked away from Diego's eyes, and for a moment, I think he might've seen the fear in mine before I could hide it. My mind immediately blasts through the possibilities, but it doesn't take long, because there's really only one conclusion.

One of the guards managed to get a distress call out before he was taken down. And now there were more cartel soldiers inbound. From where? And how long had they been on the road? And how many of them were coming?

Didn't matter. Our timeline just got massively truncated.

Which means if I falter—if I can't convince Diego of my mercilessness—I won't have the time to convince him with other, less repulsive methods.

Should I ask Diego how many are coming, and from where?

No. I don't want him to think he's got the upper hand. From his perspective—provided I can convince him I'm the devil I claim to be—I am the one with all the power in this situation. I can't afford to relinquish that edge.

"Roger that," I say, casually, as though I hadn't just received a report about our incoming doom. "Have Branch work on that."

There is a bit of confusion in Menendez's response, but he's smart enough to roll with it. "I'm on it."

My question to Diego hangs in the air—*Do you believe me?*

His eyes narrow, catching a whiff of something he interprets as weakness. An opportunity to exploit. His lips part, and I know he is going to challenge me. I can't let him get the words out. To say them will only make it more real.

I seize him by the face before he can speak and smash his head back against the wall, cracking the plaster. He winces and yowls, his challenge ruined, and I work my body closer to his, so I'm hovering over him, like a beast about to feed.

I have to do better than just pretend. I have to *be*. I have to make it real in my mind.

I think of the photograph of the Pizzuti family. Pretty wife. Two kids. When I'd viewed the photograph for the first time, I'd wondered if something was wrong with me that I felt almost nothing for them.

But now I make them mine. In an instant, she becomes my wife, and they become my children. They have been taken from me. They have been tortured. They have been violated. I soak myself in mindless wrath—the wrath of a man who would burn the whole world and everyone in it to get back the people that he loved.

I wrench Diego's face towards his children. They are frightened by the violence. They, at least, are convinced that I am capable of monstrosity. I stare back at them with heartless, seething eyes, cheek to cheek with Diego.

"Who do I start with? I'll let you choose, Diego. Which of your children do you love the least? Which one will I start cutting into? Huh?" I shake his head to hide the tremors I can feel working their way into my hands. "Pick one." I shake him again. "Pick one!"

Vaguely, I register Branch's voice saying that he's moving to the top of the mountain to get eyes on the nearby highway.

"Fuck you!" Diego snarls, then starts yammering to his children in Spanish.

I slam his head into the wall again, then erupt from my spot beside him. I take a step towards the children and they all wail and shy away from me, but they are too paralyzed with fear to get up and run.

I yank my own knife from its sheath on my plate carrier. "Maybe I pick for you." I point my knife at each kid in turn. Then I settle on the girl. "How about your daughter?"

"Don't you fucking touch her!" Diego rasps.

I stalk over. The girl squeals as I seize her by the hair and haul her out of line with the others. Her brothers scream and try to grab at her flailing legs, but they are numb with panic and can't get ahold of her. The girl weighs almost nothing. It's just so terribly easy to ram her small frame into the ground, in the middle of the atrium. I drop onto her back, my weight crushing the air out of her lungs and cutting off her screams.

I look at Diego while I work. His eyes are no longer peering. No longer trying to find my weakness. They are consumed with his own. With his daughter.

"Where are the families, Diego?" I ask as I wind the girl's hair around my fist, torquing her head so she's facing her father.

He looks at her. He looks at me.

Pity is only a memory for me. Compassion a long-dead dream.

I put the tip of my knife just under the girl's eye, and she goes very still.

Diego and I stare each other down.

My mind has splintered, but I cannot show it.

"Try me, motherfucker," I growl.

Don't make me do this.

"I'm gonna cut this pretty little eye out and make one of her brothers eat it, how's that sound?"

I won't. I can't.

I don't have another option.

"Where are the families?"

"No!" Diego barks, as though denying this reality. "No!" As though his will can compete with mine.

I am willing to do this.

I can't cross that line.

I will burn the world down.

I will burn myself down.

I ease the tip of the knife into the girl's flesh. Blood wells. Her eyes rocket wide and she tries to pull her head away from the steel, but I won't let her. She shrieks.

"STOP IT!" Diego roars, desperate pleading cracking his voice. "They're here! The families are here! I have them here!"

CHAPTER 17

I GO WEAK.

My mind feels like an overstretched muscle, rebounding and contracting on itself.

I pull the knife point out of the girl's flesh. It'd only cut into the top layer of her skin. Her screaming dies off as the pressure releases, and she gasps and whimpers. The tip of my knife trembles.

I whip my head to Diego, who is staring at his daughter, fresh tears welling in his eyes. "Hey!" I shout, because I don't want him to see how badly the knife is shaking in my hand.

He looks at me. "I swear it," he snarls. "They're here."

"Where?" I demand, and I know that I cannot speak in anything but monosyllables or he will hear the quaver in my voice.

"Let her go!"

"*Where?*"

"The last building!" Diego shouts at me, jerking his head. "The equipment shed, next to the winery! Let her go!"

I don't let her go. Not yet. I can't. This could be a bluff.

I look desperately at Marty. His face is schooled, but I know the man better than Diego does, and I can see the horror in it. He looks at me like he doesn't recognize me. I don't blame him.

I nod to him, unable to speak. He blinks, refocuses himself, and realizes what I need.

He keys his comms. "Dez, drop what you're doing and go to the equipment building next to the winery. Diego claims the families are inside."

"Traps," I croak, then skewer Diego with another promise I hope to God I do not have to keep. I hazard more words, but speak them rapidly to hide the shake in my voice. "If this is a trap..." I tap the knife point against the bloody little slit below the girl's eye.

Diego wilts, openly weeping now. "No trap."

"Keep an eye out for booby traps," Marty warns them anyways.

Then there is silence.

My body quakes as though wracked with a terrible illness and I've just spent the last twenty minutes puking my guts out. It feels like there's no strength left in me. I wonder if I'm even capable of standing at this point.

My leg muscles are jumping, and I know that the girl I have pinned to the ground can feel that, whether it registers with her or not. But I don't think Diego can see it.

"Let them go," Diego begs, the strength gone out of him too. "Please. You don't need them. You can do your business with me."

"If they're here," I say, my voice coming out strained as I try to control it. "Then we won't have any business left."

The comms open up, and I hear heavy breathing, followed by Branch's voice: "I'm at the top of the mountain, guys. I got four pairs of headlights coming down the highway from the north. They're moving at a good clip. We got maybe ten minutes before they're crawling up our ass."

Here's a thought that hadn't occurred to me until right that second: If our seven families are here, then how the hell are we gonna get them off this mountain before the rest of the cartel shows up?

We didn't have transport for seven families. They'd have to hoof it. But were they in any shape to do so? And could they get off this mountain before it was swarming with cartel?

For a half a beat, I almost hope that Diego is lying to me.

"How many of the families are here?" I ask the man.

"All of them."

"How many?"

He falters, and I can see he's trying to remember.

What an incredible piece of shit. You don't even remember how many families you're currently holding hostage? Just another day at the office for a cartel warlord.

All his victims must run together in his mind, I think, very righteously, while I hold a ten-year-old girl down with a knife to her eye.

I'm still not sure if I would've done it or not.

I was able to channel evil so well that a man intimately familiar with it was fooled, and didn't push me over that line.

But I think that says something about me. Doesn't it?

"There are..." Diego begins, hesitantly. "Five women. And seven children."

My mouth opens, but my words jam up because I'm trying to do the math in my head, matching the number of children to the number of women, but no matter how I cut it, it doesn't come out to seven families.

I readjust my grip on the knife, and the girl sobs.

"There was supposed to be *seven* families," I say, my voice low and dangerous.

Diego doesn't respond. I suppose because it wasn't really a question.

Then there seems to be nothing more to say. I can't think of a question, and Diego just sits there, alternately staring hatefully at me, and piteously at his daughter. Everything is up in the air, and I'm just waiting to see where it all lands, because I don't have a clue what I'm going to do next until I know what all my problems are.

Then Menendez breaks the silence over the comms, and even before he speaks, I can hear voices in the background. The voices of women and children. When he does speak, his voice is tight with relief and triumph.

"We got 'em, Abe. We got 'em."

"Shit!" the words just comes out.

I should feel relief, and triumph as well. But all I feel in that moment is terror and urgency. I lurch upright off the girl, stabbing a thumb into my PTT. "Dez, get me a headcount ASAP. Branch, you with me?"

"Go with it," he transmits back.

"The second those vehicles are in range I want you to start taking out engine blocks. Whatever you can do to slow them down, you got me?" I spin to Marty. "Pantry."

"Pantry?" he says, mystified.

"Yes, the pantry! Get the kids in the kitchen pantry! Move!"

He jolts into motion, his M249 held in one hand as he starts waving his hands at the kids as though they are leaves to be swept up. "Go," he commands them as they begin to squeal and cry, not knowing what's happening. "Into the kitchen!"

"What are you doing?" Diego demands, as I drag the girl up and shove her towards her siblings. "Leave them out of this, you sonofa—"

Everything this motherfucker did—everything he just put me through—comes out of me in the form of violence. I launch myself across the atrium and ram a front kick straight into his chest with all the energy I have, sending his kneeling form crashing back into the wall with a woof of breath.

"Shut up!" I roar at him. And kick him again.

Actually, less of a kick, and more of a stomp to the chest.

I don't know what else I say. I'm sure you can imagine. But I just keep kicking and stomping him in the chest, and I hope that one of the kicks ruptures an internal organ and he dies in agony in his children's arms.

All my mad yelling has coated my lips and beard and mustache with spittle, and I take a breathless step back from his pummeled form, swiping a wrist across my mouth. Diego groans and coughs. I've never hated a creature so immensely in my life. It actually kind of surprises me. I don't usually lose my shit like that.

Getting some modicum of control over myself, I sheath my knife, then grab him by his wrist restraints and drag him towards the kitchen, his arms torqued back in a direction they're not typically meant to go.

Good. I hope his shoulders break.

As I drag his spluttering form into the dark kitchen, I make another transmission, heaving for breath. "Dez. We need a vehicle to get off this mountain. What's in the garage? Did you clear the garage?"

He must be busy with the hostages, because it takes him a moment to respond. In the meantime, I drag Diego up to the kitchen pantry where Marty is standing at the door, his M249 leveled at the children inside. He looks at me with a curious expression.

"The fuck are you doing?" he demands. "Just put him down."

I know he doesn't mean "release him." He means put him down—like a rabid dog.

I ignore Marty and pull Diego into the doorway of the pantry, then kick him repeatedly to get him clear of the doorframe—like a mess I'm trying to cram in an overflowing closet. The children cry out for their "papa." But this is the only mercy he'll ever get from me. And I'm only doing it because of them. I'm not gonna leave three kids alone on a mountain.

I'm not a monster.

I slam the pantry door on their crying faces. It is an outward-opening door, which is why I thought of it as a place to hide them. I only remembered it because an outward-opening pantry struck me as a bit of a design flaw in an otherwise immaculately constructed house.

"Watch them a sec," I bark at Marty, then run into the dining room.

Menendez finally comes back as I'm snatching up one of the dining room chairs. "Abe, we got five women and seven children. There's a big-ass Suburban in the garage. I think we can all cram in there."

"Find the keys, and get everyone loaded up. We need to be off this mountain five minutes ago."

I hustle the chair back to the pantry and ram it under the doorknob. Between Diego's restraints, and the chair pinning the door closed, they should stay trapped for a good bit. At least long enough for us to get the hell out of there.

"Shoulda just killed him," Marty growls.

“Let it go, Marty,” I say, immediately heading for the front of the house. “Come on.”

As we reach the front door, Branch transmits: “Vehicles are in range, nearing the base of the mountain. Engaging.”

“Copy, Branch—we’re gonna need to use the road out, so try to keep that lane open for us.”

I hope he heard, but I don’t request a response, because it’s more important that he starts poking holes in engine blocks. And maybe some faces.

Me and Marty erupt out of the front of the house.

EZ is sprinting headlong across the compound, moving towards the garage on the far right. To the left, Lucky and Menendez are hustling a pathetic gaggle of women and children out of the structure on the end. Even with only the moon and two weaponlights to illuminate them, I can see they are in a sad state. Their clothes are filthy. Their hair is lank. Their faces are gaunt with stress and lack of food. They move with the shuffling gait of the sick, and the terrified, and the overwhelmed.

I charge towards them, snatching my flashlight off my rig and clicking it on. The white light plays across their faces. They squint away from it. Tear-stained cheeks. Sobs reach my ears. Most of them are crying in some combination of relief and fear. A few seem struck dumb, moving on autopilot.

Right as I reach the first of them—a middle-aged woman with a teenage boy clinging to her like a toddler—I realize my face is still a rictus of violence and rage. I put the brakes on myself. I can still move with a sense of urgency without freaking these people out any more than they already are.

I need to start thinking like a human being again.

I need to *be* a human being again.

I try to smooth the ire out of my voice, but it still comes out as a mean-dog growl in my ears. "It's okay. We're getting you out of here. Go to the garage at the far end." I point to it. "We have a vehicle waiting."

The woman and teenager—Tina and Blake Burton, I'm pretty sure—stutter to a bewildered stop. I've confused them. They're half-starved, scared out of their minds, and probably incredibly sleep deprived. They can't handle complicated commands.

I grab Marty and push him to the front of the column. "Lead them to the garage."

He starts backing up, waving the women and children on. "Follow me. It's alright. Just follow me."

He speaks with the kindness and gentleness I was unable to dredge out of my own voice. Hearing him in that moment, I don't think anyone would believe he'd just stabbed a kid to death a half hour before.

"Follow him," I tell the line of ghostly figures, pointing and waving my flashlight in his direction like a cop directing traffic. "Follow him. It's gonna be okay. We got you now."

Dear God, how am I going to get them out of this alive?

The Burtons—wife and son. The Mitchells—ex-wife and daughter. The Paulsons—wife, daughter, and son.

Then I see the Pizzuti's. Tracy. Kinley. Gauge.

My knees wobble a bit. I don't know why. Maybe because they were the only ones I had a picture of. Maybe because I was friendlier with Pez than the other refinery workers.

Or maybe because I pretended, for that short, hellish moment, like they were my own family.

Before I can think about how unwelcome it might be, I've grabbed Tracy by the shoulder. She recoils a bit, but seems too stunned to do much else. I relax my grip on her and force a grin that I hope doesn't look manic.

"Good to see you, Tracy Pizzuti," I say, and there's just the slightest hitch to my voice.

She blinks at me.

I pat her shoulder. "Pez is waiting for you back in Texas. We're gonna get you back to him." *Don't fucking say it, you asshat.* "I promise."

God, I'm such an idiot.

Then her face breaks. Tears come pouring out. She throws her arms around me. Surprised, I awkwardly pat her back as she sobs into my neck.

It is only then that I realize that her kids—Kinley and Gauge—have linked hands with a third kid about their age. A boy I can't place. But he's not one of the Pizzutis.

I pull Tracy gently off of me, catch her eyes, and nod to the boy. "Who's that?"

She looks at him, but seems unable to speak.

I realize we've stalled out at the back of the line, and start moving towards the garage while I talk, trying to pick up the pace. "What's your name, son?"

"Noah," he says.

My guts tighten, already picturing his father's face. He'll be so relieved to get his son back. And so devastated to have lost his girlfriend.

"Noah Feldman?" I ask.

"Yeah?"

I swallow and put my arm on his back, spurring him and the Pizzuti's on. "Come on, Noah. We're gonna get you back to your dad."

A big engine roars to life. Headlights blast the darkness away. A black Suburban with a ridiculous lift-kit surges out of the garage and jerks to a halt, EZ in the driver's seat with the windows rolled down, shouting: "Load 'em up! Let's roll!"

Then Branch transmits, his voice tense. "Abe, I got 'em stalled out about a quarter-mile from the mouth of the road. But I'm on my last rounds here, man. Y'all need to pick up the pace. I can't hold 'em off forever."

Shit.

How are we gonna get Branch off this mountain?

CHAPTER 18

DESPITE THE ENORMOUS BULK of the Suburban, five men in combat gear *do not* fit inside with four women and seven children. But one of us does—EZ, in the driver's seat, currently taking the narrow, switchback mountain roads with entirely too much gusto.

"EZ, slow the fuck down!" I yell through the passenger window at him.

Yes, *through* the passenger window. Because, when it became apparent that we all weren't going to fit in the vehicle, me, Marty, Lucky, and Menendez heroically decided to grab onto the roof rack and ride on the runners *outside* the vehicle.

In retrospect, we probably could've figured out how to get us all inside. But we didn't really have time to play human Tetris. Still, I regret my decision as EZ drives us along a curve, and the big knobby tires are dusting the very edge of the road, beyond which is nothing but a straight drop.

I stare down at it. "Oh, Christ. Oh, Jesus." The trees to either side are close to the road, and I'm just waiting for one of them to swat me off the side of the SUV. I squash myself as close to the vehicle as I can. My faith in EZ's driving abilities is made worse by the fact that he's killed the headlights.

In the front passenger seat, Carrie Mitchell sits with her daughter in her lap, looking bewildered in the blue glow of the dashboard lights. Then she does something very odd. She reaches out and grabs me by the front of my belt.

The fuck?

"I got you," she says in a clear, strong voice, her eyes earnest and determined.

I blink, but I'm not so brave as to brush off a little extra security at that point.

"Thanks." I almost make a crack about buying her dinner first, but then remember—I don't know what the hell's been done to these women in their captivity. Or their children. Besides being off-color, it really isn't the time for jokes.

EZ apparently disagrees. "Anybody like monster truck rallies?" he calls out to the passengers in general, daring to take his eyes off the road to glance behind him.

No one responds. He presses on anyways, letting a haggard smile cross his face. "This is just like that. Just like a monster truck rally!"

I realize he's trying to distract them.

One of the kids starts crying.

My earpiece shushes with the sound of heavy breathing and running. It's Branch. "Just fired my last shot. Took some dude out that was trying to get everyone to break cover. Don't know how long that'll convince 'em to stay put, but I'm getting the hell off this mountain. I need a rendezvous."

"Standby a sec, Branch," I strain into the comms, trying to think.

EZ takes a turn a little sharper than advisable. The back-end gets loose. He swears and corrects, getting all four tires back on the road, but not before going way too close to a tree. I see it coming and yelp, thrusting my body against the door while Carrie Mitchell pulls vigorously at my belt.

The tree smacks the oversized sideview mirror and scuffs the back of my armor.

"Goddammit, EZ!" I roar at him.

"Sorry."

"I got you!" Carrie Mitchell repeats.

Branch. Gotta pickup Branch somehow. Except we're three-quarters of the way down the mountain, and he just left the top. On foot.

Then I remember Isabella.

With everything that had happened at the vineyard, she'd completely slipped my mind. But she's still back at base camp, trapped inside the Toyota.

My brain races for a solution. I'd be a liar if I told you I didn't consider leaving her at that point. We got the families, and we need to get them out of cartel territory as fast as humanly possible. They are the mission. They take priority over Isabella.

They take priority over me, too.

I duck my head to look at EZ hunched over the wheel. "EZ—don't fucking look at me! Watch the road! Just listen! You remember that abandoned city we passed by, just before the convenience store outside of Pancho?"

"Yeah."

"You need to get these people to that city."

"Branch can't hoof it that far!"

"I'm not—just shut up and listen."

"Listening."

"When we reach the bottom, I'm hopping off. I gotta go back and get Isabella anyways. Branch will meet me there at base camp. You take the families to that city. You stay there for twenty-four hours, not a goddamn second longer, you got that?"

EZ's starting to look concerned, but he nods. "I got it."

"If we don't meet you there in twenty-four hours, get these people back to Texas. We'll find our own way."

I turn and look at Menendez, who's hanging on my side of the vehicle. "You hear all that?"

He nods, his expression just as worried as EZ's.

I open the comms again. "Branch, you copy?"

"Go ahead," he gasps out, mid-run.

"Get back to the 4Runner. I'll meet you there. We'll rendezvous with the rest of the squad later. How copy?"

I'm sure he has reservations, but he's got too much going on at that moment to voice them. "I copy. Meet you at the 4Runner."

The road is leveling out and starting to straighten. We've reached the bottom of the mountain. I peer north through the trees as EZ picks up speed and we hurtle towards the highway. I catch little flashes of what I guess are headlights in the distance. Those cartel boys aren't far away.

I need to get off this ride before we're exposed on the road.

"Stop here!"

Thankfully, EZ is gentle in his application of the brakes. We roll to a stop. I start to dismount, but Carrie's still latched onto my belt. I glance at her hand. Then at her.

"I'm getting down, ma'am."

She blinks incoherently, caught up in the escape. Then computes what I said and jerks her hand away. "Sorry."

"Thanks for keeping me safe," I offer up, then hop down. I look at Menendez. "Avoid contact, Dez. If the cartel tracks you to that city, don't wait for us. Just keep these people safe—that's priority number one. Me and Branch'll figure out a way home."

"Roger that. Hey. How you fixed on ammo?"

I pat my spare magazines. Realize I never even had to reload during our takedown of the compound. That seems strange to me, but at least I still got most of a combat load-out.

I give Menendez a thumb's up. "I'm good. Go on. Get out of here."

"Hold up!" I hear Marty's voice from the other side of the car. Then the rattle of his SAW's ammo belt as he hustles around the front of the Suburban. "I'm—"

"No." I put a hand up, shaking my head. "We're not doing the hero thing. Get back on the truck."

He doesn't stop. Comes tromping up to me.

EZ leans across the center console, all worked up. "What're you doing, man? We gotta go!"

Marty doesn't even look at his friend. I'm about to start shoving him back to his position, but then I see something that stops me. I see moonlight glimmering in his eyes. They're wet.

Maybe it was just the wind in his face. But the tightness around his mouth tells me it's something else.

"Abe," he says, with a slight thickness to his voice. "Let me go with you."

I'm so damn shocked that I don't say anything for a moment.

Menendez steps forward. He seems to sense what's happening, though he doesn't yet know the full extent of it. "We need our most casualty-producing weapon, brother."

Marty blinks and his eyes clear. He looks down at his M249. Then he shucks it off. "Here. Switch with me."

Menendez hesitates with a distasteful look on his face. I don't blame him. Everyone loves to have a SAW on their side, but no one likes to carry the damn thing. He quickly relents with a huffy sigh. "Fine." He gets his own rifle off and they swap weapons. Marty hands over his spare ammo pouch, but he doesn't need Menendez's rifle mags. The M249 was designed to accept those same magazines, and Marty's already got four strapped to his armor.

"Hey!" EZ calls from the driver's seat.

Marty looks at him and they hold eye contact for a silent moment. Seems like EZ had other things he wanted to say, but what he winds up going with is, "Do me a favor and bust those brake lights for me, will you?"

Me and Marty both lope to the back of the Suburban where Marty uses the bolt-cutters like a club to smash through the brake lights' outer plates, then the bulbs themselves.

When the vehicle's completely blacked-out, Menendez hops back on the runner. He gives me a nod. "We'll see you soon."

Then, without further ceremony, the Suburban drives off, and me and Marty hustle into the darkness, heading south for our base camp.

We keep up a good clip, not needing to be so cautious as we had when we'd approached the mountain vineyard. But I do stop frequently to orient myself and to listen for gunfire.

I never do hear any. So I guess EZ got them around the cartel soldiers without a firefight.

On one of these stops, checking my pocket compass with the redlight filter on my flashlight, I eye the man with me. We're huddled close to mitigate anyone—or anything—from spotting the red glow. His eyes are up, pulling security while I check our heading. He notices me looking at him, but doesn't hold my gaze.

"What's this about, Marty?" I husk, looking back to my compass, then judging the terrain ahead. I think we've drifted a little east of our intended bearing.

"What do you mean?" he asks, feigning ignorance.

"Don't play dumb. You know what I mean."

He's quiet for a time. I adjust my position to correct our heading, then aim myself for a little hill in the distance, barely visible in the moonlight. I'm pretty sure that's where our base camp is. Maybe two miles out.

When he speaks, it's a bit defensive. "Didn't wanna make you go it alone. No matter how much of a badass you think you are, you need help. I'm here to help. You're welcome."

I kill the light and pocket the compass. "First of all, I know I need help, but I didn't want to ask. So thank you. My chances of survival are much higher with you here. Second of all, you're full of shit and you know it. But whatever. You do you."

He says nothing in response, and we get moving again.

The sky to the east is just beginning to flush when we make it back to base camp. We approach cautiously, but nothing looks out of place. Our extra gear is still where we left it. The Toyota sits motionless, all of its windows intact, which is a huge relief to me. Somewhere in the last mile, I'd become convinced that we'd arrive back to find the glass punched out by primals, and Isabella in pieces.

I'm still kind of having a hard time accepting how little primal attention we're getting out here. But maybe the cartel's done a decent job of eradicating them. That doesn't make me feel any warmth towards them, but I'm glad they made my life a little easier.

I approach the back of the 4Runner and peer inside, still somehow worried about what I might find. But Isabella is there, and awake, and the second she sees me looking in, she jolts and issues a yelp of fear. Then she recognizes me. Then she starts yelling.

"Abe! You asshole! Get me out of here!"

I can't help but smile as I move to the tailgate and pop it open. She doesn't stop yelling at me. As the tailgate opens, it just gets louder.

"Get me out of this shit! My leg's been cramping for hours! Who does that? Who leaves a fifteen-year-old girl tied up in the back of a car all night? I pissed myself, you asshole!"

"Alright! Okay!" I hiss. "Bring your voice down."

"I'm not gonna bring my voice down! I've kept my voice down all night, and now you're gonna—"

I clamp my hand over her mouth. She glares at me from over my dirty fingers.

"I'll put you right back in there, restraints and all." I smile to soften my words. "Now. I'm sorry for leaving you. And you can cuss me out to your heart's content. But do it quietly. Do you understand?"

She nods.

I remove my hand.

She continues, albeit at a whisper. "I'm so fucking mad at you. You have no idea how mad I am."

"Oh, I've got an idea."

"You see this?" she hisses the second I cut her wrist restraints off. She's pointing to her crotch. Her pants are soaked, practically down to the knee. "You smell that?"

I do, but just set to work on her ankle restraints.

"I had to sit and stew in my own piss since, like, *midnight*! I told you I wasn't gonna do anything bad or run off! But no, you had to be a hardass and tie me up in the back." She stops as I stand up straight again, the zip-cuff around her ankle cut. She swallows. Takes a breath. "Got any spare pants?"

I scoff, then turn and look at Marty, who's back from the 4Runner a few paces, watching with some amusement. "Hey, kick out a bit and watch for Branch, yeah?"

He nods and heads off.

I turn back to Isabella, folding my hands on the buttstock of my slung rifle. "So, you're gonna come out calling me all kind of names, and then you're gonna demand my spare pants?"

"I wasn't demanding," she says, sullenly. "I was asking."

"Mm. Didn't sound like it."

She glares. "May I *please* have your spare pants."

"They won't fit you."

"I'll make it work." She thrusts her hands at her crotch again. "Unless you wanna smell this all up in your car. Is that what you want?"

Sighing, I pull my daypack off my shoulders and set it on the ground. I've gotta dive deep into the main compartment, unsettling my nice, tight packing. I come out with my spare set and toss them at her. "Here."

She smiles with poisonous sweetness. "Thank you."

She heads to the far side of the vehicle for privacy.

"As long as you promise not to piss in them."

"Sure. As long as you promise not to leave me tied up all night."

I don't make that promise. So I guess we're at an impasse.

While she changes, I retrieve some paracord from my pack and measure out a length.

"Where's the rest of your guys?" she asks after a moment. And you know what surprises me? She sounds genuinely concerned. Which doesn't make all that much sense to me. Maybe she's getting a bit of Stockholm Syndrome.

"They're fine. We're going to meet them."

She comes out from around the vehicle. The pants are ridiculously baggy. She's rolled up the cuffs. I hold the length of paracord out to her. She looks questioningly at it.

"You can use it as a belt," I say. "Like a drawstring."

She shuffles over and begins threading the paracord through the beltloops. As she works, she glances at me. "What happened? Why are you split up?"

I regard her thoughtfully for a moment.

She frowns. "What?"

I guess it can't hurt to tell her about the mission at this point. She can't ruin it now. "You know, Isabella, we didn't come down here just to kill Mexicans, despite what you think."

She snorts. "Okay."

"Up in Texas, there's an oil refinery. The *Nuevas Fronteras* cartel took it over. We took it back from them. Then they found the wives and children of some of the workers there, and held them hostage. Threatened to kill them if they didn't fight us or sabotage the refinery. We came here to find those wives and children and get them back."

Her fingers slow as she listens to me. She ties the two ends together, cinching the waistband tight so that it folds over on itself to fit her. Her eyes come up, but don't quite meet mine. "I didn't know that," she says, quietly.

"I didn't tell you."

"So...you found them? In the vineyard?"

"Some of them. We were too late for the others."

She makes a face, and I know what's coming next. "I'm sorry for those people. I never claimed the cartel was good." She looks sharply at me. "But if you think that justifies what you did to my uncle?" Her eyes start to well up, but her face is all cold fury. "Or to Angel? Or to the doctors?" She shakes her head, the tears spilling. "It doesn't. And if this is some sick, twisted version of an apology for everything you've done to me and them, then fuck you. I don't forgive you."

We stare at each other. Her face is defiant and hateful. Mine is impassive.

I lean in. She's trying so hard to be tough that she refuses to lean away, so I get my face real close to her ear. Then I whisper: "I. Don't. Care."

Then I lean back and inspect her face. She's quaking with rage. It pours over me, but I don't feel it. I don't feel a goddamn thing.

I point to the 4Runner. "Go sit in the backseat and stay out of my way."

Fists balled at her side, with her chin and lower lip quivering, she turns and limps on her broken ankle back to the Toyota. She ignores the makeshift crutch, which is still sitting against the back bumper. She rips open the back door and sits inside, arms crossed over her chest, breathing furiously through her nose.

I start packing our gear into the back of the SUV.

We don't say another word to each other.

I'm just finishing up clearing out our base camp when the comms open up and I hear Branch whisper over the line. "Marty. If that's you, raise your left hand."

I peer out into the woods, but don't actually expect to find anything. Ever the stalker, Branch is probably sighting at Marty from a hidden position, but unable to properly identify him.

After a moment, Branch's voice comes again, louder and much more relaxed. "Hey, there, Buddy."

"You better not have been pointing a gun at me," Marty replies over the line.

"Of course I was. You'll get over it."

The sun is completely up and daylight is pouring through the trees, hot and humid. Marty and Branch emerge from the brush. Branch has his sniper rifle stowed in its drag bag, which is strapped to his back, his carbine in his arms. He looks dirty and exhausted, but smiles when he sees me.

"Marty fill you in?" I ask as I approach.

"Yeah, man." He gives me a fist bump. "We ready to get the hell out of here?"

"That's the plan. Hey." I put my hand on the back of his neck and give him a friendly squeeze. "Fuckin' stellar work up there, Branch."

His smile broadens. "I do what I can, Boss. Lot easier when it's a righteous mission, you know?"

I smile back, but it is ever-so-slightly strained. I can almost feel Isabella glaring holes in the back of my head. "Toss your shit in the back and grab some water."

Branch nods, and starts for the 4Runner, then pauses and looks back with a curious expression. "Oh, hey. On infil, what got y'all held up at the corner of the house? I couldn't see what was going on underneath that awning. Had my heart kicking."

Peripherally, I see Marty look at me, but I don't look back.

I feel like it's not my place to tell it. That's Marty's skeleton, and his closet. He can decide when and if he wants to let it out.

I shake my head and give Branch a flippant smirk, like it's nothing but a thing. "Just a hiccup, man. Come on. Let's get rolling."

CHAPTER 19

THE AVERAGE VEHICLE'S GAS tank is designed to hold enough fuel for roughly three hundred and fifty miles of travel. Of course, there's a lot of variation there, depending on fuel efficiency, terrain, and driving style.

None of those variables are in our favor. We're moving in broad daylight, so I've been keeping the pace slow and cautious, which isn't great for gas mileage. And we're going over uneven terrain. And we're not driving on roads, but overland. And I keep stopping to let Branch glass the horizon ahead for any sign of people that might see us—cartel or otherwise.

Gas has become our most precious resource.

I've been watching that damn gas gauge like a college kid with five bucks in their checking account. Every hash mark it touches, and then slowly slips below, feels like a physical pain in my chest.

The 4Runner is our only way out of this place. It is our lifeline. And yet I find myself berating it like a stubborn mule.

"Come on, motherfucker," I whisper at it. "Come on, you worthless piece of shit."

The low-fuel light comes on.

"You bitch," I hiss, clenching the steering wheel.

Everyone is already aware of my new gas gauge obsession, so no one questions me. They know our spare gas cans are empty. They knew it was going to be a long shot that what was left in the tank would get us to the city.

"Still got thirty miles after the light comes on," Branch observes from the backseat. I flick my gaze to the rearview to give him a salty look, but then realize he's talking to Isabella. She's been quiet, but the concern is written all over her face. With her busted ankle, she knows she can't keep up with us if we run out of gas.

"Where you think we're at?" Marty asks from the front passenger seat.

I grimace, giving up on the gas gauge, because it doesn't matter now. "Best guess?" I check our heading on the 4Runner's built-in compass, then the trip odometer, which I zeroed out when we left base camp. "I think we're a bit north of Pancho right now."

"Okay," he says, with a hopeful note in his voice. "That's not bad. We might still make it."

I don't think we will, but I don't say that. We've been winding our way generally north, and I'll need to start guiding us northeast if we want to find the city. If all went well with Menendez and the rescued families, they should already be there. Which means the clock on our twenty-four hours has already started.

If we don't make the rendezvous, we'll be walking back to Texas. And I don't give that prospect a high chance of success.

We drive in tense silence for another fifteen minutes before I pull to a sudden stop.

I lean forward, peering through the windshield and looking northeast. Marty follows my gaze. Branch eases into the space between our seats and glasses what we're looking at with his spotting scope.

I hold my breath, hoping he won't confirm what I suspect.

The hiss of air through his pursed lips does not sound good. "Yeah. That's Pancho."

Me and Marty swear in unison. I'd hoped we were further along than that, but the settlement sits there, maybe two miles northeast of us.

I start to drive forward again, following an old, overgrown farm road, but Branch says, "Hold up." I stop again. After a moment, he continues. "Word must've gotten out. I got two technicals on the road. They're moving. Just give 'em a minute to get outta sight."

Marty fidgets in his seat. Then he speaks quietly, as though the cartel patrols might hear him. "Hey. Abe."

"What?" I grunt, not taking my eyes off the horizon line.

"Maybe we should let Isabella out here," he suggests.

Isabella erupts from the back, jutting between the two front seats. "What? No!"

Marty twists to face her. "You can make it to Pancho. It's not that far. It won't be comfortable with the crutch and all, but you can do it."

She's shaking her head vigorously. "Are you insane? I can't go back there! They'll recognize me. And the last time they saw me, I led Angel into an ambush. They'll know I've been working with you guys."

Marty raises a placating hand. "Look. Just tell them you got ambushed by one of the other cartels, but you got away and have been hiding. They'll believe you."

"They won't." She plucks at the loose combat pants on her thighs. "Wearing a pair of men's camouflage pants? And isn't this camouflage American?"

"You can say—"

"They won't buy it!" she snaps. "They'll be suspicious, and they won't believe me."

"Well, change back into your other pants," Marty says.

"I threw them away," she mutters.

Marty considers this. Looks at me.

I shake my head. "She's right. She goes in there, they'll kill her as a traitor. Or worse."

He gives a pained sigh and settles back in his seat.

I glance at the gas gauge, like I told myself I wouldn't. The needle is below E now. The trip odometer says we've eaten up ten of the maybe-thirty miles we've got left in the tank.

"Okay," Branch says. "I think we're clear. Get us out of here."

I drive north, and a bit west, trying to give Pancho and the patrols around it a wide berth. We're following the navigable terrain, which means we're not driving in a straight line. For every two miles we drive, we're only getting maybe one mile closer to our destination.

"At least we're on the right track," Branch says, trying to be positive.

No one responds.

Twenty minutes later, I stop again. We're approaching a road that cuts across our intended path, running east-to-west. The trip odometer tells me we're within five miles of empty. I am agonizingly aware of every single shudder in the engine, wondering if it's the engine's last gasp on fumes. But I can't just go barreling across the road. It's slightly raised from the brushy fields around us, and it looks well-traveled.

"Check it, Branch," I order.

After a few moments of him scanning in both directions, he says, "All clear. Cross it."

I'm much more encouraging to the Toyota as I ease her towards the road. "Come on, baby. You got this. Just get us a little further."

She wallows a bit in some loose sand at the bottom of the road's shoulder, and I have to give her a goose, whispering love and hate to her. The tires get purchase again. She starts to climb up onto the road.

Then the engine coughs.

"Don't do it to me, baby," I urge, rocking in my seat as though my body weight can have any affect. "Come on! *Come on*!"

The engine surges as it finds some last little bubble of gas to inject. The tachometer swings high for a moment. Then abruptly plunges. The engine stutters. Jerks. And dies.

"Aw, no, come on you selfish whore!"

The 4Runner rolls back into the ditch and comes to a sad, lifeless stop.

Fuck. My. Life.

This is possibly the worst place for the damn thing to give up the ghost. Our vehicle, camouflaged or no, is jutting up onto the shoulder of the road, standing out like a giant zit on a nose. Its back wheels are in the ditch, so there's no chance of us pushing it either. One of the patrols is bound to spot it. And then they'll start tracking us.

Question is, how long will it take them? And can we get enough of a head start that we can evade them?

"Alright," I snap. "That's it. Everyone out. We're on foot from here, and we need to get distance between ourselves and this goddamn piece of shit."

"I can't keep up with a broken ankle!" Isabella protests.

I kick my way out of the door, sparing a harsh look back at her as I exit the vehicle. "You wanna sit here instead and wait for them to find you? Execute you as a traitor?"

She realizes there isn't another option.

Luckily, I'd tossed her crutch in with her before we left base camp. For all the good it'll do.

We unass the vehicle and move rapidly to the backend. I pop the tailgate, glancing at the horizon to the east—the most likely direction a patrol will come from. "Branch, keep an eye on that road for me. Marty, help me stuff our packs with as much water as we can fit. Ditch anything nonessential. Guns and ammo only."

I don't need to tell them that we're not far from the farmstead we'd camped at a few nights ago. Which means we're not just in cartel territory—we're in primal territory as well.

I absolutely hate leaving all our gear here. It's hard enough to come by as it is, and now we're just gonna leave it in the hands of our enemies? Besides that, it'll be like a damn calling card, telling the cartel *exactly* who tore their shit up.

So much for trying to blame it on another cartel faction.

Briefly, I consider blowing up the 4Runner and our gear. We've got a little bit of C4 left, and a few grenades. But that'll hurt us more than it helps. We need to rack up distance before the cartel finds our starting point. Blowing the vehicle will put a fireball and a black cloud of smoke in the sky, which will only draw them in quicker and diminish our head start.

As I zip up my daypack, now stuffed with a spare water jug and a few extra MREs, Isabella nudges up to me.

"Hey. Gimme a gun."

"No."

"Why not?"

"Because I don't wanna get shot in the back of the head." I swing the pack onto my shoulders.

Isabella glares. "You've got my word, Abe: if I shoot you, it'll be in your face."

"Nice. But the answer's still no." I grab her by the shoulders and bodily turn her north. "We're moving out."

"Yo!" Branch calls from where he's crouched on the side of the road. "Contact! Dust cloud!"

I whip my gaze to the east and see it: A little tan smudge on the horizon, heading north, as though it was coming from Pancho. It's pretty far away, but I see what I think is the outline of a small pickup—a technical—and a guy in the back bed, manning a machine gun.

"Go!" I urge Isabella, pushing her. "Get across the road!"

Marty sprints across and posts up in the brush on the far side, while Branch stows his spotting scope in his pack and shoulders his rifle.

Isabella's progress is rushed, but pathetically slow as she stilts her way up the rise to the road. "Don't push me! That's not helping!"

I glance to the east. Is it my imagination, or is the dust cloud slowing?

"I think they've seen us," Branch says, then scuttles to the other side of the road, moving low to limit his profile.

"Alright," I grunt, letting my rifle hang and grabbing Isabella up. She yelps and curses me, but I ignore her, slinging her over my shoulder. My torn oblique lets me know it's not pleased with this development. I mentally tell it to shut up and do work.

"Go!" I snap at the others as I mount the road and cross it.

They hustle into the brush on the far side.

I take another look to the east and I know that Branch was right. The dust cloud is gone, because the vehicle has slowed. Probably because they've seen a suspicious object jutting up from the shoulder of the road. Which means we've got less than a minute before they're on our ass.

Branch has his carbine in his hands but he's looking back at the Toyota with a pained expression as I hustle past him. "My rifle," I hear him groan.

"Leave it—doesn't have any ammo anyways!"

"I'm leaving it," he snarls, but he's clearly not pleased to lose such a fine weapon.

He takes up the rear position while ahead of me, Marty slams through the brush like a bulldozer. Which is nice, because it leaves a path for me to follow, but it's bad because it'll be obvious which way we went.

"Marty!" I huff out. "Don't blaze a fucking trail!"

He doesn't respond, but he starts to wind through the bigger stands of brush, rather than plowing through them.

I hear the growl of an engine. Look behind me and see that we've only made it about a hundred yards from the road, and the technical is rapidly approaching. This isn't going to work. We have no head start. We cannot evade them.

"Get down!" I suddenly decide, and immediately sling Isabella off my shoulders. We need to get low or we'll be spotted.

Ahead of me, Marty stops and sinks to a knee.

Branch sidles up next to me in a crouch. "We might be able to take 'em."

I nod, then get Marty's attention and motion him to come back.

Isabella's now sitting on the ground, about as breathless as I am. I can't really blame her. Being carried is almost as exhausting as carrying someone.

Marty duck-walks up to us, then rests on his knees, peering towards the road. The brush is high around us, and we can't see the technical, but we can all hear its engine getting louder.

"We don't have time to evade these ones," I rush the words out. "But if we take them out, we might have a chance to evade the next ones. We gotta assume there's more coming, so we're gonna hit 'em hard and then get out." I point to Marty and Branch. "The second that vehicle comes to a stop, shred it." I pat the two grenades on my rig. "I'm moving in closer to blow it and anyone that manages to hide on the other side of the road." I look at Isabella. "You need to stay small and quiet and hide."

"What? I don't—"

"You need to shut your mouth. I know you hate my guts, but right at this moment, we're on the same side. Do what I say and you might see tomorrow. Now get in the brush and hide. Don't move. Don't make a sound."

She looks suddenly more scared than she was before, as though the urgency of my tone has bled through to her. Maybe made her realize how close we all are to getting our skulls ventilated. She scoots backward, taking her crutch with her, and balls herself up inside of a bush.

"Spread out," I say, moving off the path Marty beat through the brush.

I move as fast as I can at a crouch, my ears straining for the nuances of engine and brakes. It's still getting louder, but the direction of the noise is rapidly coming abreast of our position. I start curving my way towards the road. I've got a good arm, but that doesn't mean I can pitch a grenade a hundred yards.

I hear the technical downshift.

I stop where I am, shouldering my rifle, and take a few rapid breaths to oxygenate my blood.

I hear the slight squeak of brakes.

I slowly raise myself, my thighs burning as I hold myself in a half-squat, my head and rifle just above the level of the brush.

Small technical. Single cab. One guy with an M240 in the back. Driver. Passenger.

The machine gunner is aiming at the 4Runner.

The passenger's side door is already open when the vehicle rocks to a stop.

Then all hell breaks loose.

The passenger's door sprouts a multitude of holes, the window shatters, and the guy getting out twitches and screams, falling to the pavement with one leg still in the cab.

I've already got my reticle on the machine gunner and I fire, one-two-three-four-five, then let up when I see the guy fold like he's been gut punched. His hand is still gripping the M240 as he wilts, and the machine gun swings wildly upward and blats out a dying burst.

I can hear Marty and Branch still firing to my left, their rounds pummeling the cab and pulverizing all the glass. I start sprinting forward of the firing line, shucking a grenade into my support hand. Through the open passenger's door, I can see the driver flailing. I don't know if he's been hit, but he manages to get his door open and spill out the other side.

The technical starts to roll forward, then crunches into the fender of our abandoned Toyota.

And it suddenly hits me—the technical might be our ticket out of here.

I'd expected there to be more guys, and I didn't think we'd handle them so quickly, so I'd thought blowing the damn thing up would be necessary. But now there's just one lonely guy on the other side of the road. I can chuck a few frags at him, blow him to bits, and then we got a new ride—and an M240 to boot.

It all seems like a gift from God, and I remember Branch's words about our mission being righteous...

Then I see a little black thing go arcing through the air from the far side of the road.

There is some small, childish part of me that thinks, *Maybe it's just a smoke grenade.*

The black object doesn't get far. The guy that tossed it was definitely not an all-star pitcher.

So where does it land?

Right underneath the technical.

I watch my gift from the heavens jerk as the grenade detonates, its tires practically clearing the ground as gray smoke and fire flash from underneath it. For a moment, I'm so stunned that the guy ten yards from the truck couldn't manage to get the grenade over onto our side of the road, and that it just happened to fall right underneath the technical, that I have the surreal thought that maybe *I'd* tossed the grenade without thinking it through.

But no. My grenade is still in my hand, pin still in place.

I'm still running towards the road.

And I am pissed.

A second childish thought: *Maybe it's still drivable!*

Orange light flares from beneath the technical. Then comes the secondary explosion as the gas tank ignites.

You gotta be kidding me.

I'm closing within a dozen strides of the road now. The technical belches flames and black smoke, creating a visible column in the sky that no other patrols within ten miles are going to miss. I want to get out of there, but I don't want this one last cartel soldier taking potshots at our backs as we run.

Besides. He blew up my gift from God. So fuck him.

I key my comms as I reach the shoulder of the road. "Check fire, check fire!"

Marty and Branch have already stopped shooting at that point, but you never can be too careful when you're crossing your buddies' lanes of fire.

I mount the dirt berm of the road, my support hand clutching both the grenade and my rifle's foregrip. The burning technical and our 4Runner are nose-to-nose, creating a wide V. The last guy is in that V, I think.

I angle to the right of our 4Runner, pulling the pin, letting the spoon fly off and counting to two before I lob it. It sails through the air and lands neatly on the far side of the two vehicles. There's a cry of alarm, and then an explosion.

I hit the far side of the road, sliding down the berm on my ass, and skid to a stop on my side, rifle trained beneath the underside of the SUV.

I see a man with no legs crawling towards me, wailing.

Then he sees me. His eyes go wide and his screams die in his mouth.

I fire twice into that shocked face, and he slumps.

I heave myself up, then skitter around the backend of the vehicle, covering the dead body until I'm ultra-sure he's done. Then I look at the technical and start thinking about time, and the column of smoke still rising from it, and what I might get out of it before it's fully engulfed in flame.

My eyes land on that M240, and I very briefly consider the pros and cons of taking it. I love a belt-fed weapon. But I hate the extra thirty pounds.

In the end, fire superiority wins out. It always does.

I transmit as I run up to the bed of the burning technical. "Marty. Branch. One of you grab Isabella and start moving north. Split up. Get distance."

Marty responds in the affirmative and I jump into the bed of the technical.

The flames have fully consumed the cab now, and they're licking out of the broken back glass, right where the M240 is posted. The fire is ungodly-hot and I flinch away from it as I force myself forward. I need to get that weapon before the ammo box starts cooking off.

I take a few deep breaths of the scorching air, then move in, squinting against the stinging smoke. The machine gun is secured to a swivel base with a simple latch pin. I spit on my fingers as though to snuff out a candle and dive in. The heated metal burns me anyways, but I get the latch pin undone, then rip the M240 from its base.

The ammunition belt rattles out of its can, and I decide it's a good day, and maybe this is still a gift from God, because it looks like most of a two-hundred-round belt.

The weapon is searing my fingers. I curse as I vault over the side of the bed, then sling the weapon on the ground. I blow and spit on my fingers as I take a glance at the eastern horizon. I can't see any other patrols coming. Yet.

I bend and start patting different areas of the weapon to see what's scorching and what's tolerable. The receiver is hottest, since that's where the flames were mostly touching it, but the barrel isn't bad. I grab it by the muzzle in my support hand and shimmy off the side of the road.

I cut a path west along the shoulder for about fifty yards, then plunge into the brush at an angle, heading northwest, and deliberately leaving a trail behind me. I hold this course for about three hundred yards, then stop, dropping the machine gun again.

Our radios have great range. We should be nowhere near the limit. But paranoia's a bitch.

"Comm check—you guys still got me?"

"Branch copies."

"Marty copies."

I test the machine gun again, finding that it's cooled enough that I can carry it on my shoulder. I get it situated, looping the ammo belt around my neck to keep it from snagging on the brush, then I point myself north and start thinking evasively.

I start moving again, this time more carefully, letting my trail fade, rather than come to an abrupt stop. Another hundred yards and I start being very intentional about where I put my feet. It slows me down, but that's the price of covering your tracks.

I keep checking behind me. I'm deep enough into the brush that I have to strain my neck to see the road, though the column of black smoke is still obvious. Moses could've led the Israelites through the desert with that damn thing.

I'm maybe a mile off the road now. I don't see any other patrols approaching the scene of carnage. I start curving my way north, and then northeast. Up ahead, I see the edge of a forest. That's where we'll really be able to make up some distance.

"Hey," I transmit. "You guys see that forest up ahead?"

"Yeah, I see it," Marty says, sounding very winded. I think he might be carrying Isabella.

"I'm in it," Branch reports. "Want me to hold up?"

"Negative, keep going. Stop if you come to the edge of the forest, but otherwise, let's keep moving for another thirty minutes before we rally up."

Ten minutes later, I make the trees and pick up my pace, curving a little further towards where I think the others are. After a few hundred yards, I'm rewarded with the sound of movement and a quiet female voice: "Put me down. I think I'm gonna puke."

I head in that direction. The sound of movement stops, but it's replaced by retching.

I clear a patch of brambles and see them, thirty yards ahead. Isabella's doubled over, leaning on her crutch and heaving. Marty stands next to her, looking back the way they'd come.

"Marty!" I whisper-shout. "It's Abe. Coming in."

He whips towards my voice, his rifle up, but relaxes when he sees me emerge from the foliage. Then he grins when he sees the M240 I'm carrying.

"And you brought me a present!" he says, looking like a kid at Christmas.

CHAPTER 20

We link up with Branch about forty-five minutes later. By then, it's getting on 1700 hours. We have two more hours of daylight to keep moving, but Isabella is flagging hard. We take turns carrying her piggy-back, and alternate that with slowing down to let her limp along on her crutch.

We use those slow-moving times to cover our tracks better. We move through forests and overgrown farmer's fields, and everything is flat and coastal-plain sandy.

I know we're heading northeast. But I have no idea where we are in relation to the city we're trying to find. We haven't crossed a well-traveled road since the one where our 4Runner shit the bed.

Even taking turns carrying Isabella, after another hour, she's done in.

I won't lie—my dogs are barking too, and my side is so stiff, I can barely bend at the waist.

"I gotta stop," Isabella wheezes, leaning on her crutch and looking like she'll keel over if she takes another step. "I'm sorry. I just...I gotta stop."

"It's okay," Marty says, giving her back a little rub.

I look at him curiously for a moment. He seems to have done a complete one-eighty since the assault on Diego Beltran's compound. It's not hard to figure out why. I've seen guys do shitty things. I've seen what the guilt does to them. Sometimes they get meaner to try to justify it and rob it of its power over them. Sometimes they try to absolve themselves, as though they need to prove that they're still capable of human compassion.

I know the feeling. And being the shitty human being that I am, I tend towards the former.

I look around us. We're in the middle of yet another brushy field, left fallow for years on end. Maybe a half mile ahead, there's another stand of forest. I've been keeping a pace count, and estimate we're about seven miles from where we left the Toyota. I would've been more comfortable with ten.

I catch Isabella's eye, then nod towards the forest ahead. "Can you make it to those trees? I don't wanna sleep out in the open."

She drags her beleaguered gaze over to look at them. Then makes a sound like she's dying.

"Come on," Marty says. "I'll carry you the rest of the way." He hoists her onto his back with a groan. "Hop on the Marty Express. Toot-toot." He immediately shakes his head as he starts out. "Sorry. I get weird when I'm tired."

"So fucking weird," she mumbles into his back.

I look to Branch. "Go on with them. I'm gonna double back. Confuse our trail."

Branch looks me over clinically. I think I'm doing a good job hiding my pain and exhaustion, but apparently not. For his part, Branch looks like he could keep going through the night. He shakes his head, then jerks it towards Marty and Isabella's retreating figures.

"Nah, man. I'll do it. You go take a load off those old bones, huh?"

"Bah. Fuck you." But he can tell I'm not arguing. I give his shoulder a tired pat as I pass him, following the others. "You're a machine. When I grow up, I wanna be just like you."

He smiles and starts to head out.

"Hey."

He looks over his shoulder.

I draw a circle in the air. "Keep an eye out for primals, too. I don't know how far we are from the farmstead, but we need to assume we're in their territory."

His eyes get a bit more circumspect. Then he nods and heads off.

I don't think I've been this tired and sore since the Project Hometown selection process.

Yes, yes. I know I'm supposed to embrace the suck. But me and the suck have had a very long, monogamous relationship. Every once in a while, I fantasize about having a more open relationship and maybe getting some hot food, and a shower, and a warm bed.

Instead, I eat a cold MRE, fearing that heating it up might make the scent of the food stronger. My skin is coated in a slime of body oils, dirt, and random bits of organic material. My bed will be the base of a tree.

We hydrate voraciously.

Isabella is too tired to speak, and after shoving a cold MRE entrée down her throat, she simply rolls onto her side and passes out. She is snoring softly within thirty seconds.

Me, Branch, and Marty huddle in the fading twilight. The sky is overcast, promising a pitch-black night. Thunder rumbles in the distance, threatening to add another layer of discomfort.

It doesn't even matter. We're only stopping for three hours, just to take the edge off. I don't know how much time we have left to meet up with Menendez, but it isn't long.

I look at my watch. "Alright. It's 1930. I'll take first watch. Branch, I'll get you up in an hour for second watch. Marty, you take third."

"Any idea where we're going?" Branch asks.

I blow out a breath that flaps my lips. "Shit, man. Can't you use your Cherokee senses to find the way or something?"

He manages a tired smirk. "I guess that means 'no'?"

I rub my face. "We'll start heading east. Hopefully hit the main road that we took south to get to Pancho. Follow it until we find Dez."

"How many miles you estimate?"

I shrug. "Twenty to the road, maybe? Another twenty to the city? That's my best guess, anyways."

Branch contemplates this for a moment. "Forty miles, huh? And we need to cover it in...what? Twelve hours?"

"I don't know when Dez started the clock. If he didn't run into trouble, he might've been in the city by mid-morning. So, to play it safe, I was thinking we try to hump it out in ten hours." I grimace. "Even that might be cutting it close."

Branch raises an eyebrow. "Fifteen-minute miles for forty miles, no stops? That's doable. For us."

He lets that hang there.

Marty shifts where he's sitting. "What're you saying, Branch?"

Branch glances over at Isabella, who is still snoring. "She can't keep that pace."

"So we'll carry her," Marty says, resolutely.

Branch looks uncomfortable. "Yeah, okay. I'm just saying..."

"What?" Marty snaps.

Branch kind of recoils, then frowns at his teammate. "Look, man, she's a hundred pounds of dead weight, and we need to haul ass. Be awful shitty if we didn't make the rendezvous because she slowed our pace by thirty seconds per mile."

"Then we don't slow down. Stop being a pussy, Branch. When've you ever been worried about your ruck time?"

"I'm not worried about *my* ruck time," Branch says, then looks pointedly at me—which I resent the fuck out of. Then he glares back at Marty. "And when did you get so soft on the girl? Are you really willing to risk getting left behind in cartel territory for her ass?"

I see the way Marty tenses up, and I know I should interject. I know why he's gone soft on Isabella, but, again, that's his story to tell, and I don't think he wants to tell it yet.

"Alright," I say, waving a hand between them like a ref stopping a fight. Then I point at Branch. "First of all, you don't need to ever worry about *my* ruck time, jackass. I'll be fine. Second of all, I'm on first watch, so it don't make a difference to me, but y'all are burning through your rack time, so maybe you should both just shut up and go to sleep."

Branch narrows his eyes at me. "So..."

"We're not leaving her behind," I state. Then I snuggle my rifle to my chest and lean back against my chosen tree, looking out into the growing darkness.

"Okay," Branch sighs, rolling over onto his side. "Whatever. Wake me in an hour."

"Fifty-five minutes, now," I grouch at him.

"M-hm."

Marty makes a few huffy noises and lays back, irritably adjusting the links of his new machine gun's ammo belt, as though he's fluffing bedding. He uses his daypack as a pillow and closes his eyes.

It's not so hard to keep mine open. For the first ten minutes anyways. Then it becomes a struggle to keep them peeled. I knew guys on deployment that'd take the hot sauce from an MRE and drip it in their eyes to keep themselves awake. I'm not quite that desperate, though.

The hour slogs by, blessedly uneventful.

By then, I've gotten myself pretty comfy where I'm at, and I don't want to get up, so I find little bits of woodland debris to throw at Branch until one of them hits his face and he wakes up with a snort.

"You're up, Branch," I whisper.

I keep my eyes open long enough to see him sit up with his rifle in hand. Then I let them droop closed, and I'm out like a light.

"Abe."

I'm instantly awake. It feels like I just closed my eyes, but when I blink the sleep out of them, I see it's Marty on watch. It's so dark I only identify him by his bulk, and can just barely see the whites of his eyes, staring back at me.

Then I hear it: A distant bark.

I roll to my knees, my first thought being of primals...but no, that's not right.

"That a dog?" I hiss.

The outline of Marty's head bobs in a nod. "They're tracking us."

I swear and get stiffly to my feet. Shit. Maybe I was just spouting off bravado when I told Branch I'd be fine. It appears my body strongly disagrees. This bullshit is a young man's game, and I'm past my prime. But that irritates the hell out of me, and my hate and discontent gives me some energy.

I kick Branch in the foot. "Branch. Get up."

I check my watch. It's 2145. Poor bastard only got fifteen minutes.

He rolls up. "What? Fuck. I just laid down."

"I know. They've tracked us. They got dogs. We need to move.

He's up in a flash.

Marty is already over by Isabella, shaking her awake. "Hey. Isabella. Come on. We gotta get moving."

"Are you serious?" she slurs, a distinct whine in her voice like she's on the verge of crying. "No. It's still dark."

She must've thought we were sleeping the whole night.

Marty takes her arm and starts hauling her upright. "They're coming. They're close. We gotta move."

I'm standing there, my brain like an old diesel engine: Coughing, stuttering, warming up, then revving and picking up speed until it's racing. Not exactly zero-to-sixty in three seconds, but I've always been more of a semi than a sports car.

Then I drop to my knees and unsheathe my knife. I stab it into the dirt where I'd been laying, then snap my fingers at Marty. "Hey. Gimme the C4, detcord, and detonator." Then I look at Branch. "Gather me up everyone's grenades. Put 'em in my pack."

Then I start digging.

Isabella's up now, her makeshift crutch stuffed under her arm. Branch gathers grenades. Marty rips through his own pack and comes up with our last bit of explosive equipment. He takes it over to me and pops a squat, while Branch stuffs the grenades into the pack that's still on my shoulders.

"What're we doing here?" Marty asks, handing me the C4, detcord, and detonator.

"*You're* taking Isabella and getting out of here. *I'm* gonna fuck them up a bit. Try to slow them down. Hopefully take out their dog."

You know something weird? I don't think twice about killing the men. But the dog? Man...that sucks.

I feel Branch tugging the zippers on my pack closed. Then he gives me a pat on the shoulder. "You got four frags in there. Front compartment with your spare socks."

Dammit. My socks. I should've changed them when I had the chance. If I make it out of this alive, I'm gonna have athlete's foot like a motherfucker. Which seems like a silly thing to think of, given the circumstances. But you have no idea how hard that shit is to get rid of without anti-fungal creams.

"Thanks," I murmur, taking my irritation out on the hole I'm digging. I pause long enough to look up at them.

"Go north one mile, then cut east. Get as much distance as you can. Don't slow down—I'll catch up."

Marty pushes the M240 into Branch's arms. "You take this. I'll take Isabella."

There's no more discussion. Branch takes the machine gun, and Marty gets Isabella on his back, with his daypack slung on his chest. Then they move out. In the darkness, I think I see Isabella looking back at me.

"What about Abe?" she whispers as they disappear into the woods.

"Don't worry about him," Marty says. "He'll be fine."

I gotta admit, I find myself a little touched by her concern. Less so by Marty's pronouncement of faith in me, because he said it like someone just telling a kid what they need to hear to be calm. But I'll take what I can get at the moment.

I dig my hole. Not deep. Just enough to conceal the single brick of C4. I cut the brick lengthwise, make a uli knot with the detcord, then cram it into the cut and smush it all down like a putty sandwich. This goes in the hole, which I cover up with dirt, pat down, and then sprinkle some leaves on it.

Then I pay out detcord as I hurriedly backpedal. We didn't have a lot left, and I only get about twenty feet out of it. I stare at the end of the detcord, wracking my brain for some way to MacGyver a delay fuse. I rapidly come to the conclusion that I can't. This is gonna suck.

I start covering the detcord in leaves, running calculations in my head. One pound of C4 at the base of a tree. I'll be positioned twenty feet behind that tree, taking cover behind another. I probably won't die. I might get a concussion. I'll definitely blow out my eardrums.

I hear a man call out a short, corrective syllable. Possibly talking to the dog.

They're getting close. Maybe a hundred yards out.

I take a moment to peer through the trees. I don't see any lights.

Do they have NODs?

If so, maybe I shouldn't blow them up.

Nah, fuck it. It's just me and an unknown quantity of cartel soldiers. I need some shock and awe on my side.

I hustle back to where I buried the C4. I have determined that I'd like to mitigate the impending loss of my hearing. It's kind of an important sense when you're trying to escape and evade.

I dash my hands through the loose soil, pinch off a corner of the C4, then cover it back up again. As I move back to my detonation position, checking that the detcord is adequately camouflaged, I split the wad of C4 into two, grape-sized pieces.

I go prone behind the tree that I fervently hope will shield me enough from the blast that I don't get a TBI, and then cram the two bits of C4 into my ears.

It's entirely illogical, but I find I'm wildly uncomfortable with handling a detonator while there are two, tiny explosive charges on either side of my brain.

I leave them loose for now, so I still have some hearing.

I take a moment to get myself situated. I nab the four grenades Branch put in my pack. I've already got two on my rig. Two go into my right cargo pocket, and the other two I hold in my right hand. Then I take the detonator in my left.

I focus on my breathing. I wait. I listen.

My pulse keeps hammering. I realize how thirsty I am. My body feels shaky and threadbare.

Box breathing. My heartrate slows. Slightly.

I hear movement. They're not being quiet. They're chasing us, not trying to sneak up.

Someone shouts a single word in Spanish. Then repeats it twice more.

I hear the panting of a dog. Snuffling. Whining.

I peer around my cover. I can see shapes in the darkness, but little detail. There's seven of them. I can make out the dog and its handler easy enough—they're up front, rapidly approaching where we slept, the dog smelling all our gathered scents and pulling the man holding its leash. There are four guys behind, jogging to keep up. Two guys in the wings, kicked out maybe fifteen yards on either side.

My heart starts pounding again as I prioritize targets.

The dog closes within twenty yards of our camp. I ready the detonator, then ease my hands to either side of my head, using my thumbs to push the C4 in tighter. The world gets muffled and quiet.

But I still hear it when the dog starts barking.

At me. It knows I'm close.

The dog's handler hauls back on the long leash. Snaps a command, but I'm pretty sure it was to the others, because they stop, about ten yards out from my surprise gift. The handler starts speaking in excited interrogatives to his dog, who just keeps yapping.

Poor pup. He doesn't know his handler's an evil cunt. He's just doing what he's been trained to do.

There's a lesson in there somewhere, but I don't have time to parse it.

They get closer, the handler controlling his dog's pace a bit more now, getting cautious since his canine is alerting on something. I realize the dog isn't scenting the ground where we laid. He's more interested in the ripe scent of me, freshly wafting from behind the tree.

That dog knows exactly where I'm at. And it wants to chew on me.

The handler pulls to a stop, the dog going ape-shit at the end of the leash. Looking at the man, I see the faintest glow of light around his face, and realize he is, in fact, wearing NODs. Then I realize he's also looking right at me.

I don't see when the handler releases the leash. All I know is that the dog's manic barking is replaced by the scramble of its paws across the forest floor.

I shut my eyes, open my mouth, and hit the detonator.

CHAPTER 21

I've got almost twenty years in the military. All of them in combat MOSs. Five in CAG. Three in the apocalypse. I've been around plenty of explosions.

I've just never had a pound of C4 go off twenty feet from me.

It feels like being in a head-on collision. The blast smacks the sense right out of me. The sound of it isn't so much a noise, as a massive, sudden pressure in my head. I think I lose consciousness for a second, because the next thing I perceive is some sort of rumble—felt rather than heard.

I am confused by this. I'm confused by everything.

Then reality bleeds in just in time for me to see a tree slamming to the ground.

It is oddly silent, but I feel the impact through the dirt.

The explosion felled the tree. Smoke and dust are everywhere. I smell blood. Feel it trickling through my mustache, and taste it on my lips. My nose is gushing.

I need to move.

Things are not fluid. I can't just say "get up, Abe." Where before my body would have moved on autopilot, now every motion requires a deliberate mental command.

I stare at one hand, still holding two grenades. Then the other, still holding the detonator. Let go of the detonator, Abe. My fingers open and it drops. Put that hand on the ground, Abe. Now push yourself up, Abe.

Am I really moving this slowly?

Onto my knees.

Get on your feet, Abe.

Then I'm up. Something feels off. I realize my pack is hanging weird on my back. I leer at my right shoulder, seeing a frayed bit of fabric where there should've been a shoulder strap. The explosion tore it right off of me.

Rifle. Get your rifle.

No. Grenades. You have grenades. Use those.

I watch my hands come together. Fumble with the pin on one. I should be moving while I do this. Yeah. Moving is good. Get those feet into motion. I start moving to the right. It feels like a stagger, but I think I'm actually moving faster than that. I manage to get my index finger into the pin's ring, and yank it. Then I hurl the grenade into the cloud of smoke.

I'm moving faster now. Brain had a bit of a hiccup, but it's getting back on track now.

Cover. I need to get down, or get behind a tree.

I go to a knee behind a thick trunk.

My chest aches. I realize I'm not breathing.

Really, Abe? I have to tell you to breathe?

Breathe, asshole.

The ground shakes as the grenade goes off. I hear nothing but a muted *thump*. I reach up and claw the bits of C4 out of my ears. A tiny bit of hearing comes back to me, but not much. Just enough to hear someone screaming, but it sounds like I'm hearing them from underwater.

I need to move again.

This time my feet get going more or less automatically.

I de-pin the second grenade as I sprint. It takes a bit of fumbling and I realize I can't feel my fingers. That's not great.

I lob it, spoon and all. I almost shout "Frag out!" but then remember it's not smart to give your enemies warning. But hey, at least I caught myself—my brain's coming back online after a hard reboot.

I take two more strides then dive to the ground.

BOOM

I grab my rifle. Time to do work.

I come up, moving laterally to where I believe the enemy to be. I search for targets, but there's too much darkness and too much smoke.

Then a shadow moves. There's no one out here but combatants, so target ID is not required. I pump five rounds into the shadow and am rewarded with another muted scream. I give it three more to be sure. My rifle is suppressed, but even so, I don't hear a damn thing—just feel the recoil against my cheek.

Then I start getting return fire.

Advantage—with my suppressor, they can't see my muzzle flash, but I can see theirs. Three little twinkling lights in the darkness, maybe twenty yards from me.

Disadvantage—I can't hear the zip of the rounds, so I have no idea if they're actually shooting *at* me, or just spraying the woods in a panic.

I play it safe and slide into a prone position behind a tree.

I feel bullet impacts hit the trunk.

Yeah, they're shooting at me.

Alright. Okay.

I roll onto my side, trying to stay small, and grab a third grenade from my chest. I de-pin it, then blind-fire around the base of the tree until my rifle's bolt locks back on an empty mag. Then I lean out just enough to get a good wind-up and hurl the frag in the general direction of my enemies.

I roll back into cover and conduct a rapid reload. Good to see some autopilot coming back.

BOOM

I'm up again, moving diagonally to their last known position. Crashing through brush. Searching for movement or muzzle flashes.

Another twinkling light—at the same instant that something slams into my chest plate, knocking the wind out of me. Spall shreds the underside of my chin. I gasp and stagger, searching for cover while I try to keep those muzzle flashes in sight. They're still shooting at me. Something snaps across my left ass cheek.

I hit a tree, almost head on. Scramble to get it between me and the shooter. Try to get my breathing back. I touch my ass cheek and feel a wet hole in my pants. Nonsensically, I think, *Somethin' jumped up and bit me in the buttock*. In the moment, that is weirdly amusing to me. But also kind of terrifying.

I've been shot before. Scares the shit out of me every time. You never know when it's going to be The One.

This frail human body, with all its veins and capillaries.

God, don't let me die from an ass wound.

I lean out, sighting down my rifle.

Another muzzle flash, and the side of the tree explodes, sending bark and splinters into my face.

I yelp, then roll back into cover, but I don't stop. I roll right to the other side of the tree, transitioning my rifle to the other shoulder as I go. The second I see my red-dot line up with those muzzle flashes, I fire, and I don't let up until I register no more muzzle flashes.

Then everything is oddly, eerily quiet.

Because I'm deaf, or because everyone's dead?

I lay where I'm at for a handful of breaths, my eyes scouring the woods for any semblance of movement.

Something shifts across the ground about fifteen yards in front of me. I fire five rounds at it, then stop and reassess. No more movement. I give it a few more beats, then ease up to a kneeling position. Still no movement out there. No muzzle flashes. I strain to hear, but I'm still getting nothing.

I lean out of cover, then duck back in. Like a clownfish, in and out of an anemone.

No one takes the opportunity to shoot at me.

I pick a tree about ten yards from me and sprint to it.

Still no shooting.

I dare to flash my weaponlight—just one strobe, and I don't get shot for it. That little glimpse of light shows me a body curled up not far from me. I think they're dead. I move out of cover again. Approach the body. Give it a kick.

No response.

I kneel over it and see he's wearing NODs. I yank them off his head. Mine now. Except, there's really no purpose putting them on. I don't have a laser aiming device on my rifle, which means I can't shoot accurately with them on.

They're dual tube, and since I won't be wearing them, I decide not to toast the natural night vision in both of my eyes. Instead, I hold one of the tubes up to my left eye. The woods around me comes into focus. Monochromatic, phosphorous white. Pretty crisp. These are high-end.

Several IR lasers become immediately apparent as I scan my environment. They don't move. They are attached to the rifles of dead men. I count four of them. I complete a full, three-sixty sweep of the woods. Spot another dead body. With the one at my feet, that makes six.

The dog and his handler were pretty close to the blast. Their bits are likely scattered around a ten-yard radius of the felled tree.

Elation hits me and my chest bucks with an unuttered giggle.

Then I get the shakes. Hard.

Shit. I can't believe I'm still alive.

All the near-misses flood back into my brain. All the moments when they almost punched my ticket. A dozen instances where centimeters and milliseconds were the only difference between me, right now, with working lungs and pumping heart, and me as one more sack of dead flesh.

In the moment, it feels so improbable, I can only chalk it up to providence. There *must* be a God, and he must want me alive, because I sure as shit shouldn't be.

Okay. I take a few shuddering breaths. No more of that. Get your head on straight, Abe.

When I can control my shaking hand a little better, I give the woods another scan with the NODs.

That's when I see headlights.

I lower the NODs, confirming that it is naked white light I'm seeing, flickering through the trees. Yeah. Those are definitely headlights.

Hm. Jumped the gun a bit on God liking me.

I picture some middle school girl plucking petals off a flower and saying, "He loves me, he loves me not." I think being in combat is kind of like that. At alternating moments, you either feel like the luckiest person on earth, or that the Universe is fucking you in the ass.

I think I'm still a bit loopy from that explosion.

The headlights aren't moving directly at me, but kind of at an angle to my left. They're maybe a couple hundred yards from me. I don't think they're actually in the woods. I think they're in the field of brush we crossed to get here.

I slip my left hand through the head-strap of the NODs so they dangle off my wrist, then check my rifle. I swap out the mag, stowing the half-empty one in my dump pouch. It just so happens the dead guy I'm kneeling beside was using an AR platform. I strip him of his magazines.

The headlights have stopped moving.

Someone calls out into the woods. I think they're calling someone's name.

Whoever he is, he's not answering.

The sound of car doors opening and closing.

I bring the NODs up to my left eye again.

The headlights flare the image, but I make out two shapes moving on either side of them.

I look off to my left. The nearest edge of the forest is about fifty yards from me. I've got a few moments where the newcomers likely won't be able to see or hear me with all the trees between us, so I stand up and take the fifty yards at a run.

I stop at the woodline and lean out, scanning with the NODs again.

I can just make out the brake lights of the vehicle. I'm more or less broadside to it now, on its passenger side. I get low in the brush and start moving towards it. I stop every few strides to scan the woods.

There are two guys in there. Neither of them have NODs, but they're both armed. They're moving cautiously in the direction where all their buddies are laying. They're about parallel with my position now, and I can see their faces in profile. I hold my position until they move past my line, and I can see the backs of their heads.

Then I start slinking through the brush towards the vehicle again.

I've got a full view of it now. It's an old Mexican police pickup—the kind with roll bars over the bed so a whole squad of Mexican police could stand up back there. But no one's in the bed.

It's a crew cab—four doors. The back windows are tinted and I can't see inside. But both front windows are open. I see only a driver.

I'm feeling lucky again.

I work my way towards the vehicle until I'm about ten yards off the passenger's side door. The guy behind the wheel is leaning forward, craning his neck around, trying to see what's going on inside the woods. I take a peek myself, and can just barely make out the backs of his buddies. They're about a hundred yards away from the truck now.

I think about maybe trying to keep it stealthy and take the driver out with my knife. I decide I really don't want a physical confrontation in my current state.

I rise up out of the weeds, my rifle shouldered and start creeping my way closer to the truck, keeping my reticle on the driver's temple the entire time.

I'm about five yards off the side of the truck when my foot snags some brush, rattling the weeds. He whips around to look at me, eyes wide with alarm.

I put one round through his face, then sprint around the back of the truck. Clear the bed to make sure no one's lying down back there—it's empty. I rip the back left door open, prepared to dump my mag at anyone inside. There's no one.

I'm sure the guys in the woods heard my shot, suppressor or no, but if they're calling out to their friend in the driver's seat, my busted ears can't make it out.

The driver is slumped against his open window. Brain matter is drooling down the door panel. I yank the door open. His body topples out all on its own.

Then I do hear a shout from the woods. It sounds questioning, like they're not sure what's going on. I leap into the driver's seat and slam the door. The first thing I look at is the fuel gauge. Almost a full tank.

God loves me after all.

A bullet *thunks* into the hood of the truck. I swear and duck down behind the engine block. Another round smacks through the windshield, leaving a spider-webbed hole a foot shy of my face.

I jerk the truck into reverse. The tires skid as I stomp on the gas pedal, then find purchase, and the vehicle lurches rearward. I cut the wheel, hit the brakes, shift into drive, and jam the accelerator. The back glass explodes. The truck jumps violently as it hurtles across the rough terrain.

I feel bullet impacts thwacking through the truck, chasing me as I get distance.

They taper off as I haul out of range, driving recklessly through the brush around the northern edge of the forest.

It is only then that I remember my team, my comms, and the earpiece dangling from my collar.

Wrestling the jerking wheel with one hand, I push the earpiece back in. I hear a wet, squelching noise. Dab my earlobe with a finger that comes away bloody. That's to be expected. It reminds me that I need to address the hole in my ass cheek sometime soon, but I got bigger problems at the moment.

I key my radio. My voice is a dry, croaking rasp. "Branch. Marty. You guys copy?"

It's Branch that responds. "Holy shit, Abe, is that you? You sound fucked up. How bad are you hurt and where are you?"

"Uh..." I hazard a glance in the rearview. By the glow of the headlights and the dashboard, I realize I am indeed fucked up. My face and beard are coated in blood from the nose down. It's trickling out of my ears. The whites of my eyes are almost entirely red from broken blood vessels. The seat of my pants is wet and squishy. "I'll make it. Thanks for asking. How are you?"

What the hell am I talking about?

I shake my head, and don't even let Branch respond. "Stop where you're at and look back the way you came. Look for headlights." I start manically flashing the high-beams. "I got us a truck."

The Universe has pulled its dick out of my ass.

For now.

CHAPTER 22

I'M CRAMMED IN THE backseat now with Branch, my pants pulled down to my thighs. I don't like the way Isabella is leaning on the center console from the front passenger's seat, staring at my exposed ass with a mix of revulsion and fascination.

Branch swears as the truck hits a hard bump. He jostles into my wound, causing me to groan.

Branch pulls the little flashlight out of his mouth and snarls towards the front. "Marty, you mind slowing the fuck down for thirty seconds so I can patch this man's ass?"

Marty's behind the wheel with the headlights off and the NODs I stole on his head. "You fucking high? I'm not slowing down."

Branch elbows the back of his seat. "Then could you try not to hit every fucking ditch in Mexico?"

"I can't see the ditches through the weeds! Just deal with it!"

"Motherfucker," Branch murmurs and then gets himself in real nice and tight with my rear end, bracing himself on it to mitigate the jostling. "It's not too bad," he says to me, his tone changed to friendly encouragement. "But you got three holes. Went into your left cheek, exited near your crack, and tore a bit off your right cheek."

"Technically, he's got four holes."

Me and Branch turn our heads to stare at Isabella. Even Marty turns his goggles on her for a moment, his mouth slack beneath them.

She blinks, innocently.

"Do you fucking mind?" I say to her.

"What? You guys are always saying fucked up shit."

"Yeah, well..." I reach out and push her back. "Look somewhere else."

"Oh, like I've never seen a dude's ass before?"

"You're sure staring at it like you haven't."

"I've never seen a dude's ass *with bullet holes in it*."

Marty nudges her with an elbow. "It's a nice ass, though, isn't it?"

"Gross," she sneers.

I see an opportunity to get the privacy I so desire. "Yeah, well, don't fall in love, Honeybuns. You're too young for me."

It works. She turns away. Faces Marty. "So, wait. You've seen Abe's ass before now?"

"All the time. He's constantly shakin' that thing around. Probably shot himself just so he could pull it out again."

Isabella returns to looking at me. "Abe, are you gay?"

That's it. I'm done. "Next person besides Branch to say one more goddamn thing about my ass, I don't care who it is, I'm punching the fuck out of you." I look right at Isabella, so she understands. And I am completely serious. My head is killing me, and their bullshit is making it worse.

She turns back around in her seat.

"Pretty sure he's got a TBI," Marty says to her in a consoling tone. "Irritability and violent outbursts are common symptoms. So, you know. Don't push it."

"What's a TBI?"

"Traumatic Brain Injury."

Isabella's quiet for a moment. "From what?"

"Probably the explosion."

"Is that why his eyes are all messed up?" she whispers.

Marty doesn't respond. Isabella turns back around in her seat, and I swear to God, I really am about to punch her right in the face. But then I see the genuine concern in her eyes. Plus, she's not looking at my ass. She's looking at my eyes.

"I'll live," I growl at her, because that's about as nice as I can be in the moment.

"Alright," Branch says, and I feel his hands stop their operations. "I'm gonna leave it open and bandaged, just like Dez's wound, and for the same reasons. That cool with you?"

"Yeah." I start to pull my pants back up.

"Guys."

I look at Isabella, expecting some more of her nonsense. But her eyes have gone wide, and any humor has been stricken from them. She's staring out the back glass.

Immediately, Branch and I turn to look.

A pair of headlights twinkles in the distance.

Then two pairs.

"Are they still chasing us?" Isabella moans.

"Following our tire tracks," Branch observes.

I raise a hand towards Isabella to stave off the coming panic. "They're too far away to see us, and we're running without any lights. But yeah—what Branch said." I can't seem to catch a damn break. I turn back around. "We should hit the road soon, and then they won't have our tire tracks to follow."

I'd known this was likely to happen. It was the big downside in stealing the truck. But the truck has still vastly upped our chances of making it to the rendezvous.

"Problem is," I say, half to myself and half to Branch and Marty. "If they do manage to follow us, we're gonna end up leading them right to Dez."

Branch lets out an ornery grumble as he puts my IFAK back together. "Might be safe to assume they know we're Americans."

In the moment, the statement seems to come out of the blue. As I look at Branch, confusion etched on my face, I realize that my brain is still not working quite like it should. I can see the problems. But the solutions seem hazy and indistinct, where I'm accustomed to them being bright and clear.

Now, the pros and cons of all the possibilities seem to muddle together. Whatever that explosion did to my head, it's turned me strategically dyslexic.

I squeeze my eyes shut and pinch the bridge of my nose, trying to breathe the headache out of myself. "I'm sorry. I'm not following."

Branch's eyes narrow for a moment, but he's smart enough that I think he knows what's happening without me having to spell it out for him. "We're leaving these tire tracks. They're gonna lead straight to the road. The road heads north and south. They've probably figured out by now that we're not some other faction of the cartel. Which means they probably know we're Americans. Which means it won't be too hard for them to figure out that we went north when our tracks disappear at the road."

Ah. Right. Okay.

Shit.

Ideas start hitting me. Usually, I talk them out with my team. But, knowing I'm a bit addled at the moment, I take an extra second to inspect them for strategic soundness. And come to the conclusion that I'm incapable of commanding this team.

I hate not being the proactive one. I have a lot of faith in my abilities to think through situations, which leads me to have less faith in others. After all, I have a stellar track record of surviving, and a lot of other guys are dead.

But the worst thing I can do in this moment is hang onto control simply because it hurts my pride to admit that my brain is currently not capable of thinking more than a step or two ahead. This is chess, not checkers, and I'm over here struggling with tic-tac-toe.

"Alright, Branch," I say, opening my eyes again and looking at him. "I'm fucked up. You're in control. Tell us how to get out of this shit."

He blinks, his expression inscrutable. Then, like any good operator, he accepts the challenge and rolls with it. "Okay. Marty, when you find the road, head north. We're gonna continue as planned. We should be back in radio-range with Dez once we get close to the city. It's a decent size, so we've got a good chance of losing pursuit somewhere in there and not leading them *directly* to Dez and the others. Plus, once we get our comms back, we can coordinate with them and maybe figure out a better option."

The part of me that has no faith in others knowing better than me wants to poke holes in that plan. But no. I told him he's running shit. I'm not gonna turn around and start fighting over the reins.

"I'm with you," I tell him with as much confidence as I can put into my voice.

Branch twists in his seat and looks behind us again at the trailing headlights. "We've got decent distance between us and them." He turns back around. "Isabella, you know how to drive?"

She nods. "Yeah. I can drive."

Branch leans into the space between the two front seats. "Marty, when I tell you to, I want you to pull to a stop, give Isabella the NODs, grab the M240 and get in the bed. Abe, I want you back there with him. If our pursuit starts climbing up our ass, y'all are gonna discourage them." He puts his hand on Isabella's arm. "Driving with NODs is a little weird, okay? You won't have much depth perception, and you'll have a narrow field of view, so just be prepared for that."

She gets a worried look on her face, but doesn't object.

He leans further in and points to the dash. "You see the compass on the dash there?"

"Yeah."

"Just make sure it says E for east, and keep going that way until you hit the road. Then go left. Once you go left on the road, it should say N for north."

"Yeah, I know how a compass works."

"Okay, great. I'll be taking your seat when we switch up, so I'll be right there with you."

As he's been explaining this, I've been re-attaching my IFAK, checking my rifle, and making sure all my gear is where it needs to be. The M240 is in the backseat with me. I grab it into my lap, looping the ammo belt around my neck.

"Marty, I got the M240, so just go straight to the bed," I tell him.

"Roger that," he murmurs.

"Everybody know what they're doing?" Branch asks. "We need to hustle. I don't want to be stopped for long. Ten seconds, max."

I crane my neck to look behind us again. I don't think our pursuers have gained on us much.

Everyone indicates they're ready.

"Alright, Marty. Come to a stop."

Marty skids us to a halt, and then it's a mad dash.

I spill out the passenger side, lugging the machine gun with me as I scramble up into the bed. Marty meets me there a second later, and I pass the weapon to him. The front doors slam shut. Me and Marty brace ourselves. There's a pause, and I can hear Branch's voice through the shot-out back glass. Calmly walking Isabella through the motions, while Isabella keeps snapping at him that *she knows.*

She accelerates in a surprisingly controlled manner.

I take the driver's side of the bed, so my rifle's ejection port won't be spitting hot brass in Marty's face. He positions himself to my left. I briefly consider dropping the tailgate so we can go fully prone, but decide to leave it up. It's not armored, and bullets can definitely punch through, but it's better than nothing.

We've barely settled into our positions before I hear Branch call from the front: "Road ahead! Hang on!"

Something like relief floods my system. But that's dumb, and I don't let it relax me. We might be on the home stretch here, but it's far from over.

The truck decelerates and then jumps as it mounts the roadway. Me and Marty brace ourselves again, sliding as Isabella hangs a sharp left-hand turn, pointing us north. Our engine roars as we accelerate again, moving much faster than before, now that we're on level ground.

I look far to the right, and see the headlights, way back there. I mutter a curse, barely audible over the wind, then turn my head and holler through the broken back glass. "Branch! We got *three* sets of headlights now. You copy?"

"Copy—three vehicles in pursuit!"

A moment later, Isabella pushes our speed up even more.

I watch those headlights as they move through the darkness, bouncing over the rough terrain as they follow our tire tracks. There is a moment where I find myself hoping that, when they hit the road, they will somehow be dumb enough to turn south, in defiance of all expectations.

He loves me. He loves me not.

I judge we've got about a little over a mile head start on them when they reach the road.

They slow down, the headlights bunching up, and in their conjoined glow I see that they are all technicals, just like this one. Reflective decals flare in the light, and I can't read what they say, but I can intuit it well enough. More Mexican police trucks, appropriated by *Nuevas Fronteras.*

And their beds are all full. Jam packed with cartel soldiers.

Then, one after the other, each set of headlights turns, like three pairs of eyes looking right back at me.

All three cartel technicals are coming after us.

To my left, Marty swears. I glance over and see he's looking at me. I can't tell much in the darkness of the pickup bed, but there's something about his eyes that catches me and makes me suddenly worried for him.

"It's fuckin' Diego," he says.

I shake my head. "I'm pretty sure he's not in one of those trucks."

"No. I mean..." Marty looks back at the headlights. "I mean he's not gonna let us go. Because of what I did."

"Hey." I reach over and give him a jab to the shoulder, getting his eyes back on me. "Fucker was never gonna let us go, Marty. It's not all on you." I look back. "I pissed him off pretty good too. But he woulda come after us no matter what."

And, as much as I hate these cartel bastards, I have to admit...if I'd had my compound invaded, my wife killed, my son killed, and my daughter threatened in front of me? Yeah, I wouldn't let it go either.

"They're gaining on us," Marty says.

I squint at the lights. He's right. They're getting closer.

I turn to holler back at the cab. "We need to go faster! They're catching up!"

"Working on it," Branch calls back. Then I hear his raised voice, but it's unclear what he's saying to Isabella.

Then her voice shrills, and I hear that pretty clear: "I *can't* go faster! I'm gonna crash!"

As though she's trying to prove her point, we hit a nasty pothole in the road and the backend fishtails violently, forcing me to sprawl my legs to keep from tumbling.

I post up with my rifle. It's tempting to rest it on the tailgate, but when shooting from a moving vehicle, it's better to let your body be an extra shock absorber. I see Marty lugging up his M240. He doesn't have much choice but to rest it on the tailgate—the machine gun's a heavy bitch.

I judge the distance of the headlights. They're closing within five hundred yards of us. Well within range of the M240, but my rifle's comparatively-puny rounds will struggle to do much damage at this distance.

Right now, we have an advantage. I'm pretty sure their headlights can't reach far enough to illuminate us, which means they can't see us, but we can see them.

Then I think about the ammunition belt for that M240.

"Marty, you got tracers in that belt?"

"Yeah."

Shit. Well, that kind of mitigates the advantage. Tracers work both ways—they let you see where your rounds are going, but they also let the enemy see where they're coming from.

"Alright, fuck it," I decide. "Branch! We're going hot!"

"Roger that!" he shouts back.

I hunker behind my rifle, my red dot playing figure eights over the nearest set of headlights, now within three or four hundred yards. I flick my select fire over to full auto.

"Hit 'em!"

CHAPTER 23

We both open up. Marty lets it eat, trying to use our momentary advantage to its fullest extent as we send a wall of lead thundering out of the darkness. I fire three-to-five round bursts in rapid succession, targeting just above the rightmost headlight, trying to chew up the driver.

Every few rounds out of the M240 is a glowing orange streak through the night. They hammer the front of the leading truck, some of them ricocheting and spinning off into the darkness.

The lead truck swerves, trying to dodge, but we keep firing, tracking it as it jukes wildly in the road. Not sure if we actually hit anyone, or just freaked them out a bit, but the next thing I see, the truck tries to swerve too aggressively, skids sideways, and starts tumbling.

The headlights of the second truck in line silhouette the shape of the lead technical in a disastrous roll, spewing bodies out of the truck bed like candy from a busted piñata.

Me and Marty don't sit back to marvel at the carnage, but immediately pivot our fire to the second truck. The first is still barrel-rolling across the road, smashing its ejected passengers into paste, and the second truck veers around it. I see the shadow of something in the road, briefly illuminated by the second truck's headlights, and then comes a *BANG* that is somehow louder than all our shooting.

The second truck jumps as it rolls over the body it just struck.

I feel my bolt lock back to the rear.

"Down!" I shout, sweeping up a fresh mag.

The second pickup has slowed dramatically to avoid wiping out like the first, and the third technical in line overtakes it. This one came to play—I see automatic muzzle flashes like sparklers above the glaring headlights. My hearing hasn't *quite* come back enough to catch the high-pitched whine of projectiles splitting the air over my head, but something makes the back of my neck prickle.

I immediately flatten myself onto the floor of the bed. A flurry of rounds smashes through the tailgate where I just was. I snap my head to look back over my shoulder, and see fresh holes in the back of the cab.

They're right in line with the driver's seat.

I slam a fresh mag into my rifle and send the bolt home, waiting for our vehicle to start yawing in the roadway because Isabella has just been shot in the back...but it doesn't happen.

"Up!" I shout as I surge back to my knees, clear the lip of the tailgate, and bring my sights back to my eyes.

The third technical is now the lead vehicle—and it's gotten closer.

"Aim for the driver!" I bellow at Marty, as I bring my optic up and start firing at the muzzle flashes, which are continuing to shred the back of our truck—I can hear Isabella yelping and wailing, and I hope it's from panic and not pain.

They're close enough now that their headlights are splashing us. We've fully lost our advantage.

I see Marty's tracer rounds spraying wildly across the vehicle, but he's wrestling them down into the cab, pulverizing the windshield on the driver's side. The muzzle flashes are more sporadic—good, because that means less bullets coming our way, but bad, because it makes it harder for me to aim at them.

Then the pursuing vehicle just kind of gradually goes off course, drifting towards the left shoulder of the road. Me and Marty continue to hammer it as its tires leave the pavement. My rifle runs dry right as the technical tilts, and then slams to a stop in the ditch, sending a single truck-bed passenger flailing and screaming through the air. His body plummets into the brush.

Maybe it's only my imagination, but I think I hear the sound of his terminal *crunch.*

I reload again, immediately sighting for the last set of headlights—the second technical that had fallen behind. But then I register that it's *way* back there now. Is it even moving?

Marty's holding his fire.

I glare at the distant headlights. "Can you tell if it's still chasing us?" I'm pretty sure it's out of range for me, but Marty might be able to get it with the M240.

"Uh..." he says, and...there's just something weird in his voice.

I look over at him. He's peering over his machine gun. But his head is kind of lolling, like he's dizzy.

"I, uh...I can't tell, man."

I slide over to him. Grab his shoulder. "Hey. You good?"

He's still squinting over the tailgate. His mouth is slack. His eyes widen, then squint, then widen again, like he can't focus. "I can't...I can't really..."

I shake him and scootch in closer. "Hey. Look at me, Marty."

His head turns, a little slow. His eyes swim around. He frowns at me.

Then he hacks, right in my face. A nasty, wet, wheeze. And I feel warmth splatter across my face. I instinctively flinch away from it, but when I look back at him, I can see his lips and chin are stained dark.

"Aw, shit," I snap, instantly slinging my rifle to the side and getting both hands on him. "Marty's hit!" I shout towards the cab as I pull the man back off the tailgate. The machine gun slides out of his grip and clatters to the bed.

Marty's chest is heaving now. His respirations are labored and rattling.

I get him onto his back. "Where are you hit? Can you tell me where you're hit?" It's too damn dark back here—I can't see shit.

Marty struggles weakly against me, raising a hand as though to grab the M240 again. He stifles his coughing long enough to creak out, "The other...come on..."

I glance at the last vehicle again, but it's fallen even further back. "Don't worry about the other truck. Marty. You're hit, brother. Tell me where you're hit."

I rip my flashlight off my chest rig, flick it on, and hold it between my front teeth. The beam turns his skin stark white, the blood on his chin a vivid red. I work my hands across his body, starting at his chest and neck, trying to feel for holes and wetness. What I feel instead is an unnatural lump over his left clavicle. Like someone crammed a lemon under his skin.

"Oh, fuck," he wheezes, his hands hovering in the air like he doesn't know what to do with them.

I pull at the collar of his armor, now straddling his waist, but careful not to put my weight on him. There's the tiniest little hole in his shirt, and a massive amount of swelling beneath, right over his left collarbone. No blood though. And I have the stupidly-hopeful thought, *Maybe he just broke his collarbone somehow.*

I yank his shirt down with one hand, exposing his clavicle, while my other hand wrestles for the medical shears I keep snugged in behind one of my spare mags. Right on top of his left collarbone, his skin is livid and bulging, with a cratered hole right in the center of it.

No, he's definitely been shot. But there is literally *nothing* coming out of it. It's just a hole.

Without blood to stop, my mind is momentarily blank.

I need to switch mental gears. Start diagnosing.

Then I hear Branch shouting behind me, "Isabella's hit!"

I almost turn around, but then my eyes flit over Marty's face. He's staring up at the sky, mouth working like he's trying to gulp air. His breathing is getting shallower. He sounds like an asthmatic.

Popped lung. Tension pneumo.

I take the flashlight out of my mouth and shout back to Branch, "I hear you! Can she still drive?" Seems callus, but everything has priorities.

Branch doesn't immediately respond, so I refocus. I need to find the exit wound and see if there's hemorrhaging there. That'll kill Marty quicker than a collapsed lung. His armor needs to come off. I can see two large buckles, right at his shoulders.

I stick the flashlight back in my mouth and unsnap the two buckles. Pull his chest plate back and let it rest over his pelvis. Then I start jamming my hands underneath him on both sides. I can feel plenty of wetness, but I can't tell whether it's sweat or blood. So I rake my fingers across his back, feeling for the lump of chewed up flesh that'll be an exit wound, and watching Marty's face as I do.

His expression contorts as my fingers run across a sticky cavity. I pull my hands out and see blood on my fingertips. The exit wound is on his lower ribs, left side. The path of that bullet was unforgiving. It definitely took out his left lung.

I use my medical shears to start cutting away his shirt.

"Hey, shtay wiff me Marty," I say around the flashlight in my mouth. "Keep fighting. Don't shtop. I'munna patch you up."

"Just an arm!" Branch yells from the cab.

It doesn't make sense for a second. Then I remember—oh, yeah, Isabella's been hit. She's gone quiet, though. I can't hear her screaming anymore.

I take the flashlight out of my mouth and clip it to my shoulder. "Can she drive?" I demand again, pulling the cut portions of Marty's shirt away to reveal the entrance wound. I take a glance up again to assess the threat behind us.

I can still see those headlights. The last technical is definitely following us, but they're keeping they're distance. I don't like that. They're trying to keep us in sight. Possibly while they wait for reinforcements to catch up.

In response to my question, Branch shouts, "She's staying with me. Got her TQ'd. She's tough." I know that last bit was more to bolster her courage. "How's Marty?"

I reposition myself on Marty's side. "I'm gonna roll you over, okay? Ready? Here we go." I heave him onto his right side, exposing the exit wound. He groans and coughs again. I spot the hole in his back. It's bleeding, but it's an ooze, not a squirt.

No massive hemorrhage. There might be one internally, but I can't do shit about that at the moment. So my priorities are to patch the hole in his back, then treat for his tension pneumothorax.

"Uh," I shout over my shoulder, not entirely sure what I can tell Branch without freaking Marty out. I scrabble about his plate carrier, looking for his IFAK, but I can't find it immediately so I say *screw it* and rip my own off my side.

"Chest wound!" is what I finally decide to go with. "Working on it!"

Then my earpiece crackles, and a broken transmission comes through.

"Abe...arty. Branch...guys copy?... is Menendez. Anyone copy?"

I guess we've crossed into radio range. We must be approaching the city.

"Handle that, Branch!" I shout, then pull hemostatic gauze and a chest seal from my IFAK. Then I give Marty a few light slaps on the side of his face. "Hey! Marty! You're not passing out on me, are you?"

"Nuh...no..." His voice is choked and weak, but at least he's still conscious. "Can't breathe."

"I know, buddy, I'm working on that right now. Gonna get you some air in just a second. Just hang with me and stay awake." I push gauze into his exit wound and hold.

His back goes rigid against the pain and he mewls, his foot kicking against the side of the bed. "Yeah, there you go. Fuck that bed up, Marty. Kick it."

There's nothing worse than having a wounded buddy on borrowed time and having to sit there and hold pressure on a wound. Half of me listens to Marty's ragged breathing, while the other half listens to the flurry of transmissions between Branch and Menendez.

"Dez! We're in a Mexican police pickup truck, coming in hot with two wounded, and some baddies on our ass!"

"You gotta be close—we heard the shooting. Who's wounded?"

"Isabella and Marty."

"How close is your pursuit, and how many are there?"

"There's one pickup tailing us. Unknown number of hostiles inside. They're...maybe a mile back from us. They're keeping their distance. Might be waiting for backup. But I don't wanna lead them to you guys."

"Yeah, well, we got a bit of a problem here, too. Ran out of gas. We got the vehicle pushed into a mechanic's shop, so we're not exposed, but we can't go anywhere right now. Any chance you have enough fuel in your pickup for us to siphon off?"

"Yeah, we should, but we're gonna have to break pursuit first. We're driving blacked-out, but I think the truck that's tailing us has NODs, because they're acting like they can see us. Hold up—I think I can see the city coming up."

"Hey, wait! One more problem—we got a pack of primals in the city with us. Even if you break pursuit, if you come in too noisy, you're gonna draw them in."

"Shit—goddammit—how many primals?"

"Last I saw them, I counted nine. Got no idea where they're at right now."

"Roger that. Standby, Dez." Then Branch shouts into the back, "Abe! What're we doing here?"

What're we doing? I have no fucking clue. I gotta focus on Marty. "Figure it out, Branch! I'm a little tied up!"

I know I've only held pressure for maybe a minute, but I decide that's long enough. Marty's breathing continues to get shallower. I need to give him an airway. I push my knee into the gauze over his exit wound, causing his groans to go high-pitched for a moment. Then I peel the backing off the chest seal and slap it over the gauze. I roll him onto his back again—his own weight should supply some continued pressure on the exit wound.

"Look at me, Buddy," I tell him as I dive back into the IFAK for a decompression needle.

His eyes pivot to mine. He's scared.

Then I notice that his trachea is displaced—a bit off center.

Shit—that is not good. His internal bleeding is bad enough that it's created pressure in his chest cavity and pushed his trachea out of line.

I look at the decompression needle. We were lucky to get a resupply off the last Project Hometown bunker we scoured. The little medical device in my hand won't be easy to replace. And I realize in that moment...Marty's not going to make it. Not with that kind of internal bleeding. Even if I get him breathing again, his body is dumping all its blood into his chest cavity. He's only got minutes before he bleeds out.

I realize he's looking at the needle too. Does he know what I'm thinking? Does he realize I'm triaging him as terminal? A patient whom valuable resources should *not* be wasted on?

Dimly, I hear Branch transmitting again: "Alright. Dez. You got room in that garage you're hiding out in?"

"Yeah, we got room. We're close to the northern end of the city."

"Copy that. Make some room for us—we're coming in."

I feel our truck make a slight turn and realize we're heading into the city.

Marty reaches out and rests a cold, trembling hand over the decompression needle in mine. We make eye contact. He manages to shake his head. He still looks scared as shit, and that twists something in me—makes me want to stick the damn thing in him and give him a few breaths before he goes. Not being able to breathe is panic-inducing, and a shitty way to go. But bleeding out is just a numb fade—so I'm told.

"Save it," he husks, his voice barely audible. Then his hand weakly pushes the decompression needle aside, and crawls up my arm. I can tell he's trying to grab me, but his fingers aren't working well. So I lean into him.

"This is...what I get."

Dammit—I knew that's what this was about.

I shake my head. "That's bullshit, Marty. We've all done some fucked up shit. It doesn't mean..."

It doesn't mean...what?

It doesn't mean we deserve to die?

Do we? I rail against the indictment. Because don't the ends at least *sometimes* justify the means? Yes, we've all been cruel, but look at the good that we've managed because of it. Look at the families we've saved.

Doesn't that count for something? Doesn't the big picture matter?

Marty's struggling to speak. Struggling to get enough air to make words. He can't quite get there, so what he says next is only audible to me because my face is so close to his, and I can smell his bloody breath and his sour sweat. His words are just the clicking of tongue and teeth.

"Live by the sword..." he strains out. "Die by the sword."

I shake my head again and find myself angry with him. Resentful. He's done with this shitty life—he's making his exit. But we all have to keep going. How dare he try to take the fight out of us. How dare he impugn what we do, just because he doesn't have to do it anymore.

But I don't say any of that, and I don't let the anger show on my face. Because here's the big picture: This is a man's last moment. And if there's anything all of us that live by the sword are completely terrified of—even moreso than death itself—it's dying while drowning in shame, and choking on a belly full of regrets.

The least you can do for a dying warrior is make him feel like he's not going straight to hell. That the scales of his life were at least *slightly* weighted towards good. That's what I'd want, anyways. And isn't that the Golden Rule? Do unto others as you'd have them do to you?

"You made up for it, brother," I tell Marty. "We wouldn't be alive if it weren't for you. We wouldn't have gotten all those families back if you hadn't been there to help. And hey—Isabella's gonna survive. She's gonna go back to her family. And the only reason that's possible is because you carried her ass half the way here. That counts, man. If you're gonna count the mistakes, then you gotta count the good shit, too. And you did good. You did good by us, and by those families, and by Isabella. You did good. You *are* good."

In the seconds before he fades out, I can't really tell what effect my words have had on him. Because his lips peel back, and I can't tell if it's a grimace, or a smile.

His head shakes, and I can't tell if it's disagreement, or just one final tremor before he goes slack.

He dies looking right back at me, and I don't know if he ever felt absolved.

CHAPTER 24

"EZ HERE—I'M ON THE roof of the shop. Give me some white light so I can get your location."

We're moving through the city now, still blacked-out, Isabella doing her best to navigate with the NODs. I'm hovering in the shattered opening of the back glass. She was hit in the right elbow, and Branch put the tourniquet high on her arm. The wound doesn't look good. The round absolutely destroyed the joint. There's no coming back for that arm—not in this world.

Branch is hanging out the passenger's side window with his flashlight in hand. He's got it set to a strobe function and he's flashing it all over the place as we speed through abandoned intersections, heading north.

I take another glance behind us. I can't see the pursuing technical's headlights, but that's just because the buildings are blocking it. I know they're out there. Last I saw them, they were on the outskirts of the city as we plunged into it. I think they'd stopped.

Yeah, they're definitely waiting for reinforcements.

Diego Beltran is not going to let us go. He's going to throw everything he has at us. And I can't even blame him.

Not gonna stop me from tearing their shit up when they come. But maybe—just maybe—we can get the hell out of here before they do.

"Got you!" EZ transmits, his voice excited. "Okay, I think you're about two blocks west of our location, and maybe a half-mile out. Next chance you get, bang a right and let's see if I can get you on the right street to meet us."

"Roger that," Branch says, then turns to Isabella. "Slow down and hang a right when you got a clear intersection."

Something bad happened in this city before it was abandoned. I'm not sure if it was a riot, general mayhem, or a military action, but the streets are filled with debris, and a lot of intersections are walled off with jersey barriers and concertina wire. Half of the buildings look like they've been hit with artillery. Almost every abandoned vehicle we pass is a burned-out husk.

Isabella is breathing hard, and every so often she sobs. Her good hand is on the wheel, and I can see the way the tendons stand out beneath her skin as she wrestles with the pain.

"I feel faint," she says, her voice thin and taut.

Branch reaches across and vigorously rubs the top of her back. "It's alright. Stay with me. The second we get there, I can give you something for the pain."

"Fuckin' ibuprofen?" she wails, with surprising strength, then chooses an open side street and yanks the wheel to the right.

Branch and I steady ourselves, and I imagine he too is restraining the urge to cuss at her for the sudden maneuver.

"No," he says, reassuringly. "I've got some harder stuff, okay? You earned it. But you gotta get there first, because it's gonna make you pass the fuck out."

"God!" she groans, on the verge of sobbing again, and it sounds like she really wants that stuff.

I know Dez has a couple fentanyl lollipops—which, to guys that know their most likely death is from traumatic injury, is more valuable than gold ever was. Given Isabella's bodyweight, she'll take one lick and be off to La-La Land.

"Alright, slow down," Branch says as we approach another intersection. He strobes his light some more and transmits. "EZ, let me know when we're on the right street."

We go one block, Isabella now making sounds like a woman in labor as she jerks us haphazardly around obstacles. Two blocks.

"Right there," EZ transmits.

"Stop," Branch says.

Isabella slams on the brakes, ramming me into the back of the cab.

"You're directly south of us," EZ says. "Make a left and come up. I'll give you a flash. You'll see the building. There's three bay doors. Go for the middle one. We'll roll it up when you're here, and then you need to get in quick."

Branch relays this to Isabella as she mewls and pulls us into a lefthand turn. He finishes with the addendum, "Pull into the garage quick—but don't crash."

Isabella has nothing to say but a repeating string of curses.

I stand up. We're moving slow enough now that I'm worried about Dez's reports of primal activity in the city. I start scanning with my rifle up, ready to lay waste to any moving shadows.

"We're prepping our medical shit," EZ says. "How's Marty doing?"

I feel suddenly cold. I glance down into the bed where Marty's body lays.

I don't answer.

Neither does Branch.

It's like a macabre game of chicken—neither of us wants to be the one to tell EZ his best friend is gone.

I feel bad. But honestly, I don't have the stomach for that right now.

Branch never does respond to EZ. The silence must've been response enough, because as we approach an intersection, I see a flash of light from a flat rooftop, and EZ speaks into my earpiece, his voice gone hollow and dead.

"Visual. That's my light. Come on."

Isabella turns right, then left into the entrance of the building, threading narrowly between a displaced dumpster and a burned-out vehicle that somehow wound up on its side. She pulls us up to the middle bay door of three and it rattles open before she even comes to a stop.

Inside is dimly lit by a single flashlight directed at the ceiling, diffusing the glow across a space cluttered with tool chests, lifts, piles of trash, and the twelve women and children. They all watch us with that complete absence of expression unique to the utterly exhausted and disused.

Menendez and Lucky slip through on either side of the door, rifles up and scanning the dark cityscape. Their faces are grim. Isabella rolls us into the bay, then jerks the truck to a stop and rams the shifter into park.

As though she'd done all this while holding back, she lets loose a gust of hisses and groans and curses. "Gimme the stuff!" she demands of Branch. "Please."

"Just hold on for another thirty seconds."

She whimpers but says nothing.

Menendez and Lucky slide the garage door closed again. I can tell they're trying to be quiet with it, but the old thing rattles and squeals on rusty bearings. They engage the door's security latches, then turn to me.

I know what they want before they say anything.

Resting against the cab, I swallow and nod to the back of the truck bed.

They approach. Peek inside. See Marty's body lying there, face up.

Lucky winces and looks away with a muttered curse.

Menendez just stares for a time. Then he looks up at me, and his expression is no different, as though I'm a corpse too. "You good?" he asks.

What am I gonna do? Complain about the ouchie in my ass with his friend lying dead in front of him? "Yeah, I'm good, brother."

Menendez nods. Turns so he's in profile to me. Takes a huff of air as though clearing his lungs of something toxic, then transmits. "EZ. I'm sorry, my man." He holds the PTT down for another second, as though he wants to say something else, then winces and lets go.

If you didn't know EZ, you wouldn't be able to tell, but I can hear the slight thickness in his voice when he responds. "Roger that. I'm on watch."

Branch emerges from the passenger side of the pickup and walks to the back. He takes a moment to look down at Marty. Reaches in and runs a hand through the body's sweat-soaked hair. Then he puts it all behind him.

"Dez. Need a lollipop. Isabella's in a world of hurt in there."

Menendez turns and looks at him, his expression still unchanged. I can tell what he's doing. He's hiding behind a mental wall. Too much to deal with right now. No time to grieve. We can all have a breakdown later, if we survive.

Menendez reaches into the IFAK on his left hip, rummages around, and comes up with something that looks more like a fat Q-Tip than lollipop. He holds it out and gives Branch a very serious look. "Do *not* take your hands off it. Hold it in her mouth for her, and the *second* she even starts to look drowsy, take it out."

Branch nods. "I know."

He moves off to put Isabella out of her misery.

"What happened to the 4Runner?" Menendez asks.

"Ran out of gas. Had to leave the gear behind—cartel patrols were right on our ass."

Menendez eyes the pickup. "Didn't do too bad for yourself. How much fuel is left in it?"

"About three-quarters of a tank."

Lucky reappears with a siphon tube, pump, and two gas cans. The Suburban is in the first bay, on the driver's side of the pickup, but it's too far away to siphon directly from tank to tank. He sets to work feeding the siphon tube into the truck's gas tank and pumping the precious fluid out.

"Leave me a quarter tank," I say to Lucky.

Both he and Menendez frown up at me.

Menendez points to the Suburban. "We took the back seats out while we were waiting for you. We should be able to get everyone inside the Suburban. We won't need the pickup."

I shake my head. "I'm not going with you guys."

There's a whole lot of mystified blinking at that.

"Okay," Menendez says, cautiously. "Explain."

"I promised Isabella I'd get her back to her family. Their place is, what? Forty miles from here? Just leave me a quarter tank. That gives you a half-tank to—"

Menendez is already shaking his head. "The fuck are you talking about, Abe?"

I knew I was gonna get flak for this. Hell, I'm not overly excited about the prospect either. But if I don't get Isabella back to her family, then what was the point of hauling her all across the Mexican countryside? Everything we did—everything *Marty* did—to try to save her, would be for nothing.

Everything I told Marty in his last moments would be lies.

Saving Isabella was his chance at absolution. And maybe mine, too. My chance to prove that, even after everything I've done, I'm still capable of doing the right thing, simply because it is the right thing to do.

If I don't follow through with it, then is Marty really absolved?

And am I anything more than a black-hearted devil?

It might've felt therapeutic to explain all this to Menendez. But it wouldn't make a difference to him. He hasn't been in my head. Doesn't know the things I've been wrestling with. This is my problem, and my problem alone.

So I don't argue. I just say, "You heard me."

Menendez opens his mouth to respond, but he's cut off by a transmission from EZ.

"Guys, I got...one-two-three-four-*five* sets of headlights moving into the city. We're gonna have company in a few minutes. We need to...” he trails off and cuts his transmission.

Menendez and I glare at each other, waiting for him to continue.

After a moment, Menendez prompts him: “EZ, you cut out before you finished. We copy five sets of headlights incoming, and then we lost you.”

Another few seconds pass before EZ comes back, and when he does, his voice is a bare whisper. “Primals. Coming down the street.”

“Get him off the roof,” I immediately snap at Menendez, who nods quickly.

We’ve all seen the primals’ athletic abilities. Being on the roof will *not* keep EZ safe from them. Hell, the garage doors might not even hold if they get riled up enough, but you gotta work with what you got.

“EZ, get your ass back down here,” Menendez transmits, already moving towards the huddled crowd of women and children. “Everyone in the Suburban! Now!”

Then he whirls on me. “You’re being a dumb fucking cunt, Abe.”

I’m too tired to give a shit about his opinion. I’ve already decided this is what I’m going to do. If I back out now...well, that feels like cowardice.

“Just leave me a quarter tank,” I reiterate. “That’s all I’m asking, Dez. You let me head out there first. I’ll draw them off of you.”

He chews on that for a moment. Then seems to accept the tactical advantage as a peace offering.

A hatch in the ceiling clatters open and EZ scrambles through onto a roof-access ladder. He closes the hatch behind him, then, hanging from the ladder, points in the direction of the street beyond the bay doors. "Nine primals!" he calls. "Coming right at us. They know we're here."

"Must've been those rattly-ass doors," Menendez swears.

Between the pickup and the Suburban, the women and children are lining up and climbing into the SUV. Lucky is manically pumping the siphon, then stops, pulls the dripping tube from the gas can, and pushes the can towards Menendez with his foot.

"Start filling her up!" Lucky says, then immediately sets to work on the second gas can.

I clamber out of the bed. My ass-cheek has stiffened up something fierce in the last half hour. I can feel it pulling my hips out of whack. Stupid old guy shit, I know. I didn't used to be this damn fragile.

Branch is at the open driver's door of the pickup. He sees me when I get my boots on the ground and jerks his head. "Help me with her."

I move to his side. Isabella's passed out cold, drooling.

Branch gives me a severe look. "You sure you wanna do this, man?"

I ignore the question, considering where to put her in the truck to keep her the safest. I could squish her down into the passenger's side, giving her the cover of the engine block. But then any rounds they fire at me might pass through to her. And I think it'd be best to lay her down on her side. If she starts ODing on that shit, I don't want her in a position where she'll drown in her own vomit.

"Put her in the backseat," I say. "Floorboards."

We maneuver her limp form out of the driver's seat. Her head lolls and she lets out a raucous snore. Moving to the back, I go in first, guiding her head while Branch holds her feet. We get her squished in on her side, with her back to the front seats. The backseats will keep her from rolling over. Hopefully.

A rattling noise causes us to pause in our efforts.

Everyone in the garage seems to freeze. All eyes turn to the bay doors.

I can see the metal panels of the door directly behind my truck shifting up and down. The primals are outside, and they're trying to lift the bay doors. Clever bastards. They know how these particular doors open. Never underestimate primals.

The security latches hold. For now.

I climb out the other side of the vehicle, then hustle around to the driver's seat again. The truck is still running, and I take a gander at the fuel gauge. It's very slowly dipping below half a tank. This siphoning shit is taking too long.

The cartel vehicles might not know exactly where we are, but if they spot the pack of primals all clustered around some bay doors, I think they'll put it together. For a moment, I wonder if the primals might serve as a deterrent for them. But they've got five trucks, probably all loaded with gunmen, and I'd hazard a guess that some of those vehicles are technicals, with a machine gun in the back.

They'll take their chances with the primals.

Menendez slams the Suburban's side door, sealing the women and children inside. The noise gets the primals outside amped up. I hear an excited whoop and a bark. One of them slams against the bay door, as though trying to ram through it.

Menendez and Branch both shoulder their rifles, standing between the pickup and the Suburban.

Menendez glances at me. "How you wanna do this?"

I nod at the Suburban. "You all get packed up inside. Lock the doors. Make sure the windows are rolled up. I'm gonna ram my way out of this garage and take as many of those fuckers out as I can. Then I'm gonna split off and try to get the cartel's attention and lead them away from you. Some of the primals might slip in here and try to get at y'all in the Suburban—just try to hold as long as you can, then bust out and get these people back to Texas."

He nods. "I want it on the record that I think this is stupid."

"You've made that clear." I close the driver's door. The window is gone—shattered by a bullet.

EZ lopes around the front of the Suburban, then skids to a stop, eyes on the pickup truck. He can't possibly see Marty's body from where he is, and yet he looks like he's seen a ghost. Then his eyes shoot to mine.

"He's in the bed," I tell EZ.

It sounds like several primals are battering at the doors now. They know there is prey inside, and they are hungry and determined.

EZ looks conflicted. "Are you taking him with you?"

I hadn't really thought of it, but I guess I am. "I'll try to find a place to bury him."

EZ swallows. "Okay. I'll go with you."

Menendez spins on him. "No. You're not."

"Gas!" Lucky says, pushing the second gas can towards Menendez and Branch.

Branch nabs it and hustles over to the Suburban while Lucky starts refilling the first gas can.

EZ looks at Menendez and his face is immovable as stone. "Dez. We don't have time to argue. I'm going with Abe and Marty. You're never gonna convince me otherwise, so you might as well just accept it."

Menendez starts to flail his arms around in frustration, swearing up a storm.

Leaning out the busted driver's window, I call to him. "Dez. Dez. Hey."

He stops throwing a tantrum and scowls at me. "What, motherfucker?"

"Just let it go. Get in the Suburban."

He bares his teeth. No one speaks for a moment, and it is just the sound of primals snarling and huffing and slamming the bay door behind us. The metal is starting to sound stressed. Give those creatures enough time and they'll break through. We need to get going.

Menendez knows this too. Finally, he lowers his head. Takes a deep breath. Then looks at EZ. "Alright. Fuck it. You guys do what you gotta do." He points a finger at me. "Try not to do anything dumber than you already are, okay? Will you at least promise me that? That you won't get yourselves killed trying to do some hero shit?"

I raise a fist towards Menendez. He stares at it, then relents and bumps his own fist against mine. "Ain't no heroes around here, Dez. I can promise you that."

For a moment, Menendez looks like the saddest, oldest soul in the world.

"Done," Lucky pronounces, ripping the siphon tube out and letting it drop to the garage floor. He seals up my gas cap, then grabs the can he just filled and hauls it off to the Suburban.

Menendez gets into the front passenger's seat of the Suburban and closes the door. He looks at me through the window. Gives me one last nod.

"EZ," I get the guy's attention, then hike a thumb towards the bed. "There's an M240 in the back. Should have some rounds left."

EZ refocuses himself. "You want me in the bed?"

I shake my head. "Negative. Get in the backseat. I don't want primals hopping in the bed with you when we bust outta here."

"That's reasonable." He jogs to the bed.

In the rearview mirror I watch him go still as stone, staring over the tailgate at his dead friend. Behind him, the bay door rattles and wiggles on its tracks, and the whole garage is filled with animal keening.

Something gives way with a metallic *pop*, and that spurs EZ into motion again. He reaches into the bed and comes back up with the M240. It's got maybe fifty rounds left in its belt. He lugs it around and gets in the back, kneeling on the seats with the M240 sticking out the busted back glass.

More car doors slamming shut.

I look over at the Suburban. Branch is in the driver's seat. I can see Lucky taking a position in the back, though they keep all the windows up. Menendez gives me a thumbs-up.

"These windows close?" EZ asks as he gets himself situated.

"Sorry, Bud. Windows are all shot out."

The windshield is a mess too. No wonder Isabella had such a hard time navigating. I briefly consider kicking it out, but it's not as easy as you might think, and I don't know if we have the time. I tell myself it might still keep a primal from diving in the front with me. It is a small consolation.

"You ready?" I call back to EZ.

I hear the rattle of the M240's cover being lifted, the chamber checked, then the cover being slapped closed again. "Ready."

I breathe. Put the shifter in reverse. Get both my hands on the wheel. Then I hold the brake down and step on the accelerator. The engine roars. The tires shudder and chirp. Then start squealing, drowning out the clamor from the primals outside. Gray smoke billows up from the rear wheels and the scent of burning rubber hits me.

I rip my foot off the brake and put the gas pedal to the floor.

We launch backwards.

Then slam into the bay door.

And go no further.

"Fuck!" I roar, immediately shifting into drive again and rolling forward until the truck's nose is right up against the far wall of the garage.

We made a massive dent, opening a gap in the bay door through which a primal is trying to squirm through, yowling. The M240 rips out a belch of five rounds, stitching the primal up the center and leaving it hanging, twitching in the breach.

I yank the shifter into reverse again, my heart now fully lodged in my throat, and stomp on the gas again. We rocket rearward.

This time we hit it and keep going. The bay door comes apart, swinging wildly off its tracks and clattering over the hood of the truck. Bodies fly past me on both sides, bouncing off the fenders. The pickup lurches as one of them goes under our tires.

I spin the wheel one-handed, my other hand snatching up my sidearm as the pickup screams into a tight turn. I see the muscular, naked bodies of primals hurtling towards the passenger's side. Gaping mouths and feral eyes.

I fire as I brake, trying to keep them off of me while I put the truck in drive before it's even stopped rolling back. I see my rounds connect with one, then two of the primals, but they don't stop coming. The M240 chatters wildly and I glimpse tracers lancing through the darkness.

I feel the transmission wrestling to get into gear as I step on the gas a little too early.

A primal slams into the passenger's side, practically vaulting into the open window. It gets its upper half inside with me and I contact shoot it in the top of its head three times.

Then the truck drops into gear, the tires scream, and we take off like a shot, barreling into the darkness of the abandoned city.

CHAPTER 25

I TRY TO SHOVE the dead primal back out the window, but it's not budging, so I guess it's coming with us. Whatever. Maybe it'll soak up some bullets for me.

My last glimpse of the mechanic's shop shows me three or four shapes slipping into the darkness, going after the Suburban. That image still sits in my eyes like a sunspot as the truck accelerates rapidly away—I need to get the cartel's attention before those primals take to bashing in the Suburban's windows.

We didn't get off scot-free either. The machine-gun fire from the back suddenly ceases and I hear EZ yelp. A quick glance over my shoulder reveals two primals that were apparently unimpressed by me ramming them with a half-ton pickup, and are now in the bed. One of them must've got their hand on the M240's barrel, because the creature yanks it out of EZ's grip and sends it whirling into the darkness behind us.

EZ tries to snatch up his rifle, but a third primal is crawling in the back window directly behind me, and it seizes his gun hand as though it knows exactly what EZ is going to do with it.

Never underestimate these bastards.

Unfortunately, just prior to that moment, I'd realized we were heading west, and the line of cartel trucks was likely heading east, and I'd already made the decision to cut a hard left to try and cross their path and get their attention.

By the time I remember such dastardly things as centrifugal force, I'm already cutting the wheel hard to the left. EZ is pulling away from the primal that's got a hold of him, but the sudden turn sends EZ tumbling into the back passenger's side door, and the primal just seems to float in after him.

Shit.

I keep my eyes on the road just long enough to avoid colliding with the backend of an old, fire-gutted bus, then twist in my seat, knowing full well that my pistol only has a few rounds left in it.

The primal has EZ pinned—one hand keeping him from grabbing his rifle, while the other clamps down around his throat.

It doesn't escape me that the two in the bed are now both jostling to get through the back glass.

Priorities—I shove my pistol right under the primal's armpit, careful not to ram it so hard that I take my weapon out of battery. I pull the trigger, trying to direct the rounds through its chest and out its head. I get two rounds out before my pistol goes into slide-lock.

My rounds don't go where I wanted them, but they do blow the primal's shoulder out.

I stomp on the brakes, causing the tires to chitter.

The primal goes tumbling to the floorboard, writhing on top of Isabella's insensate form. But it lets go of EZ's gun hand.

It also catapults one of the primals through the back glass and into the cabin with EZ.

I snap back around to make sure we're not about to crash, see a narrow lane that's clear of blockages, and steer with my knee while I snatch a fresh pistol mag from my rig and slam in the reload.

EZ screams from the backseat, and there's all kinds of tumbling and kicking, and the back of my driver's seat is bumping violently up against me, making it hard to keep the vehicle steady with my knee.

I get a hand back on the wheel and turn just in time to see EZ, buried in grasping hands and clawed fingers, caterwauling as he wrestles the muzzle of his rifle up and starts firing indiscriminately on automatic.

Blood and gobbets of flesh spackle my face as his rounds tear through the chest of the primal trying to get on top of him. I register the one I shot in the armpit struggling to get at EZ again.

A sudden bang and scrape of rending steel reminds me to glance back at the road—I've listed to the left and side-swiped something. I don't even know what it was. I correct, then thrust my hand back into the passenger compartment. I don't want my rounds to over-penetrate the primal that's on top of Isabella, so I just start hammering the back of its head with my pistol.

I swear to God, I feel the pistol crunch through its skull, and yet the primal still whirls on me and issues a rasping bark, coughing blood into my face as it grabs my arm and traps it.

We're swerving all over the damn place. I'm losing control.

EZ hasn't stopped screaming—all one long breath of desperation. His rifle chatters again, but the reports sound oddly muffled.

I'm still fighting to keep my pistol in hand as the wounded primal in the floorboards keeps tugging at me like it wants to pull my arm off. I straighten the truck out, then twist in my seat again. The third primal is squirming through the back glass now, clawing at EZ, it's too-long teeth gnashing.

I see why his reports are muffled: The second primal in the backseat is all over him, and he has his muzzle shoved into its sternum like a spear. His rounds are blasting a gaping crater out of the primal's back. They can take a lot of rounds, but that thing doesn't have a heart or lungs anymore and it's going limp.

EZ runs out of air to scream right at the same time that his rifle goes empty.

Just a split-second of eerie, preternatural silence.

"EZ!" I scream at him.

He doesn't try for a reload. He lets go of his rifle, and the primal he had speared with it collapses onto his midsection, spurting blood all over him. The third primal is halfway through the back glass now, its neck stretching, trying like hell to get its snapping jaws on EZ's face.

I tug at my arm, but the fucker on top of Isabella won't let go. Distantly, I hear Isabella's muted cry of pain and confusion as she wakes to a nightmare.

EZ writhes away from the primal trying to get at him, gives it a hard elbow to the face, stunning it just long enough for him to snatch his fixed-blade knife from his chest. Then he rams it, underhanded, right into the temple of the primal still attached to my arm.

I feel the creature's grip on me loosen. Instantly, I rip my arm free, twist a bit more, and get my muzzle right in the face of the primal in the back glass. I pump rounds through its nose until it collapses, twitching.

"Shit!" EZ yelps, breathless.

"Fuck!" I gasp, getting my eyes on the road again, just in time to see a big pile of trash I can't avoid. The pickup smashes through it, jumping violently and sending EZ and the three primal corpses airborne. Then they all crash down again, more or less in their same positions.

I get both hands on the wheel again as the truck fishtails, and let off the accelerator so I don't go skidding into the side of a building. "Both hands" is a bit generous, since I'm still gripping my pistol, but I manage to get control again.

A high-pitched mewling noise comes from beneath the dead primal in the floorboards.

"Get it off of her!" I shout at EZ as my scrambled mind tries to take stock and think tactically about what in the hell I'm doing. We weren't going as fast as I thought we were, and we're only halfway through the city now, heading south. Hopefully still on an intercept course with the cartel.

EZ grunts and curses as he wrestles himself free of the tangle of bodies and starts trying to heave the one off of Isabella. I can tell by the sound of her moaning that she's not all the way there. Just conscious enough to be scared, even in the midst of her fentanyl haze.

The whole debacle in the truck only lasted about thirty seconds.

Is the Suburban still stationary, or did they get the hell out already?

I think about transmitting to Menendez, but he's a big boy, and right about the time I get concerned with him, my eyes alight upon the center console of the old Mexican police pickup. A police radio. A frame to hold a computer that isn't there anymore.

And a control panel for lights and sirens.

Well, if you're trying to get attention...

I don't know if the equipment still works, but I jab my fingers at the buttons.

Immediately, the dark city around us is bathed in strobing blues and reds, the siren wailing.

"Ah! Fuck!" EZ cries out. "What're you doing?"

"Tryna call attention to—"

We blast through an intersection and are damn-near T-boned.

I whip around, seeing the line of cartel pickups—five of them, just like EZ reported—coming to a screeching, jumbled stop.

Yeah, I think we got their attention.

A machine gun opens up from the back of one of the technicals, the rounds smacking our backend. EZ's in the middle of repeatedly kicking a dead primal like a bit of luggage that won't fit into a trunk, trying to get it off of Isabella.

On second thought...

"Leave it!" I shout, then explain myself as succinctly as possibly: "Meat shield!"

He lets the primal collapse back onto Isabella. She moans, but if she's moaning, then she's breathing, and I'm more worried about incoming bullets at the moment.

"Good thinking!" EZ concurs with my thought process.

Blaring through the streets like a big, shiny, aggro-sponge, I look in the rearview and see three of the technicals charging after us. The other two split off and head north.

I hate it when the enemy is smart. Why couldn't God give me idiots to battle with?

Then a little red streak from the pursuing machine gunner zips up the spine of the primal hanging in my back glass and pulverizes the rearview mirror. I flinch away as bits of plastic and glass pepper my face, narrowly avoiding a traumatic eye injury. When I blink my eyes open, the windshield is so fucked I can barely see out of it.

Maybe I should've kicked it out back at the garage.

Too late now.

EZ completes a reload on his empty rifle and squishes himself over top of the dead primal in the back glass, using its body like a sandbag. He starts returning fire as I key my comms, shouting to be heard.

"Dez! We pulled three technicals from the main column, but two split off and are heading your way! You need to get out *now*! You copy?"

When he responds a second later, I hear squealing tires and screams and gunshots in the background. "Copy! We're on the move!"

I pray they get out before those two technicals catch sight of them.

"Turning right!" I yell back so EZ has a chance to brace himself, then yank us down another side street, heading west again. I want to break contact—because I don't want to get shot—but I also don't really want to lose them, or they might run off and join the other two in going after Menendez.

What I *really* need to do is kill these motherfuckers. That's the ideal scenario.

My leg bumps up against the door as I juke around an abandoned vehicle, and I feel heavy things clank together in my cargo pocket. Oh yeah, grenades. I still have two in my cargo pocket, and one on my rig.

Both sideview mirrors and the rearview have been shot off, so I can't see our pursuit, but I figure the technicals are still behind us when EZ opens up again. Then I hear an enormous bang, almost like an explosion, and jerk my head back to see one of the technicals has planted itself in the side of a building.

I don't know if EZ got the driver, or the driver just lost control, but I'll take it.

I take my foot off the accelerator as I dive into my cargo pocket and bring out both grenades.

"Why're you slowing down?" EZ cries.

"Gonna frag 'em!" I shout back, wrestling to control the wheel with my elbows while I pull both pins, making sure to keep the spoons depressed. "Turning left!"

Then I yank us down another street, stick my grenade-laden hand out the window, and the second I straighten the truck out, I give my wrist a little flick, sending the frags tumbling behind us.

Two technicals careen around the corner after us.

Three. Four...

Incoming rounds smack the pickup and there's a disheartening *bang* as one of my rear tires gets shredded, then starts *thwop-thwopping* as the truck's backend gets loose.

Then twin *BOOMS* shake the air.

I wrangle the swerving truck.

"Shit-yeah!" EZ whoops. "One disabled! It's blocking the third technical!"

I take that opportunity to break contact again, making another right turn while EZ sends a few spite-rounds back at our pursuers.

The thumping of the chewed-up tire turns to the grinding squeal of rims-on-concrete.

I fumble for my PTT. "Dez! How you guys lookin'?"

More gunshots and wailing in the background: "We got out of the garage, but we got two technicals on our ass!"

"God*dammit*!" I punch the wheel, caught in momentary indecision.

Yes, I promised Isabella I'd get her back to her family. And no, I'm not throwing that all away. But my primary mission—the whole reason I came down here in the first place—was to save the people in that Suburban.

People that now have two cartel technicals going after them. And I don't think for a single second that Diego Beltran gives a shit about taking them alive—not that that would change my mind about what I gotta do. But it makes it a little more urgent, since I know the asshats in those technicals are just going to fire indiscriminately into that Suburban.

Honestly, that's what does it: The image of bullets ripping up mothers and their children as they huddle in the back.

I bang out another right turn, now heading back north. "Dez, gimme your location! We're coming to you!"

CHAPTER 26

It can never be easy, can it?

"Sonofabitch!" EZ roars from the back, and I know what his problem is, even as he removes all doubts: "Third technical's back on our ass!"

These are some determined motherfuckers.

But so am I.

I take my last frag off my rig, twisting to get a look behind us. I can see their headlights, plunging through the emergency-strobed darkness behind us. They're gaining on us. I just can't get as much speed or maneuverability out of the truck with the back right tire out. The only reason I'm able to keep any speed up at all is because the tire that was shredded wasn't the one the engine's power is going to.

As I struggle to keep control of the truck, dodging around obstacles with limited traction, another fusillade of machine gun fire comes from behind.

The wheel jerks in my grip as another rear tire explodes.

Yup. It's the one the engine's power is going to.

I should've known better than to jinx myself.

Our engine is screaming, but the power's bleeding out through scraping rims, and the truck is now slaloming like we're on ice.

EZ is thundering back, then reloading, dumping everything he has at our pursuers.

I manage to get the pin out of the grenade and waste no time lobbing it behind us. "Frag out!" I call.

I hear tires protesting as the technical behind us swerves around the grenade. Then, a second later, it detonates.

"No joy!" EZ reports.

I glance back to see a dust cloud settling, well clear of the technical's backend. They were too close. They got passed the grenade before it went off.

Too much to hope that they'd fall for that trick again.

Thunk-thunk-thunk!

Automatic fire rakes the cab, and EZ yelps.

"Hey!" I yell back. "You okay?"

"God-fucking-*dammit*!" he squeals, writhing around. "Hit!"

"Where?" I jerk the wheel to the left, trying to get around a jersey barrier some dickweed put in the middle of the fucking road. But the backend slews, then slams into the concrete. And the next thing I know, we're spinning.

We complete a one-eighty before grinding to a stop. Headlights flare directly ahead, turning my battered windshield into a white kaleidoscope. I realize we're tilted back, like the backend of our truck is way lower than it should be.

I kick the driver's door open and tumble out, immediately going low as I snatch my rifle up and dump my mag at the approaching headlights. The technical screeches to a stop, twenty yards away.

The jersey barrier is right there between us. I scramble for it, reloading as I go.

This time I *do* hear the whine of the bullets as they lance the air around me.

I baseball-slide into cover. My pants don't have the fancy-ass, built-in knee pads. The concrete shreds the fabric like tissue paper, and then rips the flesh off my knee. My boots hit the concrete barrier.

Shit-shit-shit!

I glance at the truck I just unassed, looking for signs of movement from EZ, but the headlights are glaring right in my face and I can't see shit inside the cab. What I do see is that the entire back axle got ripped off when I hit that jersey barrier.

Are trucks that shoddily made? Axles shouldn't just go flying off. This is bullshit.

I crab backwards along the jersey barrier as incoming fire chips the top, sending bits of concrete everywhere. I lay my back on the ground, take a breath, then roll to my left, so just my head and rifle are peeking around the side of the barrier.

The technical comes into view.

Machine gunner—still aiming at the truck.

Two guys with rifles standing just outside the passenger's side doors—still firing at the other end of the barrier where I'd been seconds ago.

As I flick my select-fire to full-auto, one of them runs dry and goes for a reload. I couldn't have asked for better timing.

I hit the still-firing rifleman with a flurry of rounds that stitches him up from hip to shoulder. He pitches backward as I transition to the second rifleman, who spots me and is so damn shocked that I've magically appeared somewhere else that he fumbles his reload.

That's the last mistake he ever makes. Should've trained harder. Come at me with some bush-league bullshit like that, I'll make it a bad day every time.

I squeeze off a five-round burst that shatters his shocked face.

The machine gunner has realized where the threat is coming from and rips his weapon around, still firing streams of tracers that whip at my face.

I roll back into cover. The ground where my body had just been shatters and sends spall and concrete erupting into my side. I get to my feet, then juke to the middle of the jersey barrier and come up firing as I move to the opposite end. My rounds send the machine gunner jolting backward into the bed, screeching.

I don't stop firing. I pump bursts into the windshield, focusing on the driver's side.

Beyond the glare of the headlights, I see someone on the driver's side bolting for the back of the vehicle.

I clear the jersey barrier just as he dodges around the back corner of the bed, his body briefly illuminated by the taillights.

My bolt locks back. I immediately sling my rifle and transition to my pistol, sprinting for the front of the technical. I go to a knee at the front fender, wincing as my shredded skin touches the gritty road. I drop to my side, pistol extended.

I see a boot.

I shoot it—one round that shatters the ankle.

The guy at the backend drops, screaming.

I put two more rounds in his chest, then two in his face.

I stagger up, pointing my pistol at the driver's window. A guy is slumped inside, the top of his head missing and his face a mess. No one else in the cab. The back door hangs open. I clear it, then clear the bed—just the machine gunner.

He's still alive.

"No-no-no—!"

Two more rounds fixes that.

I clear the back. Dead guy with a blown-out ankle. I consider a security shot, but ammunition is starting to be a concern, so I save the bullet and kick his limp head instead. No response.

Okay.

I do a quick scan, then, still holding my pistol up, I grab my rifle with my support hand, give it a quick visual inspection, then quickly holster my sidearm and conduct a reload. I've only got one spare mag left.

With my rifle back up, I do another sweep to make sure there are no more surprises.

Priorities.

EZ.

Isabella.

Dez and the Suburban filled with civilians.

"EZ!" I shout, moving back towards the destroyed police pickup. The engine's still running. "EZ, you with me?"

"Abe?" the voice sounds weird, but it's definitely EZ.

"Yo! You still in the truck?"

"Yeah!"

I move around to the passenger's side.

EZ's laying in the backseat, his eyes wide. I rip open the door. A dead primal arm flops out. EZ's holding his rifle propped against the front passenger's seat with one hand, while his support hand is pressed against the left side of his face. Blood flows freely between his fingers.

I realize why his voice sounded weird. His face is swollen, blood dribbling between his lips. I swear and move in closer, hovering over him. I don't want to take pressure off the wound, but I need to see what I'm dealing with. Somehow, the dome lights in the cab are still working, and they give me just enough light that when I pull his hand away, I can see that a round zipped him right across the mandible. It ripped out a good bit of his jaw muscle. His left ear is a mangled mess. I can see his tongue and his red-tinted teeth through a gash in his cheek.

I fully expect his carotid to squirt when I remove his hand.

It doesn't. The blood's flowing, but not shooting out. I let out a pent-up breath.

"Didn't hit your artery," I tell him.

He almost wilts with relief as I put his hand back over his wound.

"Fuck...me," he says, his words a little garbled, though he's clearly happy to not be mortally wounded.

"You get another day, you lucky bastard." I grin as I reach over his body and rip his IFAK free of his rig.

I take a glance into the floorboards, beneath the dead primal. Isabella's glassy eyes stare back up at me, and for a moment, my heart drops. Then her eyes narrow.

"Abe?" a drugged-up lilt, tinged with terror.

"Oh, hey girl," EZ slurs, dropping his hand from his rifle and reaching under the dead primal to squeeze her arm. "You're still with us."

"The fuck?" she whines, her eyes widening as she tries to focus on the inhuman face of the primal resting on her shoulder, drooling blood down her chest. "Wha—?"

I can see the panic blooming. "Ssh, it's okay," I tell her as I grab combat gauze from EZ's IFAK, then tear it open with my teeth. "It's dead. It was soaking up bullets for you. Be thankful. You're still alive."

"It hurts," she moans.

"I know, Hon." I put the combat gauze over EZ's wound, then press his hand back over it. Then I take a roll of regular gauze, eyeballing the guy and trying to figure out how I'm going to keep the bandage in place. I wind up looping the regular gauze around, partially mummifying his head.

I give it a critical look. "It'll have to do," I conclude. "Can you operate?"

EZ sits up. Spits blood. He looks a little woozy, but nods.

"Come on." I help him out. He keeps his feet steadily enough. "Go for that technical back there." I jerk my head at it. "That's our new ride." EZ starts moving towards the technical, his gait a little dazed.

I yank the dead primal out by an arm, letting it flop to the ground. Then I reach in and hook my fingers into Isabella's armpits. "Gotta pull you out, okay? Try to work with me."

She groans, and then her groan turns into a squeal as her shattered elbow bumps against the front passenger's seat. She's still pretty out of it, so her legs are floppy and, while she doesn't exactly work with me, she's not wriggling against me either.

She can't walk. Exhausted and aching, I just kind of hold her up in something like a hug. She burbles against my chest, drooling over my rig. I sigh. Then suck in a breath.

Fuck you, oblique.

"Up we go," I grunt as I scoop her into a cradle carry. Start hoofing it over to the technical as EZ clambers into the front passenger's seat.

I'm trying to go easy on her wounded elbow, but it dangles, and that must've lit off a nerve stronger than the fentanyl could handle. Her eyes go wide.

Then she vomits all over my chest.

"Ah, sonofa..." I hoist her higher so her head's over my shoulder and she won't choke. She retches weakly then devolves into shaky whimpers.

I get to the technical. Prop her up against the side of the bed. Then yank the back door open and negotiate her floppy body into the backseat. I'm in a bit of a rush, but I try to make sure she's on her right side. I push her feet clear of the door and slam it, then pull the dead driver out and take his seat.

The truck's still running. I pull it into gear as I glance at EZ. He's got his rifle posted up in the open passenger's window. "You good to go, brother?"

"Yuh," he grunts.

The truck drops into gear and I peel out, transmitting as I swerve around the broken police pickup. "Dez! You still with me? I need a location, man! We're still trying to get to you!"

"Northwest corner of the city!" Dez responds, immediately. "We're runnin' in circles tryna break contact with these fuckers!"

I consider that for a spare second or two. Do I want them to try to hit the highway and get out? No. The cartel will have a better chance of catching up and getting rounds on them if they're driving in a straight line. What Dez is doing is probably the best way to keep the people in the Suburban alive.

"Roger that," I say. "I'm heading north right now, about midway through the city. See if you can double back towards the east so I can get eyes on you."

There is a pause.

Through my open window, the night air rushes and the engine roars, and I hear the chaotic popcorn noise of a distant, rolling gunfight.

"Alright," Dez comes back. "We're heading east, but we can't stay in a straight line."

"That's fine, just keep heading *generally* east and let me worry about the rest!" Then I look over at EZ. "Hey, you think you can drive?"

He looks at the wheel. Then at me. "Yeah, I can do that, but—"

I slam on the brakes, skidding to a stop. "Take the wheel! I'm going into the back!"

He curses and, instead of getting out and going around, launches himself across the center console in a frenzy of kicking and grunting, while I bolt out of the driver's seat and haul myself into the bed where the machine gun is still posted. I grab it to steady myself. There's a decent bit of ammo belt left in the can beside the weapon.

I slam on the top of the cab. "Go!"

EZ immediately hits the gas and we roar forward with me clinging to the machine gun to keep from getting toppled into the back with the dead guy that's still crumpled there. When the acceleration levels out, I get myself situated behind the machine gun. It's not an M240 like I thought at first glance. It's actually an old-school M60.

For some reason, I find myself immensely pleased by this development.

Oh—and look! A spare ammo can!

I dip down and snag the handle, giving it a little tug and feeling the heft of a full load in there. I rip the can open and snag the first few links in the belt, then cram them into the front of my pants for a faster reload.

Which I'm going to need. Because I'm gonna let this Pig eat.

I see a flash of light ahead—headlights, glaring off the sides of the buildings, and rapidly growing brighter as a vehicle approaches. It's about to blast across an intersection ahead of us.

"Dez, I think I got you guys!" I transmit, and then keep the PTT down to talk to my driver: "EZ! Step on it! And kill the lights so those fuckers don't see us before we're on their ass!"

We accelerate again, EZ angling for an open stretch of road that's free of obstacles, then dousing our headlights.

Two blocks ahead, the black Suburban roars through the intersection, from left to right. Menendez is hanging precariously out of the front passenger's window and firing back at their pursuers. The Suburban is illuminated by cartel headlights, and in their glow I see a lot of busted glass and bullet holes that hadn't been there before.

There's something about that.

Indiscriminately firing into a vehicle full of innocent women and children.

I didn't think I really had much in the way of feelings anymore. I've felt angry, sure, but in order to feel *righteous* anger, you have to have some sort of functioning moral compass.

Maybe my compass is a little janky, but when I see bullets sparking off that Suburban, and wonder how many kids in there have been wounded…Well, the needle finds true north once again.

I am *righteously pissed*.

I lean into the buttstock of the M60.

The Suburban disappears.

I watch the glowing cone of headlights from their pursuers, shrinking as the cartel technicals reach the intersection.

I aim for the far side of the intersection and let the Pig go cyclic. Tracers lance through the night, right at the height of the technicals' cabs, and they can't stop in time. They plow right through my unforgiving stream of fire.

By then, we're nearly on them, and EZ slams on the brakes so we don't T-bone the second technical in line.

The first makes it through, but the second realizes they're being attacked from the side and swerves.

The deceleration threw my aim downwards for a beat, but I've got a lot more to say to these boys about indiscriminate fire. I jerk my stream of fire back up, chewing through their back tires, their bed, and then pounding their machine gunner as he's in the act of trying to swivel his fire towards me. He doesn't get the opportunity. He wilts and I don't let up on my fire as I shred the cab, widening my stance as EZ yanks us into a sharp right-hand turn, our tires squealing as we fall in right on the technical's rear.

The technical veers left. I continue to soak that cab with heavy projectiles, turning all organic matter inside to hamburger. EZ swerves around it as the technical plants itself into the side of a building.

I let up on the trigger right as I register the last few rounds in my belt getting sucked into the chamber.

The first technical is maybe three car-lengths ahead of us. The machine gunner in the bed can't get his weapon swiveled all the way to the rear to put fire on us. He grabs a pistol from his belt and starts popping rounds at us, while one of his buddies leans out the back driver's side window and starts chattering with an AK.

"Reloading!" I scream at EZ, while he swerves, trying to avoid the incoming fire.

I rip the second ammo belt out of my pants, flip the cover up, sweep two unspent rounds out, seat the fresh belt, and slam the cover. Haul back on the charging handle.

One of the pistol rounds clips my left trap. I yelp, more in surprise at the unpleasant tug-snap sensation, as the pain hasn't hit me yet. Then I hammer the pistol-shooter with I don't know how many 7.62mm rounds. Fuck your nine-mil, you ass. Fuck you, and fuck the guys behind you. I chew through the pistol-shooter's twitching body to get to them.

EZ's smart, and he sees the direction of my fire. He drifts to the right so I don't overshoot into the Suburban. It also deprives the AK-shooter of getting an angle on me. I pour fire into that cab, raking it back and forth, like I'm trying to fill up every cubic inch of its volume with lead. I don't want anything left inside. If Diego Beltran ever finds this technical, I don't want him to recognize the bodies. I want him to find nothing but blood pudding.

This is what indiscriminate fire looks like.

The technical starts to coast, decelerating and listing to the right, so it kind of cuts us off. EZ slows to stay behind it. I find myself irritated when I have to stop firing for a moment so I don't accidentally hit the Suburban, though they're gaining distance now as we fall behind.

That moment lets me take a breath. It smells like hot brass and spent propellant.

The technical crunches somewhat anticlimactically into a trash pile, and then rolls to a halt. I'd kind of wanted to see it explode, but I'm getting a handle on my brief flash of emotions.

No need to waste any more ammo. There's nothing left alive in there.

I don't *actually* need to disintegrate them.

Christ. What was *that* about?

I kind of lost my cool there.

EZ rolls by the battered technical. I watch it as we pass. There's really nothing to see. Just shattered glass and perforated sheet metal. I guess their headlights got shot out, because, as we roll by, the truck simply melts into the gloom.

I turn around in the bed, putting my hands on my rifle, since the M60 won't turn all the way around. I half expect to see another technical roaring up behind us, or some stubborn survivor winging out shots as a parting insult.

Behind us, there is nothing but darkness.

CHAPTER 27

We follow the Suburban out of the city, heading north.

Dez says they have to stop, but doesn't explain why. His voice is strained. Grim. My stomach is already in knots, staring at the backend of the vehicle. There are so many bullet holes in it. The rear windshield is gone, and yet I can't see anyone inside.

This is gonna be bad.

The Suburban veers to the side of the road and skids to a hasty stop. The second it rocks back, both front doors open. Dez comes hobbling out, favoring a leg and holding his support hand to his chest. But he's not worried about himself—he's focused on whatever carnage is in the back.

Out of the driver's seat comes one of the women. I realize its Tracy Pizzuti. She must've taken the wheel from Branch so he could get in the fight. She looks stunned and stricken.

EZ throws our technical into park and gets out, hustling to where Dez is pulling up the Suburban's rear lift gate. It takes me a few seconds to get out of the bed—I'm wrecked, and now that my life is not in immediate danger, my body is screaming at me. I move stiffly to the back of the Suburban.

I can hear crying. Sobbing. Wailing.

Tracy stands off to the side, both hands clutching her hair, her face a mask of horror.

Dez and EZ are hovering over someone. No one's talking.

I push in.

Huddled in the rear of the vehicle, I spot Lucky and Branch. Or what is left of them, anyways.

Lucky...dear God. He's been shot so many times. His body is slumped against the passenger side frame, his rifle dangling from limp fingers. His armor caught a lot of rounds. His spare mags are just shards of polymer and spirals of springs. The plate carrier is so tattered it looks like it's been drug across the road for miles.

His arms and legs are battered with uncountable holes. His face is unrecognizable.

Branch is on the driver's side. He's sitting up, and a woman is crouched behind him, with her finger stuck in a hole in his neck. She tried to stop the bleeding. Branch's eyes are open, but sightless. The top left side of his head is gone. His limbs are in a similar state to Lucky's.

I look behind those two dead men. The women and children are laying all atop each other. One of the children is the one that's crying so loudly. It's a little boy. His mother is petting his head and muttering soft things to him.

I count heads. I count faces. I see wide, tear-stained eyes that blink back at me and track my movement. I don't see any blood. No one's screaming about a wound. Just the one boy crying because he's terrified and saw some shit little boys aren't supposed to see.

But they're alive. They're *all* alive.

Branch and Lucky put their bodies in the way. They soaked up all that indiscriminate fire for the people they'd been sent to save.

My eyes track back to Branch, and I see that he's not even holding his rifle. He's got his pistol in his hand. It's locked back on an empty magazine. His rifle is slung to the side. It's empty too.

These guys didn't just take the rounds meant for those women and children. They fought through it. They fought until they couldn't fight anymore, and died letting their bodies be the shield for others.

Menendez reaches up to where the woman's hand is still clamped on Branch's neck, her index finger still two knuckles deep in the bullet hole that doubtlessly severed his carotid artery. I realize it's Carrie Mitchell—the woman who'd held onto my belt to keep me from falling off the Suburban.

This time she tried to help Branch.

She looks up at Menendez, her eyes so wide they seem to take up her whole face. They're scared, and broken. And hopeful. When Menendez lays his hand on hers, her eyes seem to ask if she did enough.

"It's okay," Menendez says, gently pulling her finger out of Branch's neck. "It's alright. You did your best."

She doesn't crumple. Doesn't weep. Just kind of falls back against the hump of the tire well, her dazed eyes staring at nothing at all.

EZ makes a strangled sound. I look across at him and see his hand is clamped over his nose and mouth. Eyes tight and streaming.

"Come on." Menendez pulls Branch's torso towards him. "Grab his legs."

EZ removes his hand from his mouth and grabs Branch's legs.

I notice that Menendez is missing the pinky and ring finger on his left hand. He's struggling to get a grip on Branch. Christ, we're all fucked up, aren't we? But at least I got two working hands. I step in and take his position without speaking. He relents, knowing I'm better equipped.

"We'll put 'em in the truck bed," I say to EZ.

He just nods.

We carry Branch back to the technical.

I wait for him to demand to go back and recover Marty's body from the pickup we left behind. But he doesn't. He knows we don't have time. We're in the clear, but we don't know how long that will last, or if there are more cartel soldiers coming. No one's safe until we get back to our own territory.

We place Branch in the bed of the technical. I yank the dead cartel soldier out, because that fucker does not deserve to lay next to my friend. Then we return for Lucky.

Tracy Pizzuti is wrapping gauze around Menendez's injured hand. He stops us as we pull Lucky's body out. Looks at me.

"You still taking Isabella home?" His voice is flat. Not looking for an argument. Just asking.

"Yeah."

He looks at EZ. "I know you wanted to be a part of that for Marty. But I need you, man. You're all I got left. And we're not out of the woods yet."

EZ doesn't argue either. It was different when Menendez had Branch and Lucky. The situation has changed. Menendez needs another good rifle to make sure they get out of Mexico alive. EZ knows that.

As we haul Lucky back to the technical, EZ asks me, "You gonna be straight on your own?"

"Yeah."

"You gonna get these guys back to us?"

We settle Lucky in next to Branch. Push him so his legs are clear of the tailgate, then slam it shut.

"I'll get 'em back to you guys," I promise him. "And...sorry about Marty."

EZ just stares at me for a moment.

Menendez calls back in a voice bereft of emotion: "EZ. We gotta roll."

I pat EZ on the shoulder. "I'll bring 'em home, alright?"

He nods. "Alright."

Then he jogs back to the Suburban, as I get in the driver's seat of the technical. I look into the back. Isabella is still laying there as I left her, curled on her left side, facing away from me. I see the tension in the muscles of her back. Her breathing is labored against the pain.

Shit. I realize I have no idea where the fentanyl went.

I look up to see if I can hail Menendez for another one, but they're already peeling out, leaving a cloud of dust in their wake as they head north for the border.

I park the technical about a mile from Isabella's home, and wait for her to come out of it.

I use that time to patch the hole in my trap. It's actually not bad. Stiff and sore, but it clotted on its own and stopped bleeding a while ago. So I just clean it as best I can, then slap a bandage on it. That'll do for now.

I watch in the rearview as Isabella comes out of the fentanyl haze, and back into a world of full-on agony. I know she's not high anymore when she starts to sob and hiss through her teeth. Shakily, she rises from her curled position, moving gingerly to protect her arm.

She looks around, eyes squinted against the pain. "Where are we?" her voice cracks.

I turn painfully in my seat and look her in the eyes. "We're not far from your house."

She shudders, her expression too pain-wracked to show anything but the dimmest glimmer of relief that she is reaching the end of her nightmare.

Or so she might think.

"Why are we stopped?" she asks, smacking dry lips in a pasty mouth. "Did we run out of gas?"

I wish I had some water to give her, but I don't have shit anymore except my rig, rifle, and pistol.

"No," I answer her. "We still have gas." I take a breath and adjust my position so it's not putting so much strain on my oblique. Or my wounded ass-cheek. Or my trap. "Isabella, I gotta be real with you, okay? And I need to know that you're clear enough in the head to understand what I'm telling you. Are you clear? Not drugged anymore?"

"I need more," is her response.

"I'm sorry, I don't have anymore."

She whimpers.

"Are you clear-headed enough to understand me?"

"Yes," she half snarls, half moans.

Alright. Here we go.

"Hon...you're gonna lose that arm."

Her eyes whip to mine. They are surprised, but only for a second. Then I see that I've confirmed something she was already deeply terrified of. Still, she breathes, "What?"

I can't blame her for the denial. No one just up and accepts the loss of a limb.

I reach out and very gently put my hand on her knee, close to her wounded arm. I point at the elbow. "That bullet shattered your elbow joint. Even if this was back when we had modern medical facilities and teams of surgeons, it'd take a lot to save that arm. Nowadays? It just ain't gonna happen. I'm sorry. I know that's fucked up and it's not what you wanna hear, but you need to understand something about that."

She groans as though to say *Oh, there's MORE?*

"I can take you home. But if I leave you there, that arm's gonna get infected, you're gonna go septic, and that's if you don't die from blood loss when we take that tourniquet off your arm. Your mom can't do an amputation. So, basically, if I take you home and leave you there, you're gonna die."

She cries softly for a few shaky breaths. Then glares at me—a thoroughly ugly expression with her face all contorted and snot-dribbled. "What do you care if I die? You don't care about anything."

I sigh and hang my head.

Yeah, I know. Black-hearted devil that I am.

I don't argue with her accusation. I move on to the crux of the matter. "I can take you with me. Back to my people. I mean, you're still gonna lose the arm, Isabella, but we got guys that can do the amputation, and we have medical equipment and medicine that can help you. I can't make you a guarantee, but I know you'll stand a better chance of surviving if you come with me."

Her sobs falter for a moment as she parses through what I've told her. Emotions come and go across her face, because she doesn't have the bandwidth to hide them from me. Then pain becomes the strongest expression again.

Pain and...sadness.

"I don't wanna die."

"I know you don't. I don't want you to die either. That's why I think you should come with me. I'll make sure you get the best we can give. I owe you that much."

Her head tilts back and she stares at the ceiling of the cab for a moment, huffing through pursed lips. Then she drags her wrist across her face, smearing snot and tears. Looks at me with those sad, tormented eyes again.

"At least let me see my mom again. Let me say goodbye to her."

Is that a yes? Has she decided to come with me?

I'm not sure. But for some reason I feel relieved.

I nod to her. "Yeah, I can do that."

When we drive into the little homestead, our headlamps are the only light in the dark. They splash across the front of the house. I'm cautious, casting a suspicious eye at everything—even the dirt, to see if there are tire marks from cartel soldiers coming and going.

Nothing seems amiss.

I park the technical near the front of the house and pop my door, leaving the engine running. Hopefully we won't be here long.

"I'll get your mom," I say quietly, then step out, holding my rifle, but keeping it low and non-threatening.

That doesn't last long.

The front door bursts open, and there is Isabella's mom, holding a shotgun and yammering a bunch of shit in Spanish I can't understand.

Reflexively, I take cover behind the door panel—it'll *probably* stop buckshot—and snap my rifle up. God, I don't want to kill Isabella's mom right in front of her.

"Hey! Yo!" I shout back at the woman, but this has no effect except to make her yell at me even louder and brandish the shotgun.

Shit and fuck.

Hunkered behind the door, I keep one hand on my rifle, then wave the other in the air in what I hope is a peaceful or friendly gesture, then point at the cab. "Isabella! Isabella is right here!"

That shuts her up long enough to hear her daughter calling back to her in Spanish.

The woman immediately lowers the shotgun and comes staggering down the steps like her legs are suddenly numb. I'm not overly comfortable with an emotional wreck shambling towards me with a shotgun in hand, but I'm willing to take some risks at this point.

Maybe I'm just fucking tired.

The woman breaks into a sprint as she spots her daughter in the back, illuminated by the dome lights. Me and my threatening rifle are completely forgotten. She bypasses me, heedless, and throws herself into the backseat.

Isabella yowls—I guess her mom tried to wrap her in a hug before she realized the girl's arm was wounded. Then there is a whole lot of crying and sobbing and hiccupping words in Spanish. They're both talking over each other.

I stand outside, just watching. Unable to help. Unable to speak, or to understand what they are saying. I feel pretty useless, so I just start scanning the environment for threats, because that's what you do when you're standing around, not accomplishing anything.

It takes a while. There is a lot of back and forth. I can tell when Isabella has laid the truth on her mother, because the woman starts wailing again, and though I can't understand the words, it sure sounds like she's protesting.

Isabella is remarkably calm in that moment. She gets her mom's attention again, gets her to be quiet, and speaks softly to her. I imagine she's laying out the facts, as I laid them out for her. The arm's gotta come off. If I leave her here, she's most certainly going to die. But if I take her with me, she's got a good chance of surviving.

This goes on, until it is just Isabella, practically whispering, and her mother, sniffling.

Then there is a question.

A response.

The emotion has changed. It doesn't feel like sad goodbyes anymore. I can't really tell what it is.

A rapid back-and-forth.

I'm starting to get concerned. I lean in. "Isabella? What's going on?"

The woman disconnects from her daughter, gives me a wary side-eye, then starts shouting at the house. It kind of surprises me, so I jerk a little, then look at the house, then back at Isabella.

"Isabella," I seethe. "The fuck is happening?"

She still doesn't respond, and that's getting me a little angry.

I get an answer though.

Two kids come trundling out of the house, jabbering in sleepy, worried voices.

"What is this?" I demand. "What are they doing here?"

The woman beckons them and they come running over. And the next thing I know, the woman is piling the children into the back of the truck.

"Hey. No. Get them the fuck out of there. Stop. Isabella!"

Then the woman herself gets in, sits right next to her daughter, and shuts the door in my face.

The fuck is this?

I ram myself into the cab by way of the open driver's door. I glare at Isabella. "I'm not fucking taking—"

Isabella just reaches out with her good hand and grabs me by the collar of my armor in a surprisingly-strong grip.

She pulls, but I stubbornly don't allow her to move me, so she only manages to pull herself closer to me.

"They're coming with us," she states.

"The fuck they are," I snap, then start to pull back, intending to physically extract these people if I have to. But Isabella holds on.

Her eyes, though red-rimmed and tear-streaked, are hard. "I already told you that the people in Pancho know me, and they know where I live. They saw me with Angel. They know I was the last person he was with. It's just a matter of time before Diego Beltran puts it all together and comes looking for me here. And do you think he's just going to ask my mother politely where I went? Or do you think he's going to start carving them up for answers?"

I stare at her, unyielding.

She stares back, equally unyielding.

Unstoppable force, meet immovable object.

My eyes narrow to slits, and I speak with all the meanness I can muster. "And why in the hell would you think that I care?"

Then she smiles at me. "Because I'm still alive."

I growl.

She gives my chest a shove, releasing me. "You keep saying you don't care, Abe. But you know what? Actions speak louder than words."

Then she sits back.

The whole family just stares at me.

The mom sneaks a glance at her door. Then hits the manual lock.

EPILOGUE

DAWN BREAKS OVER THE Texas plains, as I drive the lonely highway north.

I haven't seen hide nor hair of any cartel elements since the firefight in the abandoned city, but I'm keeping a lookout for them. I still can't get Menendez or EZ on comms. I hope they made it back to safety.

I *know* they made it back. Menendez and EZ—they were as determined as I was to see this mission through. I have faith in them. They got it done. And in another handful of hours, I'll see them again, and this last little knot of apprehension in my guts will let go of its grip on me.

And I'll breathe a little easier once I see those families reunited.

For a little slice of time, I made those families *mine*. I made it real in my mind. And yeah, that caused me to do some fucked up shit—or at least threaten to.

But I felt for them in that moment. And I guess I feel for them now, more than I did when Michael Pizzuti gave me that photograph of his family. I guess sometimes I just push shit away, because the menu of emotions you can feel while trying to survive in this world are mostly negative.

The mind is a powerful thing. You can control how you view the world, and through that, you can control what affects you, and what slides off your back. When I was holding Diego Beltran's daughter down and threatening to hurt her in horrible ways, I made myself believe that the Pizzuti's were *my* family, and the only emotion it gave me was rage. But that's what I needed in that moment. I needed Diego to believe I was capable of the things I said.

But I didn't do them.

And I am...relieved.

I guess Isabella was right.

Maybe actions do speak louder than words.

The dawn casts the eastern sky in brilliant orange hues. I try not to get maudlin about it, but...fuck. It's *beautiful*.

I look in the rearview mirror.

The orange light plays across four faces, making them look flushed, though they're asleep.

Except for Isabella.

She's looking back at me in the rearview mirror. She's still in a lot of pain, and it's pulled her features taut. But there is a calm in those dark eyes that I haven't seen before. Calm, as her brother and sister sleep to her right, and her mother snores softly to her left.

She offers me a tired, careworn smile.

Then silently mouths the words: *Thank you*.

I grunt and look forward again.

"Whatever," I say under my breath. "This is bullshit."

Then I quickly run a hand over my beard so she can't see me smile.

About The Author

D.J. Molles became a New York Times and USA today bestselling author while working full time as a police officer. He's since traded his badge for a keyboard to produce over 20 titles. When he's not writing, he's taking steps to make his North Carolina property self-sustainable, and training to be at least half as hard to kill as Lee Harden (his most popular protagonist). Molles also enjoys playing his guitar and drums, drawing, cooking, and cruising on his Onewheel.

Most nights you can find him sitting on the couch surrounded by his family and three rescue dogs—which he prefers to call "All American Couch Hounds" but are also commonly referred to as "Pillow Pibbles."

Want to be in the know for all things D.J. Molles?
Sign up for the newsletter.
There's a giveaway every month!

djmolles.com/newsletter

Also By D.J. Molles

The Remaining Universe Books:

The Remaining Series

Lee Harden Series

The Valley: A Lee Harden Novel

Sanctuary

The Book of Dog: A Satire

A Harvest of Ash and Blood

The Santas

Wolves

Godbreaker Trilogy

A Grower's War Series

...and more at **djmolles.com**!

Printed in Great Britain
by Amazon

48432668R00233